Amethyst Pledge

Book 1 of
The Albatar Chronicles

Leonie Rogers

AMETHYST PLEDGE

Book 1 of *The Albatar Chronicles*

The moral rights of Leonie Rogers to be identified as the author of this work have been asserted.

Copyright 2019
Hague Publishing
PO Box 451
Bassendean, Western AUSTRALIA 6934
Email: contact@haguepublishing.com
Web: www.haguepublishing.com

ISBN 978-0-6485714-5-2

Cover: Amethyst Pledge by Jade Zivanovic
http://www.steampowerstudios.com.au/

Typeset Garamond 12/13

ACKNOWLEDGMENTS

A few years ago, our writers group decided to use the word 'purple' as the theme for our next meeting. Each month, we write five hundred words using a theme, which we then read aloud and gently critique. I wrote those words, liked them a lot, and turned them into a whole book. That was where Amethyst Pledge began. Thanks to the Brook and Beyond Writers Group for that prompt.

Thanks should also go to the MATS (Muswellbrook Amateur Theatrical Society) Sound of Music cast in that year. The SOM kids, and some of their parents, read the first draft, along with some of my faithful friends. Thank you.

I'd also like to pop in a special thanks to two of my writing friends in particular. Deb and Simone, my partners in the 'Apostrophe Posse' are marvellous women, and are always ready with a grammatical solution or a reading 'ear.' They also had a big hand in the 'purple' prompt.

Many thanks once again, to Mal, who puts up with my writing, and most recently my obsession with crafting things from EVA foam. I do love you very much.

CHAPTER ONE:
BEGINNINGS

A tear tracked slowly down Kazari's cheek, as she picked up the leather belt she'd been working on the night before and began to carve the flowers onto its well-tanned length. Under her hands the leather was soft and supple, the metal tongue and buckle perfectly matched to it. Each was evidence of her father's careful skill, and her mother's touch with metalwork. And now as Kazari engraved each flower with delicate precision, she knew each was a farewell kiss to the family who'd decided to abandon her on the Day of Choosing.

She kept her eyes on the belt, blinking to clear her vision, watching the tiny curls of cut leather curve away from the belt, as if each was a piece of her regret sliced free.

She remembered last night's argument. Her mother's voice, clipped and icy – "You want to shut yourself up in an Abbey, Kazari? Forever? For the rest of your life? Away from your family and your friends?"

Kazari had been so angry. "But it's *my* choice, Mum, mine, and the Lady's." And then her voice had wobbled, annoying her with its weakness. Even now she was embarrassed she hadn't been able to remain calm. She knew she was doing the right thing, no matter what her parents wanted. "It doesn't matter what you want, not this time! I'm of age. Everyone has the right to commit themselves to the Lady's service once they turn fifteen."

For a moment the flowers blurred again, and Kazari blinked her eyes furiously, trying to ignore the hot sting as another tear tracked after the first.

She recited the words of *The Book of Service* in her mind. 'She who is called is certain, and I will not forsake her should she bend her will to Mine. When you hear the call, choose to bend and not break. Submit your will to Mine, and walk My path all the days of your life.' They calmed her, but not as much as they should have, because when she'd quoted them the night before, her mother had spat them back at her.

"I notice you didn't finish your quote," her mother had said in those same icy tones. Her mother's blue eyes had matched the coldness perfusing her voice. "It goes on: 'And though My path may lead you into darkness, and your very life become forfeit, I will walk beside you always. Those who lose their lives in My service will walk with Me all the days of eternity.' Some of those who pledge to the Lady *die*, Kazari – they die, or fall into darkness!"

Kazari knew her mother was worried for her. But it was her decision, and her own anger bubbled, struggling to escape. Her mother had no right to deny her her path.

"Didn't you listen to the last part of the quote, Mother? 'I will walk beside you always. Those who lose their lives in My service will walk with Me all the days of eternity.' Does that mean *nothing* to you, Mother? Not everyone who pledges to the Lady walks close to the darkness or loses their life. Very few of the septs ever have to confront danger. Most of the Lady's servants become Growers, or Judicars. It's possible I might become an Adviser, or a Healer, but can you see me as a Hunter, or even a Navigator? You know what my teachers have said about my schoolwork –"

The words had poured out in a torrent, stopped only when her father held up a hand.

"But some do, Kazari. Some always do," her father had told her sombrely, "And isn't it also said that 'The path of the initiate is determined only by the Lady. No-one knows your path but Her, until the moment of awakening?'"

"Of course it does, but you know what I'm good at, and pretty well everyone knows what they'll become on entry to the Lady's service. Look at Enda last year – she was a born Healer. Everyone knew it, and now she is. You saw her on her home visit last month, didn't you? And Harrod? He knew he'd be a Judicar, and he is. I'm sure the Lady knows best, but there are patterns, and they're followed in almost every case." She could have mentioned more names – people known by her family both before and after choosing the Lady's service, but she hadn't, hoping they'd begin to calm down and see reason.

She'd watched her parents exchange glances and seen their anger start to ebb. They knew they couldn't deny her her choice the following day. Tomorrow was the Abbot's annual visit, and anyone over the age of fifteen was required to present themselves to answer the Abbot's question. It was the law, and with her school friends, she must present herself for the choosing. Fifteen-year olds had more than one option, though. When the Abbot posed her question, Kazari could choose to declare herself for service, in which case she would leave with the Abbot; she could choose to state that she was abstaining from choice, in which case she was free to present herself in any following year; or she could choose to close the door completely on serving the Lady in one sept or another, by declaring she was not called. Most of the attendees the next day would choose one of the latter two.

Only one or two fifteen-year olds would choose to serve, but it was likely that some who had abstained in previous years would present themselves ready in the morning.

"Couldn't you just abstain, tomorrow?" her father had asked. "Take some more time to think. Give yourself a year."

But Kazari had heard his unspoken words – 'Give yourself time to grow up and forget all of this nonsense' – and they had firmed her determination.

Her mother had said nothing, just looked away from her

daughter, to where Kazari's two brothers were playing on the hearth in front of the fire, pretending to ignore the argument. Kazari wondered how her parents' anger now, might affect their own choices in a few years.

She carved the last flower carefully. Despite her mother's anger, and her father's regret, she was determined to choose for the Lady. She'd had long nights to wrestle with her decision, and despite her parents' opinions, she knew her choice was the right one.

Lady, how can they not see? Why don't they understand? It seemed she'd prayed the same thing over and over the last few months, as she'd tried time and again to raise her upcoming pledge with her family. Her mother had begun by ignoring her efforts. Her father had discussed her thoughts and quotations as an intellectual exercise, and her brothers hadn't been particularly interested.

She tidied the scraps of leather from her desk, smoothed the belt, now covered in delicate carvings, and set it gently on the desktop.

And now she was leaving, perhaps forever. She'd hoped against hope her parents would have become resigned to her choice. It wasn't as if she hadn't mentioned it to them over the years. Ever since she'd been tiny she'd known that the Lady had called her. She'd never suffered doubts about the reality of the Lady who looked after them all, as some of her peers had, and had never struggled with a connection to her. Kazari had no doubts that the Writings were a true record of her words at the founding of Albatar.

Some days she'd felt the Lady so closely she could have sworn if she'd turned her head she would have seen her, walking by her side. It happened most often when she was outside, but every now and then, Kazari would feel her presence as she carefully engraved another piece of leather, or rejoiced with a friend. She knew most of her friends thought she was silly, but *she* knew what she felt. At least her closest friend, Dari, understood, but *her* sister was Enda, who'd seemed destined since birth to join the Healers.

From the shelf built into her bedroom wall, she took a small bag and began to fill it with a few possessions. Information about what would happen when she arrived at the Abbey was sketchy, but she knew she'd need underwear for the journey and a couple of clothing changes. She tucked her copy of the Writings away in her bag along with the leather belt her parents had given her at her last birthday, and the bookmark Dari had woven for her from wool from her family's sheep. Its textured surface reminded her of the hours they'd spent together, helping Dari's parents with the shearing. It still had a faint lanolin smell. She breathed it in deeply, and let the scents of happy hours soothe her.

She made sure that her shelves were dusted, that her collection of leather scraps was boxed, and that the clothing she was leaving behind was neatly folded. At the last moment she stuffed her four treasured books into her bag. They just fitted, although they made it heavier than she'd have liked. Finally, she washed and dressed for the new day.

Thoughts chased themselves around her head like a cat after mice, mixing with the remnants of her confused dreams. Over the last couple of months, it seemed that Kazari's nights had only left her tired and grumpy.

Yawning, she made her way downstairs to an empty kitchen. The house was quiet and felt empty, as if her parents' disapproval had drained it of all homeliness. The morning was chilly, and Kazari stirred the embers inside the stove, feeding them another piece of wood, before filling the kettle and popping it on to boil. She drank her tea when the water boiled, before setting a pot of porridge simmering for the rest of the family. She grabbed a piece of cheese and an apple, and let herself outside quietly.

She sat on the bench seat outside the leather shop, eating her breakfast, and after delaying for a few more minutes, came to the weary conclusion that neither of her parents was going to make an appearance before she presented herself to the Abbot. The early morning light usually left her feeling energised and refreshed, but not this morning. She wasn't normally a depressive personality, but the spring in her step was missing, and the lack of the warm farewells she'd fantasised about for years left her feeling empty and teary.

She hefted her bag, settled its weight onto her shoulder, and began the lonely walk to the town centre. Her footsteps echoed hollowly as she made her way down the cobblestoned road, past the familiar houses and businesses of her childhood, and towards the unknown. As she approached the town square, others began to join her one by one. Familiar faces from her lessons in the chapel walked with family members beside them, leaving Kazari feeling even more alone as she trudged along with her bag over her shoulder.

Kaz!" It was Dari, dodging through the growing crowd around the square. "Stand with me! Oh." Her friend's eyes widened as she took in the lack of family walking with Kazari. "You told them? And it didn't go well?"

Suddenly choked up, Kazari shook her head. She felt her friend thread her arm through hers and tug her to one side. "You can stand with us until it's time then, come on." As they neared Dari's parents, she saw Gweda, Dari's mother, raise her eyebrows slightly as they neared, before breaking into a smile.

"Kazari! You're planning to declare?" She motioned towards the bag over Kazari's shoulder.

Kazari nodded, not trusting her voice.

"And your parents?" Gweda left the question hanging.

"I hope they might be along shortly." She was proud her voice stayed steady, although it nearly undid her.

"I'm sure they will," Gweda replied brightly. "It's such a proud day for a parent. Of course we miss Enda, but we know that the Lady has great plans for her. And once she's assigned to a chapel or a hospice, we hope to be able to visit."

Despite pledging to serve for a lifetime, the Lady's servants lived full lives, marrying if they wished, and serving as their vows to the Lady required. Early initiation and training kept them sequestered for long periods of time, however, once a certain point had been reached, visiting home was possible, and even encouraged. Despite what her parents had insinuated, Kazari knew the Lady's servants were a vibrant part of Albatar, seen and welcomed across the land.

Kazari wondered if she'd ever be welcome at home again. Sometimes it went like that, although most families came around eventually. She hoped hers would, but she couldn't stop herself looking around every few minutes, hoping for a glimpse of her mother or father. The crowd was growing rapidly, and it was becoming harder to see through it.

She warmed as Dari tucked her arm through hers, and for a few moments, she no longer felt abandoned.

"I've had the weirdest dreams, Dari," she said.

"What do you mean?" Dari replied.

"Rainbows, stars, colours. It was like I was drowning in them. And inside the rainbows, feelings. So many feelings that I've been waking up ill, or crying, or so tired, I've barely made it through the day."

"Do you think it's because you've been worried about your Mum and Dad?" Dari asked. "I mean, you always knew it was going to be hard telling them."

Kazari shrugged, and then shook her head.

"No, it's not that. *Those* dreams are pretty obvious. I just see their eyes." Tears threatened again, and Kazari gritted her teeth against the sadness that once again, seemed ready to overwhelm her. She breathed in and out, deeply, and went on.

"These are . . . different . . . somehow. It's as if there's a message, or a sign, or – I don't know – *something* that I'm missing." She hitched her bag a little higher on her shoulder. "I think maybe it's the Lady. Did . . . did Enda mention anything?"

"Nothing, and do you really think the Lady sends dreams, Kaz?"

"You don't?"

Dari opened her mouth to answer, but a gong rang out, and the crowd stilled. Kazari and Dari exchanged glances. It was time.

"Leave your things with us, Kaz," Gweda said. "You can get them after the ceremony. There'll be time." Kazari nodded gratefully. Standing on the dais with a bag over her shoulder would only emphasise her lack of family support. *Lady, please stand with me,* she thought. *Give me the courage I need, and the comfort too.*

She walked quickly to the raised area in the centre of the square, slightly awkwardly taking her place beside her friend. Dari gave her hand a quick squeeze. "You're doing the right thing, Kaz. I know you are."

"Thanks, Dari." She squeezed back and then turned her eyes forward. There was quite a large group on the platform, mainly fifteen-year olds, but there were also a few of those who'd abstained from decision-making in previous years. They stood in a clump rather than in lines, waiting for the Abbot to appear. This Abbot had only been raised to her position four years before, when her predecessor had stepped down citing old age. She was a tall woman, competent looking, and raised from the Hunter sept, as evidenced by the amethyst pendant glowing purple on her chest.

A stir in the crowd heralded the Abbot's approach, and Kazari's stomach wondered if she was going to be sick. She took one more look around, hoping to see at least one of her parents standing in the crowd around the square, but their familiar figures were nowhere to be seen.

The Abbot climbed the stairs to the platform, followed by a member of each of the Order's septs. Their multihued robes spun a rainbow of colour, against which the Abbot's black robes stood out starkly. Her brown eyes wandered across the group, pausing briefly here and there, before resting momentarily on Kazari where she stood to one side with Dari. She thought the Abbot's eyes tightened slightly, but immediately dismissed the idea as the woman's eyes passed on to the three standing next to her.

A few moments later, the gong spoke again and the square quietened. In the silence the robed figures chanted the ages' old song of declaration:

> *With the morning light*
> *Comes the dawning*
> *Of the Lady's day*
> *To dispel night*
>
> *Sing the songs of praise*
> *In the morning*
> *Of the day of choice*
> *Coming of age*
>
> *Set the pathway still*
> *Your choice is here*
> *To declare or not*
> *Follow her will*

Kazari exchanged a nervous look with Dari. The moment was finally here, and now, in front of her whole village, she would declare for the Lady. She knew Dari's decision, just as her friend knew hers, decisions that would set them on completely different paths. Tearing, she squeezed Dari's hand, and then turned her face resolutely towards the Abbot.

CHAPTER TWO: DECLARATION

It's the Day of Declaration," the Abbot announced. "Most of you have already decided what your choice will be, but if anyone hasn't, place your trust in the Lady, ask for her help, and follow the guidance of your heart. One by one, you will approach, lay your hand upon the Writings, and state your choice. Speak clearly, so that all may know your mind. Those who declare for the Lady will stand to my right. Those who abstain to my left. Those whose choice is to decline, will make their way back to their families after they speak."

The Abbot looked at the assembled villagers, and then swept her arms wide.

"Whatever the choices made, respect those who make them. Those who choose not to declare for the Lady still do her will. Those who abstain, know that she may yet call them to Her service. Those who declare for the Lady today may take the most difficult path, yet it is a path of joy and one that should be celebrated." She picked up an ornate copy of the Writings and called the first name in a clear voice. "Dari."

Kazari let her friend's hand go with a sense of loss, watching her walk forward and place her hand firmly on the Writings.

"I choose to decline service with the Lady." Dari's said clearly.

Kazari could hear the ring of certainty in Dari's voice as it rang clearly out across the square, and knew her friend spoke with a conviction as strong as her own. It didn't stop the feeling of loss though because, for the first time, their lives would take different paths. But knowing her friend was doing the right thing made her more certain about her own decision. Besides, she reminded herself firmly, their friendship would not be less, just different.

Name after name was called, and one by one, each person walked forward and made their choice. Kazari watched those around her chose to either abstain or decline. Time wore on, until only Kazari and one other, older woman remained. Kazari couldn't remember who she was, but her face was vaguely familiar. When the Abbot called her forward, she remembered. The woman's name was Quisil and she'd managed a vegetable stall in the market for many years. It must have been a long time since her abstention, but the woman now walked forward to place a trembling hand on the Writings.

"I declare for the Lady." A stirring of surprise swept around the square like a sudden breeze, and Kazari let out a breath she hadn't been aware she was holding. Relief followed as she breathed in again. She wasn't to be the only one to declare for the Lady today.

"Welcome, Quisil, the Lady is pleased with your choice. Take your place on my right," the Abbot said. Quisil walked to the Abbot's right side and stood, looking nervously relieved, while her work-worn hands clutched at her tunic. "And now, Kazari."

Kazari's stomach flip-flopped, and then she was walking forward, uncertain of how her legs had started moving. It seemed a ridiculously long walk, and she was very conscious of everyone watching her. And very conscious of those who weren't. She couldn't help glancing around one more time to look for her family. She didn't see them.

Taking a breath, she raised her hand and placed it on the Writings. "I declare for the Lady." The leather cover, ornately tooled, and inlaid with the tiny gems that signified each of the septs, warmed under her hand and she looked up, startled, straight into the Abbot's eyes.

"Welcome Kazari, the Lady is pleased with your choice. Take your place on my right." The woman's dark eyes crinkled at the corners as she spoke, and Kazari made her way to Quisil's side, wondering as she did so. The other woman smiled at her, and she managed to smile back as the Abbot spoke again. "Join me as we commit these two to the Lady."

The ceremony was short, and practical; a simple laying on of hands by the sept representatives while the Abbot prayed. Then, the ceremony over, the Abbot dismissed the crowd and requested Kazari and Quisil to make their goodbyes, collect their belongings, and meet her on the edge of the square. It felt almost perfunctory, but in a strange kind of way easier.

Kazari stepped off the platform and made her way slowly towards Dari's family. Her friend rushed forward and hugged her.

"You did the right thing," she whispered into Kazari's ear. Gweda also hugged her, tears glinting in her eyes.

"I'm so sorry they weren't here, Kaz, but we're proud of you. And if you see Enda, give her our love."

"I will," Kazari said, accepting her bag back from Dari's father.

"You take care, now," he said. "And give Enda this from me," he told her, giving her a hug.

Kazari nodded. "I – I'd better go." And with one last hug from Dari, Kazari turned and walked with resolute steps towards the waiting Abbot. She could see Quisil standing there already, bag slung from one shoulder, looking excited and nervous, and occasionally waving to a group of people Kazari supposed were her family.

"You're Enda's sister?" Quisil asked as she approached.

"Ah, no. Dari is, but she's my best friend," Kazari stammered.

"And your family?" the Abbot asked.

"They weren't able to attend this morning," she replied, embarrassed, and dropped her eyes. A warm hand on her shoulder made her look up.

"Some families take a while to understand the Lady's call," the Abbot said. "But your friends are pleased for you." She motioned to where Quisil's family had been joined by Dari's, and all of them were now waving at her. Kazari's eyes misted, and she waved back, thankful she wasn't completely alone at this moment, although inside she still felt the absence of her family like a gaping hole in her middle.

"Come," the Abbot said, "it's time to go. Give them one last wave, and a smile, and we'll be off. It's best not to draw these things out."

Kazari waved vigorously, dredging a smile up from somewhere, and turned to go. She'd only taken one step when she was struck in the middle and a pair of arms went around her. It was her brother, Jaden.

"Kaz! I'm sorry! I missed it, but I'll miss you too!" He wasn't really making sense, and his eyes were full of tears and his nose was running, but she hugged him back wordlessly, grateful for his warm presence, but still wishing the rest of her family was there as well. Then the Abbot touched her arm gently, and she began to disentangle herself from him.

"I have to go, Jaden, but I love you, and tell Piddy I love him too – and Mum and Dad."

"I will." His small face was determined as he sniffed, and then rubbed his eyes with the back of his hand.

"And I'll be back sometime." She saw Gweda put her arm around Jaden and apply a hanky to his face as she turned away and walked with the Abbot and Quisil to the others waiting for them. There were two small wagons and a group of horses in the convoy which had stood unnoticed at the side of the square.

"Bags in the wagons, Quisil and Kazari, and then we're off. Andiss has your horses."

"Horses?" Quisil said.

The Abbot smiled. "If you can't ride, don't worry. You'll have learned the basics by the time we reach the Abbey." She took her own horse from another black clad Hunter, and swung easily into its saddle, waving an arm towards the wagons. Kazari hurried over and stowed her bag as she'd been instructed, and then looked around. She had no idea who Andiss was until she heard her name being called again. She hurried over to a well-muscled man, also clad in Hunter's garb. He was shorter than she expected, given his voice, but exuded an air of calm competence.

"Quisil, Kazari, I'm Andiss. Meet your mounts." Two short, shaggy horses stood behind him. They looked placid, Kazari thought hopefully, as Andiss explained the basics of climbing on and steering.

"Don't worry," he said, as he gave Quisil a leg up. "These will follow the others, that's their job. Yours is to learn to stay on top. We won't be moving fast, just walking steadily, but all the Lady's servants learn to ride. We believe the sooner you learn, the better. By the time we reach the Abbey, you'll have the basics. When we stop, I'll show you how to care for your mount and its gear. Kazari, yours is called Stumpy, Quisil, yours is Happy."

After a struggle involving much hopping on one leg while the other was stuck in a stirrup, coupled with some ungainly heaving at the saddle on Stumpy's fortunately patient back, Kazari found herself looking down at her horse's neck. She perched awkwardly on the saddle, smelling the horse's rich scent and feeling the warmth of its body beneath her. She wondered what it might feel like when the beast began to move. Despite feeling as if she was going to immediately fall back off, the warmth of her horsy companion was quite comforting against the chill in the air.

Without warning, Stumpy moved, and she wobbled, reflexively grabbing for the front of the saddle. There wasn't much to hang onto, but he'd only changed his weight from one side to the other, and she relaxed her hold slightly, grimacing at Quisil, who looked almost as alarmed as Kazari felt. There was a whistle from the front of the group and Stumpy lurched forward. Kazari grabbed for the saddle again, fumbling with her reins, and only relaxed when she realised Stumpy was just following the tail of the horse in front of him, and not bolting off into the distance as she'd feared. The rocking motion was soothing, and as they wound their way out of the village, she felt brave enough to turn slightly for one last look at her home.

The pain from her parents' absence was still there, but her memory of the warmth beneath her hand as she declared for the Lady, filled that emptiness a little. Resolutely, she turned her head away, a hot tear sliding down her cheek. She was on her way. The first step of her journey as one of the Lady's servants had begun. Stumpy made a grab for some grass and Kazari instinctively tightened her knees to avoid falling off, as her body tried to balance itself on top of the movement beneath her.

***

Two days later she wasn't sure if she was going to survive that journey. She groaned as she crawled out of her bedding. The muscles in her legs screamed loudly at her, and she was forced to walk her hands up her thighs just to straighten up. Rather than being a faster, simpler mode of transport, Stumpy seemed more an instrument of torture. She crawled exhausted into her bedding each night, feeling as if she could have slept on rocks, and then struggled her way out of it, inch by painful inch the next morning.

"Can you give me a hand," Quisil groaned. The older woman had levered herself to a kneeling position, but seemed uncertain how to proceed next. Kazari reflected that perhaps fifteen-year-old muscles were easier to cope with than, what, forty-year-old ones? She hobbled over and stuck a hand out, groaning herself as her muscles protested further abuse. "Thank you," Quisil said, as she hobbled forward. "I think I'm broken. You'd have thought that years growing vegetables and lifting crates would have left me more prepared for this."

"I don't know that anything could have prepared us for this," Kazari replied darkly. She sighed, and attempted to bend over in order to roll up her bedding so that she could stow it in the wagon. Each day began the same way. They packed their bedding, ate a simple breakfast, prepared by an initiate from the Growers sept, while the Abbot read from the Writings. Then they mounted their horses and travelled to the next village. There was now a small group of potential initiates travelling with them. Kazari still spent most of her time talking to Quisil, clinging to the one last familiar part of home, but she'd gradually met all of the newcomers.

All of them seemed pleasant, but there was a sense of incompleteness, and shyness. They'd declared, they were on the first steps of their journey, but as of yet their futures were still undecided. Kazari wondered which sept she'd end up in. The Lady's servants were a colourful lot, she reflected, with their formal robes declaring the sept they belonged to for all to see, while their jewelled pendants in the same colour as their robes sparkled on their chests.

Around her, she could see that most of her fellows were also having the same issues that she and Quisil were struggling with. Those who'd already been part of the group when she'd joined it had assured her that the soreness would pass, but Kazari wasn't certain she wasn't becoming crippled for life. She'd slowly become accustomed to Stumpy's gait, and she could feel the beginnings of some of the understandings of the art of riding tickling her mind, but when she watched Andiss, or the Abbot, she realised that what she thought she knew was barely scratching the surface.

Each day, Andiss spent some time instructing the group of new declarees. It had never occurred to her that she'd need to learn to ride to serve the Lady, even though each year she'd seen the Abbot arrive on horseback. She'd always assumed that she'd be sitting in a wagon. Clearly, she'd been wrong.

"The Lady's servants must be able to go wherever she requires, sometimes at speed," Andiss had explained when Quisil had asked. "Horses are the best way. They're fast, efficient, and friendly." And then he'd demonstrated just how fast they could be, and that they could jump. Kazari couldn't imagine how he stayed on. Even the thought of moving that fast hurt her sore muscles.

Slowly, she began to warm up, and her limbs moved slightly less stiffly. She still stifled a groan as she heaved her bedding into the wagon before she joined the others for breakfast. After the morning reading, the Abbot addressed them all.

"We'll be spending another four days on the road. By then most of your sore muscles will have settled." She smiled, and Kazari realised she must have been observing the new declarees. Not much escaped the Abbot. "We have another three villages to visit, and then we'll head for the Abbey. You'll meet the rest of the group there. In the meantime, I'll be riding with each of you at some point during the next couple of days. Don't be concerned, it's part of the process. We like to get to know our new initiates."

After breakfast, Kazari noticed a new rider approaching. A Hunter, she swung her horse in beside Andiss and handed him a message. Andiss broke its seal while Kazari looked on curiously. She wondered idly how Andiss managed to stay in the saddle and steer his horse, all the while not touching the reins, as he read the message. A moment later, he sent his horse cantering ahead to the Abbot's side.

Half an hour later Kazari saw the messenger with the Abbot. The Abbot was talking, and with a nod the messenger left the column on a branching side road. She looked tired, Kazari thought, wondering what might have brought the woman to the Abbot out here in the countryside.

Later that day, the Abbot's bay horse drew alongside Kazari's shorter horse. "Kazari, how are you?"

"Sore," she admitted, looking up at the Abbot.

"Well, as I said, that will pass." There was a moments silence. "Declaration day was a bit of an emotional upheaval for you, wasn't it?"

Kazari dropped her eyes. "Yes."

"The Lady says in her Writings: 'The one who follows Me, though forsaken by their loved ones, will be repaid a thousandfold on the day of reward. She is steadfast and true, and beloved of Me.' That probably seems little comfort for you now, but I promise you that the Lady is true to her word."

They rode in silence for a few moments, while Kazari tried to figure out what to say. So many things flashed through her mind – her parents arguing with her, her little brother's hug, and Dari's friendship.

"Thank you, my lady Abbess," was all she could manage.

"Kazari, although you are correct to use my title in public, among ourselves you may call me Ailani. Ailani means 'first' or 'chief'. But it's an informal title, and it's to be used only when you're with others of the Order, and at all times at the Abbey."

"I would be privileged, Ailani," Kazari said carefully. "And I'm usually called Kaz, by my friends."

The Abbot, though garbed as a Hunter, was much warmer in person than she could ever have imagined. Kazari had always imagined that Hunters would be taciturn and reserved, possibly unfriendly, because of their role as Albatar's protectors.

The Abbot smiled. "I hope you'll find a true home with us here, Kaz. Now, have you thought about the sept that you believe the Lady has in mind for you?"

"I'm pretty good at growing things, and I have done well in reasoning and logic at school, however, I haven't had any firm indication from the Lady." She frowned worriedly. "Should I have had?" She played nervously with her reins, and when Stumpy snorted she relaxed her hands.

"No, not at all. The Lady will make it clear before the day of your initiation. Sometimes our initiates come with a clear leading from the Lady, and occasionally an initiate thinks they should be in one sept but the Lady has other ideas." She smiled, and Kazari had the impression she was enjoying a private joke.

"She will? How?"

"We'll explain when you arrive at the Abbey, but the Lady always ensures you end up in the right sept, even if it's not quite what you expected. In the meantime, I can see that you and Stumpy are getting along well. Make sure you take every opportunity to learn more about riding from Andiss. And please, feel free to ask him any questions you might have, or address any concerns." She smiled once again, and then rode off towards Quisil.

Kazari's heart felt lighter as she watched the Abbot's mount move away. The Abbot wasn't what she'd expected, but she seemed somehow more . . . real now. She wondered how the Lady would show her her sept. She ran them through her mind. The Hunters, charged with the protection of Albatar, and the fight against the gorgones. The Judicars, who administered justice across the land. The Growers, who tended to the fields and orchards, and grew the medicinals. The Advisers, who taught and sat at the right hands of the city and village lords, and even the Kings and Queens of Albatar. The Navigators, who explored the lands and seas, and guided caravans and travellers. The Intercessors, who prayed, often administered the Lady's chapels, and were frequently teachers; and the Healers who, in the Lady's name, ran the infirmaries and ministered to the sick.

She'd always felt somewhat inclined towards the Growers or the Judicars, but apparently the Lady would make it obvious to her somehow, probably within the next few days. She wondered how she'd know. Although the process of declaration was well known, how people ended up in certain septs was unknown to the general public, apart from 'the Lady directs us,' which Kazari had always felt was somewhat vague. She supposed she'd always thought it would be something like a personal choice or more likely, perhaps, an examination of some sort during the early days of initiation.

She rode on, looking around, as Stumpy's familiar pace slowly began to soothe her sore muscles. It wouldn't be long now, and all the speculation in the world wouldn't change the outcome. She did wish she had some kind of inkling about her future though.

Chapter Three: Before

Kazari woke in a strange bed. She woke instantaneously, feeling rested and alive, but wondering what had woken her. Then the bell rang again, and she realised she'd heard it on the edges of the strange dream she'd just had. The dream had been full of confused colours – rainbow hues swirling around her. It had been similar to, but more vivid than the dreams she'd had before declaring for the Lady. There'd been a voice too, but she couldn't understand what it had been saying, and just when it seemed to have been on the verge of becoming understandable – the sound of the bell had woken her.

Pushing her hair off her face, she struggled to a sitting position, seeing the others around her doing the same thing. They were her travelling companions, those she'd met along the way since her declaration for the Lady. Her eyes were caught by her bed's curiously carved bedhead. Seven gems, obviously representing the seven septs, made an arc across the top of the wood. Last night they'd sparkled in the lamplight as she'd collapsed tiredly into the bed's soft embrace. This morning they flickered and glowed in random patterns. She wondered what they meant and, if they continued, how she'd sleep with their flickering. Looking around the bunk room, Kazari could see that each of the other bedheads was the same.

"Up, please," said a commanding voice. "Use the washrooms, and then dress. You'll follow me to breakfast once you're all assembled. Quickly please, you have a lot to learn in the next few days."

Kazari looked around for Quisil as she headed for the washrooms to make her ablutions. It had been late when they'd arrived at the Abbey, and during the confusion of arrival, she'd lost track of the woman. She couldn't see her anywhere, so washed quickly.

Rummaging through her meagre possessions, she realised she was on her last set of clean things. Everything else smelled strongly of horse and woodsmoke. She made her bed, tucking the white sheet and grey blanket in neatly, and fluffed up the pillow as her father had taught her. A pang of homesickness and regret struck, and she tried to distract herself by re-plaiting her curly hair. As she separated the strands and wove them together, she felt as though the last vestiges of home were deserting her. The memory of Jaden's arms tightening around her threatened to bring her to tears again.

"Follow me," their guide said, attracting their attention. "And as you walk, look around, read the stories on the walls, and feel the history of your people surround you."

The walk was quite long, but Kazari didn't notice, fascinated by the unfolding story in the wall art. Some of it was ancient, worn down by the passing of time, while other parts seemed quite new, all done in a variety of styles. Through it all, the rainbow hues of the seven septs shone. Gems hung at the necks of the major characters, and their faceted faces bathed the candidates in many hues. She wondered how the gems maintained their steady glow, but eventually decided that it didn't really matter, and allowed herself to be drawn into the familiar story.

She saw the creation of Albatar, born of the destruction of the world during the Gorgone War, and now protected by the Lady. She was reminded of the great battle that had raged between humanity and the gorgones – destroyers of minds, souls, and physical bodies. The War had occurred because humanity had lost its way after the founding of the world, had forgotten the Lady's gentle songs and her loving kindness;

and had brought destruction upon themselves by craving things and power rather than following the Lady's teachings.

The first mural reminded the candidates that greed was born of selfishness. That the gifts of the Lady were for the good of all – wealth and prosperity were there so that all might share – not so that one might rise above another, controlling and manipulating those beneath them for their own profit. Personal wealth was not wrong, but it was important it was to be used for the good of all.

The next mural showed the Second King. He'd begun as a ruler adored by all, but that very adoration had led him to believe that he was better than everyone else. In his quest for aggrandisement and more power, he'd opened a gateway to Beyond, allowing the first of the gorgones into the world.

A stark painting showed the beginnings of the disaster. It was charcoal black, full of hidden ghouls and ghosts, preying upon the unprotected minds of an unsuspecting people. It was followed by a montage of the creeping danger, as greed and hatred spiralled out of control, right up until the reign of the eleventh King, when the rampant greed of the people allowed the first of the greater gorgones through from Beyond. It was quickly followed by others who took corporeal form, and the Gorgone War began.

Against the backdrop of disaster, the gem pendants of the Lady's servants shone brightly. Where the gorgones marauded, the Hunters and Navigators fought them and guided those who wished to follow a better way to safety. Where people turned from their wickedness, the Judicars, Growers, and Intercessors led them into the Lady's ways. The Advisers remained to guide them. The Healers strove alongside the Hunters and Navigators wherever there was need, often giving their lives to protect the sick and injured.

A final montage showed the Navigators leading the faithful through the mountains and into the Lady's sanctuary – Albatar. There, the faithful built a home far from the ravages of the gorgones, but even Albatar was still assailed by the gorgones at times, despite the mountainous boundaries and icy passes that protected it from the outer world. Rarely did Kazari's people venture into the outer world. They hadn't abandoned it, Kazari knew. Every ten years, a group from the Abbey left Albatar to serve in the wider world, seeking those who wished to learn a better way. Some returned; most did not, but some of those they'd contacted did. Small trickles of people regularly found their way through the mountains to safety in Albatar, guided by the Lady and her Navigators and Hunters who patrolled the borders.

As the group entered the dining hall, Kazari saw that the walls were covered with images of those rescued. They were depicted in general terms – tall, short, fat, thin, old and young. People of many races and many ages, yet all one within the Lady's domain.

At the head table, the Abbot rose. "Join me in giving thanks to the Lady for her bounty." All those in the room stood and sang their thanks. Kazari was swept away in the sound of the massed voices. The words were familiar but the tune was not, so she didn't sing but just listened and let the words run through her mind, conveying her own gratitude.

As they sat, she found herself seated between two other youngsters, and opposite a man wearing the aquamarine pendant of a Navigator. He was old – very old, she realised, but clearly not decrepit, as she found his keen blue eyes surveying her and her companions with interest over the large porridge pot on the trestle table.

"Welcome, candidates," he said, smiling at them. "Don't stint on your breakfast. You've a busy day ahead." He picked up a ladle and began filling bowls. "And I'll be spending part of it teaching you what you'll need to know in three days' time when you're initiated. Here – eat." He waved a bowl at the boy on Kazari's left, and then filled another.

"Thank you," she said as he handed it to her. "I'm Kazari."

"Oh yes, the Abbot mentioned you," he said. "I'm Elliam."

The Abbot had mentioned her? "Mentioned me?" she asked nervously.

"Yes, said that you'd had the gumption to declare even without your family there." He ladled another bowl and handed it to the girl on Kazari's other side. She could feel both her companions listening avidly to Elliam. "Well done. You must feel the Lady's call very clearly."

Kazari blushed.

"I'm sure it was no clearer than anyone else's," she mumbled, and then blushed again.

"Ah but it takes a bit of gumption to declare and not abstain," Elliam went on. "Most years we get abstainers from prior years joining us. A lot of them bowed to their parents' wishes and abstained, and then declared a few years later. What about you two?" He waved the ladle at the boy and girl on either side of Kazari.

"I abstained last year," the boy said. "But this year my parents realised that I wasn't going to change my mind. I'm Abel, by the way."

"Charla," the girl said, pointing to her chest. "Mine were just proud. It must have been hard for you two."

"This year was fine," replied Abel, "But if I'd gone last year it might have been very different. Good on you, Kazari."

"Call me Kaz," she replied, and looked up at him. "It wasn't much fun. I'm hoping they'll have forgiven me by the time I get to see them again." She spooned up some porridge and blew on it to hide her embarrassment. It was thick, filling, and warming. She smiled at Abel and Charla; it was nice to talk to someone her own age. Further down the table, she could see Quisil, chatting enthusiastically with several older candidates. She liked the woman, but she was a lot older than Kazari. Perhaps she, Abel and Charla might end up in the same sept. The thought warmed her.

As the morning meal drew to a close, Andiss stood. Kazari wondered where the Abbot had gone. Her place at the top table was empty. "Welcome to our new candidates. Today marks the first of your three days of preparation. After breakfast, you'll join us all in the sanctuary for Morning-song, and then you'll proceed to orientation. Elliam, would you stand up please?" The elderly Navigator stood and waved a hand. "Elliam will take you through the procedures for the ceremony itself. For now, you just have to know one thing. Many of you will have arrived with preconceived ideas of which sept you will join. This is *not* a foregone conclusion. You may have noticed the bedheads in the candidates' hall?"

Kazari nodded with the other candidates.

"The Lady chooses your sept, not you, nor even any of us. It may well be the one you've wanted or believed was for you – it often happens like that. However, just as often, the Lady has something else in mind. She knows your path, and she will not choose wrongly. Over the next days, you will dream – dreams of colours – rainbows perhaps, or gem studded jewellery, or even the night sky sprinkled with multihued stars. It varies from person to person. But one morning you will awake, knowing your sept. Your dreams will have told you, and the gemstone above your head will be lit so that all will know that the Lady has spoken."

Well that explained the dream, then, Kazari thought. She wondered what the Lady would choose for her. She'd thought perhaps she was suited to be a Grower, or a Judicar, but it didn't sound that simple. And what if she ended up in a sept she didn't want? What if she ended up as an Adviser? She couldn't imagine being confident enough to provide advice to anyone, let alone Albatar's secular rulers, despite what she'd told her parents. Heavens, she wasn't confident enough to advise *herself* half the time.

She exchanged surprised glances with Charla and Abel, and wondered if they felt as unsettled as she did.

A mug of something hot was placed in front of her as Andiss continued. "Be aware that the Lady's choice is final. You may withdraw from the Abbey if you find her choice unpalatable, but if you do, it is as if you have chosen not to declare. You are still part of the Lady's people, but you will *not* become her servant." There was a finality in his voice that surprised Kazari, but which she supposed was appropriate. And then she began to worry what she might do, if she found the topaz, or the amethyst, or the aquamarine glowing above her bed. They were septs she'd never considered. Andiss spoke again.

"Each intake, the Lady makes certain choices. There are patterns. There is always at least one Hunter, and always two or three Navigators. Do not be fearful if these are choices you've not considered – the Lady only gives the choices you are suited for. The rest are usually evenly distributed between the other septs, except for the Advisers. The Lady chooses them most carefully. Sometimes it is several years between choices. And throughout Albatar, in all the Lady's Abbeys. the same proportions hold true."

All around her, Kazari could hear hushed whispers from her fellow candidates. Clearly, it was not what they'd expected either.

Lady, help me dream the right dreams, she thought. *And help me want the right things.* And what would her parents say if she reappeared only a week or two after she'd left against their wishes? She almost panicked at the thought.

Lady help me! The prayer became a mantra as she moved through the day. Every time she was with one of the other candidates, the subject came up. It flavoured every conversation, and as they prepared for bed that evening, Kazari could see more than one candidate apprehensively eyeing their headboard.

"I think I'm almost scared to go to sleep," Charla said as they washed together. Her bed was several rows over from

Kazari's, somewhat to her regret, because she'd found the other girl's company reminiscent of Dari's.

"I'm tired though," Kazari said. "Do you reckon they worked us so hard that we'd have no choice but to sleep?"

"I think you're probably right," Quisil said, passing behind them. "I can't imagine why they'd have us doing some of the things we've done today otherwise."

Kazari nodded, smiling ruefully. They'd been taken for a long walk around the Abbey – several times. And they'd been marched through the Abbey's winding corridors and twisting passages from one end to the other. After that they'd scrubbed the sanctuary and polished all the candlesticks, despite their already gleaming cleanliness. That had been between the lessons provided by Elliam. And the meditations! Every two hours, they'd been required to sit quietly in the sanctuary for half an hour, praying and asking the Lady's guidance.

She was almost as tired as she had been when they'd arrived the previous night. She brushed her hair again, enjoying the feel of the brush moving through her long locks. It wouldn't be long until they'd be gone. It was part of the ceremony, now only two days away.

"We won't be as tired tomorrow, though, Elliam said we'll spend most of the time in quiet contemplation instead of working all day," Kazari sighed. "What if we don't find out tomorrow – how will we sleep then?"

"Who knows," Charla said. "Maybe the meditation will help?"

"Hmm," Kazari replied, slightly sceptically. "Did you dream last night?"

"Sort of. It was a bit confused though."

Kazari nodded. "Mine too. It was full of colours, and a voice."

"Did it say anything?"

"The bell drowned it out," Kazari made a face. "I'm guessing that I didn't miss anything because nothing was glowing in the morning."

"I wonder if anyone already knows?"

"If it didn't look so obvious, I'd take a quick jog around the bunk room now," Kazari said.

"Ha!" Charla said. "I bet it's the first thing everyone does tomorrow!"

As Kazari pulled her covers up, the lantern light showed nearly everyone looking nervously around the room at the bedheads they could see. None of the ones near her were lit with anything more than random flickers. She tilted her head back and looked at her own – the same. Maybe she'd know in the morning.

"Lamps out, now," Elliam said from the darkness. "You'll be woken by the chime in the morning. Sleep well." She heard the suspicion of a chuckle in his tone and as she blew out her lamp, she was tempted to make a face in his direction. Chiding herself for being childish, she rolled onto her back, and tried to compose herself for sleep. It was difficult.

Eventually, she rolled onto her side and tried not to look at the flickers of the multihued gemstones around her. It didn't work, but she discovered that if she unfocused her eyes and relaxed her body, the shifting colours were mesmerising and quite relaxing. She sighed and hoped she'd eventually fall asleep.

The following morning, she struggled out of a dream of stars falling from the sky. They'd begun multihued, but towards the end of the dream, only one remained. It was purple, glowing and vivid. She sat bolt upright, sweating, and swung around to look at the gems on her bedhead. They were still flickering, and she sighed in relief. Perhaps she'd dream a different colour the next evening. Perhaps that was how it worked. In the next bed over, an emerald shone steadily from the headboard above the sleeping form. Clearly, the Lady had chosen the girl to be a Grower.

She looked around. About a third of the bedheads were lit with steadily glowing gems. She could see people stirring around her. Nearly every one of them twisted around to look at their own gems as soon as they were awake. She saw sighs of relief, occasional sighs of resignation, and once an exclamation of "Yes!" She looked around to see Abel, three rows over, grinning at her.

"What lit?" she mouthed at him, mindful that the waking chime hadn't yet sounded.

He beckoned her over, and she slid out of bed and tiptoed towards him, trying not to wake anyone else. The aquamarine gem glowed brightly from his headboard. "Aren't you a bit frightened?" she asked. Navigators patrolled the borders, close to any gorgone incursion, when they weren't guiding caravans or traders.

"A little," he admitted, "but it's what I've always wanted."

"I'm still waiting," she said. "Maybe tomorrow." And then tried to dismiss the purple star from her mind. It was only the second night anyway. Perhaps she'd dream of green trees, or the blue of a deep lake tonight.

As she breakfasted, the image of the vast purple star filled her mind. It had been a very vivid dream. "I beg your pardon?" she said in response to what had clearly been a question from Charla. "Sorry, didn't sleep well."

"I was just wondering whether you dreamed last night, Kaz. Abel said he dreamed of the ocean, and of glacial lakes, and then of starlight and storms. When he woke he already knew."

"Sort of," Kazari admitted, "but it was still confused." Well it had been confused, until the last star. "Mine had lots of coloured stars," she went on, deliberately avoiding mentioning the purple one at the end. "What about you?"

"Well, I did dream, and there were colours, mostly blue and white, and icy," Charla frowned. "I wonder if that means I'll become an Intercessor, or a Judicar?"

Across the table, Elliam was listening. "The colours can vary. I saw a glacial river, myself. But that was after two solid nights of dreaming of snow and ice and water. Until your dreams are consumed by the colour, you won't know. I'd wake each morning horrified by the thought of becoming part of the Judiciary. I was extremely relieved to wake with the aquamarine lit." He wriggled his eyebrows at Charla and Kazari. "Don't worry. All the worrying in the world won't hurry the Lady, or change her mind." He applied himself to his porridge, and Kazari looked at the aquamarine suspended on its chain from Abel's neck.

His hand kept reaching up to touch it, almost as if he was still surprised it was there.

"By the way, don't worry about not being able to sleep again," Elliam said. "We're breaking your meditations up with shifting rocks today." Charla groaned and Kazari made a face, while the old Navigator laughed into his porridge.

Later, she sat cross-legged in the sanctuary on a cushion as Elliam had taught them, trying to still her mind. A ring of gemstones behind the altar flickered with gentle light. She focused on them, then let her eyes relax, letting the flickers of light lull her slightly. *Lady,* she prayed, *please* . . . But the words seemed empty. She didn't know what she was entreating the Lady about. Elliam had said that the Lady made her own choices, and that sometimes those choices didn't fit a candidate's expectations. She took his words as comfort – he'd thought he might end up as a Judicar, but instead he'd ended up as a Navigator. Perhaps the purple star meant nothing at all.

She wriggled slightly on her cushion, trying not to disturb Charla next to her. The other girl was motionless, eyes closed and face serene. She envied her composure. Sighing silently, she returned her gaze to the flickers again, letting the emotion within her take the place of a formal prayer. The Lady would understand. Of course she would, but even as she closed her own eyes, flickers of amethyst tickled the edges of her vision.

Later, at dinner, she looked around surreptitiously, trying to see what colour gems hung around her fellow candidates' necks. Despite her childish awe at the Lady's Hunters, she'd never considered that the Lady might want her as one. She hoped against hope that one of her fellows would already be wearing the Hunters' amethyst, but no-one was.

Chapter Four: Ceremony

The haze of purple on the edges of her vision receded more slowly this time. Each time Kazari woke, it took longer. Now, on the third morning, she lay there quietly for a few moments, willing the haze to subside before she rose. She didn't want it. Didn't want the issues that came with it – or the responsibilities. Perhaps if she pretended she'd fallen asleep again, no-one would ever know.

She knew it was a stupid hope, anyone awake would already know. Three nights in a row, and the gemstone on the head of her bed would be glowing brightly.

"Kazari." The voice was gentle, and she thought she heard a hint of compassion in it.

Kazari opened her eyes reluctantly, to see the Abbot sitting by her bedside, hands clasped in her lap, and cloak spread on the back of the chair. Warm brown eyes looked down on her, slightly saddened. "So, it's to be you, Kazari."

"Does it have to be?" she asked.

"You know the rules, Kazari. The ceremony will be tomorrow, and then your group will proceed to sept initiation."

"Why couldn't it have been emerald? Or even sapphire?" she asked plaintively.

"Your gemstone is yours, not because you want it, but because of who you are," the Abbot told her. "Our choice is whether to serve or not, but the terms of that service are not ours. They are determined by the Lady. She knows our hearts."

Kazari pushed herself up, looking directly at the woman in front of her. The amethyst pendant hung, vividly violet, upon the black of the Abbot's clothing. She was clothed now as Kazari would one day be – leather boots, black form fitting shirt and trousers topped with a black leather jerkin. A matching belt, hung with sheaths, sat snugly around her waist, and Kazari could see the arm guard around the Abbot's left forearm peeking out from under her sleeve as she leaned forward to push Kazari's hair gently off her forehead.

"I did not wish for the amethyst either, Kazari, but now, I am glad."

Kazari looked up, surprised. It was a rare admission to hear that from the head of her Order.

"No-one wishes to become a Hunter, but the Lady sees more than our mortal eyes. One day you will know that the Sapphire of Justice, or the Emerald of Growth would not have served either you, or the Lady, as well as the Hunter's Amethyst."

"But the road will be hard, Ailani."

"Kazari, the road is always hard, no matter your path. Life tests us all, but the Lady walks with us to end of our journey."

Kazari nodded soberly. The Abbot's words rang true, even if her heart quailed at the thought of the trials ahead.

"If you're ready?" the Abbot said.

Kazari nodded slowly. "I will try to do my best, then." As she said the words, she hoped she'd be able to live up to them.

She bowed her head and the Abbot slipped the purple pendant over her head. Her course was set.

Across the room, she could see Charla, looking as stunned as she. The golden topaz of the Advisers sat on its golden chain on her chest, and the head of the Adviser's sept sat at her bedside. Their eyes met, and Kazari could see that her new friend's eyes were wide with shock. Maybe being a Hunter was easier than being trained to advise the rulers of Albatar. Or perhaps not. Or perhaps they were only two sides of the same coin.

On the day of initiation, Kazari woke early, too on edge to sleep long. Her eyes were scratchy, and her brain frazzled. She pushed the white sheet and grey blanket back and swung her legs heavily over the edge of the bed. Around her, she could see her fellow initiates stirring sleepily. One, a tall boy on the end of the row of beds was sitting, staring into space with his head in his hands. The girl next to Kazari snored gently, the air whistling softly through her lips. Kazari envied her her composure, along with the green gem winking from the head of her bed. She looked back at her own headboard, wincing as the amethyst gem glowed serenely back at her, matching the one swinging from its leather thong around her neck. Her stomach clenched briefly, before she breathed out slowly and forced herself to relax.

The waking chime sounded, and she pushed herself to her feet to begin her preparations. Hastening to the washroom, she washed carefully, making sure her hair was clean and combed, glancing at it briefly in the tiny mirror above the sink. It was a farewell of sorts. She fingered the dark curls wistfully. They'd taken a long time to grow, but she'd known she'd be sacrificing them once she'd set herself on the path of the Lady's service.

The room, as prescribed, was silent. Each initiate went about their morning tasks in silence, bound not to speak again until the evening meal. Kazari laid her white inductee's robe on her freshly made bed. The soft weave stood out sharply against the dull grey blanket, and she felt her stomach quiver once again. The bell gave a single chime, and she dropped to her left knee, bowing her head in prayer as Elliam had instructed.

Help me, please, Lady, she beseeched, *for I am afraid that the path is too hard, or that I might prove too weak.* Her prayer echoed silently inside her own mind, and for a moment her resolution wavered, but then she squeezed her eyes shut more tightly, and breathed out deliberately, lifting one hand to touch the amethyst on her chest. It warmed briefly under her touch, and tears sprang to her eyes. It had been a long time since the Lady's presence had been so close and so clear. Her hand tightened, and she let the tears slide slowly down her cheeks. Elliam's instructions to them all had been precise – emotion was to be embraced today. An initiate must come before the Lady and her Order, free of pretension, free of concealment, and true in purpose.

Kazari might still wish that another gem had lit for her, so she was free to express her misgivings, and to demonstrate honesty as she pondered her future. As an initiate, she must come before the rest of the Order freely sharing of herself, so that they in turn, might share freely with her. She felt naked and vulnerable, despite her clothed state. She kneeled on the hard floor, praying, until the chime sounded again, and then she shed the clothes that still smelled of home, for the final time, and replaced them with the white robe.

The stone floor was chill beneath her feet as she stood, hands clasped behind her back as she'd been taught. From the corners of her eyes she could see other pale faces, and a few trembling knees. She wanted to look around, but she kept her eyes forward as she'd been told to. The waiting drew out minute by minute, and Kazari's toes began to feel like little lumps of ice. She stilled an involuntary urge to shiver, by willpower alone, and tried to relax her shoulders.

"It is time, initiates," a voice intoned. "Until the next chime, you have your last opportunity to depart and return to your old lives. Pray fervently, think wisely, and consider carefully. The way of the Lady is hard, but once your feet are on her path, there is no turning back. It is no shame, even now, for you to discern that her way is not for you. If such is your choice, speak no words, but simply depart by the red door. Your clothing will be returned, and you may leave this place freely."

Kazari prayed. Prayed as she'd never prayed before, seeking, searching her heart, and wishing with all her might that the choices before her might be taken away, but the amethyst on her chest warmed once again, and, as tears welled in her eyes once more, she knew her choice was made. She took a slow, ragged breath, and then closed her eyes briefly, allowing the tears to trickle warmly down her face.

A flurry of white distracted her. The girl with the emerald gem hurried past, and Kazari caught a glimpse of a panicked face and staring eyes. Her peaceful slumber of only an hour ago was now meaningless. There was the quiet snick of the red door opening and closing, and then she was gone. Once again, time passed slowly. Twice more, the red door opened and closed, and just when the waiting had become almost unbearable, the chime sounded again.

"The Lady awaits you. You will follow the diamond lights into the sanctuary."

Relieved that the waiting was over, Kazari filed into line behind the boy from the end of the row. He was very tall, she realised, and his sapphire glowed a bright, deep-blue upon his chest. She felt tiny, behind his height, as they walked at the prescribed pace, following the lights ahead.

The hallway outside was cold, and Kazari wondered if she'd be able to feel her toes at all by the end of the ceremony.

"Keep the Lady foremost in your thoughts," the voice intoned, and she blushed, and tried to concentrate on things more appropriate than her cold toes. The diamond lights lit one by one as they paced, each stride measured and solemn. As they neared the sanctuary, Kazari felt the beginnings of a nervous flutter in her stomach, and she had to concentrate to keep her mind from flitting from possibility to possibility.

The initiates knew the formal responses to their vows, but the form of the ceremony was unknown, as was the training ahead. They knew the outcomes of their choices – what they would become once they were trained – but nothing of the process itself, except it was long, and arduous.

The last diamond light before the sanctuary remained unlit, and the line paused outside the huge, ironbound doors. Kazari took a deep breath, letting it out slowly as she waited, and tried to ignore her now frozen toes. A Hunter. That was her future. It would be a future filled with challenge and hardship, that she knew for certain. Hunters were legendary, the most skillful and bravest of those chosen by the Lady, yet they faced the greatest dangers that her people knew, and Kazari had never considered that the Lady would choose her, a short, chunky girl, to become one.

They had told them that there was always at least one Hunter chosen from each initiate group in each Abbey – but her? She wondered what would have happened had she chosen the red door – would someone else have had to take the amethyst? Or would this group have been without their Hunter initiate? So many questions buzzed around her head, and this was not the moment for them. She should be more reverent, more solemn, not giddy with too many thoughts. She tried to compose herself again, trying to focus on the Lady, while her mind wondered how Charla, Abel, and Quisil were faring.

The last diamond light lit with a brilliance that eclipsed all the others, and the great doors swung open as the drum began. The timbre was deep, measured, and solemn. In time with the beat, Kazari followed the tall boy into the sanctuary. She'd been there before, but not like this. The enormous room was lit only by the brilliance of the glowing gems set around its perimeter, and it was full of the Order, divided by gem tone, standing in sept ranks, under their sigils on the sanctuary's walls.

Kazari was unable to prevent herself from seeking out the Hunters, standing below the crossed knives near the altar. They were the smallest group in the sanctuary, black robed and solemn, but even now, they seemed imbued with the potential for movement, and several bore obvious facial scars, while one leaned on a crutch. Her stomach clenched, and her knees quaked again, wondering what they thought of the girl in white who bore the amethyst of their calling.

Or even what the others around the room thought. What her parents would think when they heard – the names and septs of the new initiates were posted in every village and town after the ceremony. The beat of the drum was joined by the sound of massed voices, singing in tight harmony. Kazari had harboured no illusions that she would be chosen to join them. Her voice had been described as 'passable', but her pitch had been called 'execrable,' with a grimace for emphasis, by the music master in her village. Still, she could enjoy the delight that the music, despite its solemnity, brought and felt her spirits rise as they sang of the Lady's goodness.

As the initiates lined up before the altar, the music stopped, and another chime sounded. This one was deeper toned, and possessed a resonance that seemed to linger in the air. Kazari felt herself drawn into the sound until it was singing through her whole body, and the gem on her chest began to vibrate in time with its harmonics. Her mind stilled, and at last her thoughts ceased their scattered scrabbling.

"Stand in the Lady's presence, initiates, and prepare to take your final vows." The words sank one by one into Kazari's heart, and the seriousness of the moment struck her to her core. Her life would no longer be her own, but one completely dedicated to the Lady's service. Where she sent her, Kazari would go, and what she commanded, Kazari would do. She would be tied irrevocably to the Order until the day of her final breath – and for a Hunter, that might be sooner than some.

Focused now on only the moment before her, Kazari heard the voice at a distance. The chime's sound seemed to be one with her body, and her eyes were drawn inexorably to the light above the altar. The great ring formed of all the gem tones of the Order spat brightness as they illuminated all at once. The whole sanctuary filled with the glory of the Lady's presence, woven in the light of her gemstones. The amethyst on Kazari's chest warmed, and the choir's voices rang exultantly through the air, and then she was lost in the wonder and the beauty of it all. Nothing had prepared her for this moment.

A voice rang in her mind. "Do you, freely, and of your own will, vow your life in service to Me?"

"I do." The response burst from Kazari with a passion she hadn't known she'd owned.

"Will you be My Hunter, forever and always, forcing the darkness back, and preserving this land from its enemies?"

"I will."

"Will you promise to stand fast in the face of evil, bringing My light to the forsaken, and fight even to your last breath to protect those under your care?"

"I will." And she would. She had no idea how to, or even whether she ever would, but Kazari knew in that moment that she was the Lady's Hunter forever.

"Then you are Mine, joined with Me, and you will serve and learn among your brothers and sisters from this moment on."

The light died, and Kazari fell to her knees, exhausted and trembling, yet still full of the wonder of the Lady's immediate presence.

"As you have promised, you now belong to the Lady. Please kneel and pledge yourselves before your peers."

Kazari looked around, slightly startled. She wasn't the only one on her knees, but there were still many initiates standing. They kneeled to join their companions and then all bowed their heads. Footsteps sounded on the stone floor, and then the voice spoke again.

"Begin."

As the first lock of her hair fell to the ground, Kazari felt an almost physical wrench as with each snip the ties to her old life; her family, her friends, her school, was severed. Each new snip sounded loudly in her ears as waves of her hair fell to the cool floor beneath her knees. Once again the drum sounded; this one was higher pitched, snapping its sound through the air like a whip crack. Again the tears fell, almost in time with her gleaming curls, severing Kazari's ties one by one until the last lock fell, and her old life was just a memory.

It was gone more than figuratively. Until the Abbot decided it was time, Kazari could not see her family or her friends. Until the day she was confirmed as a full Hunter, she would remain separate from them, set apart by the Lady's will. The air was cool on her exposed neck, and Kazari shivered. She felt inadequate, alone and feeble, weak in her body, and limited in her mind, until the warmth of the amethyst reminded her of the glory of just a few minutes ago.

She wondered if it would remain warm forever now, but a faint hint of amusement in her mind both startled her and suggested otherwise. She almost toppled over, and was hard-pressed to keep her hands where they should be, and not grasping the gemstone. The warmth remained, though, as the voice spoke once again.

"Stand, and turn, and let the assembly see you as you now are, part of us all, and pledged to the Lady, now and forever."

Kazari stood stiffly, and then turned, and for the first time was able to look around at the assembled Order. The choir, in its rainbow hued robes, sang, as the initiates stood, and she looked out at the sapphire bearing Judicar, the emerald garbed multitudes of the Growers sept, and the white clad priests of the Lady's Intercessors. The smaller septs stood, no less confidently than the larger ones, in the robes of their gemstones – the golden topaz, bright aquamarine, and ruby red of the Advisers, Navigators and Healers. Only the black clad Hunters stood slightly apart, their amethyst pendants the only brightness among the unrelieved black of their stark uniforms.

"Before you stand the initiates, now our brothers and sisters in truth, welcome them into your midst!" The voice spoke in ringing tones, and from each sept, robed figures strode forward to welcome their new members with an outstretched hand. Kazari found her hand being clasped by the Abbot herself. "Maintain your silence initiates, until your sept gives you leave to speak. Return with them and follow their directions. In the name of the Lady, you are welcomed into our fold. Remember your vows and stay true to them always."

The Abbot turned on her heel and beckoned, and slightly dumbfounded, Kazari followed her towards the rest of the Hunters.

What seemed like a multitude of questions buzzed in her mind again, but as instructed, she remained silent, although she had to clench her teeth to stop some of the questions bursting out. She felt as if every eye was upon her as she marched down to the Hunters. They stood there silently, watching, and Kazari quailed once again under their combined gazes, yet the warmth of the amethyst reassured her slightly. It was as if the Lady walked with her.

She straightened her shoulders and tried to walk confidently behind the Abbot. With each step, the light within the sanctuary dimmed, until they were walking in almost complete darkness. The Hunters' black robes blended into the dimness until all that was left were the glowing pendants around each Hunter's neck. As Kazari approached, the group closed around her and then she found herself facing the Abbot by the wall, just below the sigil, but shielded from the other septs' views. The light was faint, and amethyst, illuminating only the wall.

"Watch, Kazari. And then follow." The Abbot took her pendant and placed the bottom of the gemstone in a tiny indentation in the stone wall, directly below the sigil, and then the stone on which she and Kazari stood, moved downwards, softly and silently, and they vanished into the pitch blackness.

CHAPTER FIVE: SURPRISES

Momentarily panicked, Kazari was hard-pressed not to let out a squeak of fear, or to clutch at the Abbot's black robes as they descended. The air was chilly, and her own white robe swirled upwards around her knees, raising goosebumps on her skin. The descent into darkness seemed endless, and she wondered whether she'd plummet to her death if she took a sideways step, but then the Abbot spoke softly. "You are safe, Kazari. We're in a shaft, not standing on a pedestal."

Kazari let out the breath she hadn't been aware of holding, and blushed, momentarily glad of the darkness that hid her red face from the head of her Order. Her amethyst pulsed slightly on her chest, and she had the impression of amusement. Once again, she lifted her hand to it, wondering. Would she always have such a sense of Her now? She wished she could ask, but the injunction against speaking hadn't been lifted, and would not be, until the end of the day when they met to eat and celebrate together.

Finally, the ride into the darkness stopped, and the Abbot showed Kazari how to exit the shaft using her pendant. "Each sept has its own chambers below the sanctuary. They're places where each sept can tend to its own, meet privately, and where we finish the induction process."

Finish the induction process, Kazari wondered. What more could there be? Suddenly she was nervous again, apprehensive of what might be ahead of her. In response, her pendant warmed again, and she was comforted. Stepping out of the shaft into the lantern-lit vestibule beyond almost blinded her. The vestibule opened into a long corridor, and the Abbot urged her forward, even as she squinted painfully against the brightness. By the time she'd reached the end of the corridor and was ushered into a chamber, smaller, yet just as impressive as the sanctuary above, her eyes had finally, thankfully, become used to the light.

This time there was no music, just the sound of water as it fell, drop by drop, from a golden starburst set into the wall into shallow pool cut into the floor of amethyst below it. The whole chamber gleamed softly amethyst. The Hunters stood in serried ranks on either side, sombre in their black robes, yet welcoming with their pendants glowing brightly.

"There is another entrance, just outside the sanctuary," murmured the Abbot when Kazari started with surprise. "Andiss will show you the access later. It can accommodate larger groups."

She followed the Abbot past the silent ranks, wondering what might happen next. They stopped beside the basin, and stood silently, as drop after drop fell into the water below. The sound was mesmerising in its measured tones, and Kazari felt as though she was falling too – falling into its sound, and into the silence. She had no idea how long she'd been standing there just listening, when the Abbot spoke once again.

"Welcome, Kazari. Welcome into our lives and into our hearts. Our sept is small, but closely bound. Each sept has a different way of sealing their initiates to their fellows. A Hunters life is often transient, and as a result every moment of our time on this earth is precious. Each time we go out to fight for the people, we are reminded that the Lady asks us to place their security above our own, and that we must do everything we can to ensure their safety."

Kazari nodded soberly.

"Our lives are not easy," the Abbot continued, "and the Hunter's path is a hard one. Yet it is not a joyless one. Our time together is precious, which is why we make each step in an initiate's training meaningful."

Kazari looked around at the black clad figures, all standing with their hoods hiding their faces, and wondered exactly what the Abbot meant by 'joy'.

"Kazari," the Abbot said, speaking directly to her, "this is our most sacred place, created for us and given to us by the Lady herself. It is here we bring our initiates for training, and our elders for their passing into joy. Here tonight, you will become a Hunter, not just in word, but also in deed."

A chill struck through Kazari's soul. In *deed?* She was untrained, and until three days ago she'd thought she might become a Judicar, or perhaps even a Grower, but never a Hunter – what exactly did 'in deed' mean?

"In a moment, Andiss will release a sucker in this chamber. It is for you to deal with, and for you alone to destroy."

Kazari's thoughts raced – a sucker? Suckers took the life from people – took their joy, their hope and their love, and also their flesh, leaving great gaping holes in both their bodies and their minds. They were only lesser gorgones, but were more common than many others, and she had no idea how to deal with one. She almost opened her mouth to speak.

As if she'd asked the question, the Abbot went on. "This is the test required of all initiates. Be strong, be sure, and depend on the Lady. For only with Her by your side will you succeed." She stepped forward and handed Kazari a knife. Its edge gleamed like a ribbon of violet, and the grip was bound in black leather strips. Kazari held it awkwardly, unsure of what to do with it, hoping she wouldn't cut herself, while trying to stop her legs from trembling. She shot a glance around the chamber, but the hooded figures stood impassively, as two walked forward, carrying a box between them.

Her bare feet on the stone floor felt strange, almost separate from her body, and the knife in her hand wobbled as she fiddled with her grip, trying to figure out if she should hold it up, down, or just out. A murmur of sound, and the robed figures had somehow moved to line the walls.

As the box was placed in the middle of the chamber, the Abbot rested a hand on Kazari's shoulder. "The Lady chose you. She will not desert you now." Then she too stepped back against the wall, and nodded to Kazari, waving one hand at the two Hunters near the box. They stepped back and then one of them raised the door, and a small, black nightmare rushed out.

Kazari, hissed in a breath, trying to dispel the terror that invaded her mind. Her hand on the knife became sweaty, despite the chill, and she could almost see the miasma of despair that surrounded the sucker. Her free hand clutched involuntarily for the pendant at her breast, even as her mind screamed *"Lady, Lady! What do I do?"* How she was able to prevent herself from screaming the words aloud, she would never know. How on earth was she to deal with the thing? She'd never even seen one before – only pictures in her schoolbooks.

The sucker hissed and skittered around in a tight circle on its eight legs. The two stalk-like eyes on the back of its head scanned the hooded figures that ringed the chamber. Then it saw its prey – lit by the glowing walls, standing there uncertainly, clothed in a flimsy white robe. Without hesitation, the nightmare crouched and began to stalk Kazari.

Lady! Kazari screamed silently, almost incoherent with fear. The joy and hope she had felt only moments before evaporated, leaving behind only a shadow of sadness and dismay. It was as if the sucker had stolen everything that gave her strength, leaving a black cloud that smothered her, dragging her down. Her rational mind knew it was the sucker, but that didn't make it any easier to deal with, when all she wanted to do was run as far and as fast as possible. She felt her knife hand drop uncertainly, and gritted her teeth, forcing it up and out, fighting desperately to remember the joy she'd so recently felt as the choir sang.

The sucker paused, as though considering, then charged. Kazari fought simply to breathe as it flailed a tentacle towards her. She ducked its swing, desperately trying to avoid the barb on the end, and swung her knife towards it. Sweat stung her eyes, and she blinked it away, frantically trying to clear her vision, while trying to ignore the despair, loneliness, and desperation that beat at her mind. Kazari's mind skittered away from the creature, looking for somewhere, anywhere, to hide – away from its all-pervading fear and desolation.

The Lady! I must remember the Lady, Kazari thought frantically, struggling to concentrate through the cloud of despair that enveloped her. She blinked, trying to keep her eyes on the beast, which was advancing step by step towards her, stalk eyes now boring relentlessly into her own, its tentacles undulating in waves, probing the air between them. *Lady, if you wish me to hunt for you, you must help me now!* she begged. But then she remembered the Abbot's words. "Be strong, be sure, and *depend* on the Lady."

But what does that mean? Tears, rather than sweat, stung Kazari's eyes this time, and a tentacle barb got through, scoring her across the left arm with a line of fire. She spun away from the creature, panting, wondering desperately if she'd be helped if the creature looked as if it was about to kill her, and how many initiates actually died during this test. *"Lady, how am I to be strong and sure? I am untrained, without skills,"* she pleaded fruitlessly as she swiped at the sucker with her knife, this time, managing to sever a probing tentacle. The creature beat at her mind with renewed strength, almost swamping her under a fresh wave of despair and she struggled futilely, trying to find the free air of coherent thought. *"Lady! I cannot do this alone! Please, please, show me what to do! Help me!"*

And then the answer came, echoing in her mind. *"Depend upon Me, Kazari. Lean on Me. Trust only in Me, and not in yourself. Be still."* It was a voice – a voice insider her head? She nearly dropped her knife, but something drove her on.

Almost disbelieving, Kazari blocked another tentacle strike, and ducked away from the sucker once again. *Was that really the Lady?* Her legs were trembling, and blood was now dampening the sleeve of her white robe, dripping off her elbow onto the floor. Revolted, she realised that the sucker had paused in its attack to slurp at some of the drops she'd shed as she moved.

Then, stilling her mind, she lowered her head as she remembered the dazzling illumination from the ring of gemstones – that moment when the Lady's voice had sounded in her ears as well as her mind. And at that moment her heart filled with such love that it threw the sucker's despair away from her in a burst of feeling so intense Kazari almost sobbed aloud. The sucker was stunned, and in that moment, Kazari knew what to do. She dodged forward, and with one stab, thrust her knife unerringly into the sucker's vitals.

The creature let out a long hiss, and as the Lady's love washed through the room the sucker collapsed onto the floor of the chamber in a puddle of muddy fluids. And then the creature was gone and Kazari was alone, panting, sweaty, with the knife clutched in one hand and her pendant in the other, while blood trickled off the point of her elbow onto the floor.

"It is done!" the Abbot proclaimed. "The Lady has shown her favour."

The sound of soft clapping echoed from around the chamber as those watching celebrated in an outpouring of relief.

"Kazari, step forward to the basin, and wash your wound," the Abbot continued. "It is honourable and right to have shed your blood for the first time in this chamber. Something we all have," she added with a small smile.

Kazari stepped forward, wondering, and placed the knife awkwardly on the edge of the bowl, then cupped her hand to wash the wound now throbbing on her arm. The cool water calmed its heat, and she rinsed her hands, noting absently that the dirty water circulated away somehow, then dipped both hands in and washed the sweat from her face, and rinsed the knife.

"You are now sealed to the Lady, as one of her Hunters," the Abbot said, "Andiss will bind your wound, and then you will don the garb of the Hunter for the first time. Retain the knife – it is yours now and will be a reminder of when you knew nothing and relied on the Lady for everything. That reminder will stand you in good stead when all seems lost."

Kazari nodded. She understood that defining moment very well now.

She was never alone. Never without the Lady, even to the point of death. She picked up the knife and watched the light glint along its length. It was a tool, but also a reminder of her own weakness. Perhaps one day she might have the skill to wield it as it should be wielded. Andiss finished his bandaging and then went and stood beside the Abbot.

"Kazari, discard your white robe."

Surprise almost made her drop her knife. She was to stand there in only her underwear? In front of everyone?

"We've all done this, Kazari. In the field, unneeded modesty will handicap you, and slow both you and your companions down. Discard it now, as you discard your robe. Instead, put on the practicalities of the Hunter's life as you dress for the first time in Hunter's clothing."

Kaz gritted her teeth and pulled her robe over her head, unable to hide a wince as her new injury voiced a complaint.

She wondered how many of the Hunters standing silently inside the chamber were men, and felt ashamed as she blushed again. Once the robe was off, she stood there awkwardly, clutching it, and trying not to drape it in front of herself. Changing clothing in groups might be a Hunter thing, but it certainly wasn't a part of everyday life where *she'd* come from.

Even worse, Andiss stepped forward, indicating that she should give her robe to him. She thought she could see sympathy in his eyes, but she knew that her face was burning as she handed the robe to him, and tried to pretend that standing in her underwear in front of lots of people was a normal part of life.

"Receive now your first Hunter Blacks," the Abbot said. Two Hunters stepped forward, one holding her new trousers, and one her new shirt. A third stood behind, carrying a pair of leather boots and warm looking socks, with a leather jerkin slung over his arm. The woman with her new shirt helped her into it, demonstrating how to fasten it, and then the other held the trousers towards her. Kaz stepped into them carefully, trying not to trip, and then tucked her shirt into them as the woman nodded approval.

They were very comfortable, and Kaz wondered how they'd known what size to provide. She wriggled her frozen feet into the new socks, revelling in their warmth, and then pulled the boots on and did the laces up firmly. Finally, she slipped into the leather jerkin, feeling it settle across her shoulders as if it had been tailored for her. Perhaps it had, she thought.

"The belt," the Abbot said, and another Hunter stepped forward and handed Kazari the belt. She slipped it through the loops on her pants, pausing to string the knife sheath on its smooth length and then buckled it up firmly as the Abbot motioned to the knife. "Dry it well and then sheath it. It is yours forever, to be worn every day. A Hunter keeps her first knife forever."

Kaz nodded and complied. Dressed for the first time in severe black, her amethyst on its thong around her neck, she felt different. She still knew nothing – nothing except that the Lady was with her – but that was enough. She would have time to learn.

"Hunters – what say we all?" the Abbot intoned.

"She is ours, one with us, and with the Lady," replied the massed voices.

"Welcome Kazari," the Abbot said. "You are now a member of the Hunter sept. You will live the life of a Hunter, share with your Hunter brethren, and serve the Lady along with your fellow Hunters. Together we strive against the darkness, protecting our people in the name of the Lady, to our last breath."

"To our last breath," repeated the others, and as the Abbot nodded, Kazari repeated the phrase softly to herself. "To our last breath."

It felt as if it was a solemn seal, a promise, and understanding at last, she said it again with more conviction. "To my last breath."

"It is done, then," the Abbot said. "You may speak, and we will all welcome you. Welcome, Kazari, welcome." She smiled, and threw off her hood, as around the chamber others followed suit.

"Th – thank you," Kazari stammered, and then one by one, each Hunter came forward to welcome her with their name and a smile.

CHAPTER SIX:
TIRED

Kazari's first evening as a Hunter exhausted her. The day had been eventful, full of solemnity, joy, an unexpected fight, and an overwhelming welcome. The celebratory dinner was noisy, exuberant, and delicious. After a full day of silence, Kazari found herself almost reluctant to speak — a complete contrast to her normal sociable nature. She sat among her fellow Hunters, enjoying the food, but longing for her bed.

The day had been a weird mixture, but inside her heart, she still wondered at the closeness of the Lady's presence. Never before had she heard her voice so clearly, and never before had she believed so fervently in the Lady's power. Today she'd seen it, felt it, and heard it. As she ate, the unfamiliar pressure of the knife sheath on her thigh underlined the different path that her life would now take.

For several years, Kazari had known she wanted to serve the Lady, but she had never seen herself as a Hunter. She had imagined herself as a farmer, tending the fields of specialised medicinals and foods or, perhaps even more so, as a legist, bringing order and the law to the masses, moving from village to village, dispensing the Lady's justice.

Never had she imagined herself fighting suckers, patrolling the borders, or defending the outlying villages against the intrusions of the greater gorgones. Even now, surrounded by her new companions at their long table in the communal dining room, she still felt as if it was simply a weird dream.

"Kazari, you're not eating much," the Hunter on her left said.

"Sorry, wool gathering," she replied, "it's just all . . . " she waved a hand vaguely.

"It can be a bit overwhelming at first. Thought I'd be an artist Intercessor myself, creating murals on sanctuary walls all across the country." The woman beside her was forty-ish, tough and weathered, and wore her weapons with the ease of long familiarity. Kazari couldn't imagine her as anything except a Hunter. "Really?" she said surprised.

"I know – I don't really look the artistic type, do I? But I can still draw. Nowadays I mostly use my talent on the Order's maps, or adding illustrations to the bestiaries."

"Bestiaries?" Kazari asked curiously.

"The books that tell us what the gorgones look like and how to fight them. I'm Javon, by the way. I spoke to you during the formal welcome, but I'm sure there were too many names to keep track of."

"There *were* a lot of them," Kazari said, forking up another piece of meat.

"Well, let me get you started, then. To your right is Andiss, of course, and you'll be bunking with both of us to start with, and Sendar over there." She indicated a tall young man on the opposite side of the table.

Sendar looked up at Kazari and grinned. "Don't worry, I don't snore – I leave that to Andiss."

"We share accommodation?"

"We do," replied Javon. "It's part of being a Hunter. If you find a life partner, then you share with them, but otherwise we bunk together in groups of four."

Kazari wasn't sure whether she should be relieved or intimidated by her new bunk mates. Andiss was the Abbot's second, and Javon was clearly an experienced Hunter. Sendar looked closer to her age, though, and he looked nice. She savoured another mouthful of meat, appreciating the tenderness and flavour. Now that she was eating, she realised how hungry she really was.

"Does that mean that I move in with you tonight?" she asked, after she'd swallowed.

"It does. And that's one reason we're all sitting together. Once you'd been chosen, the Abbot let us know. Your bed's all ready and waiting for you, and we moved your personal belongings over earlier."

"You did? Thank you!" She'd thought she'd lost her keepsakes. All they'd been told was to leave them in the chest near their beds.

"The Lady requires much of us, but she doesn't require that we leave everything behind. She understands the need for memory and family. One day you'll see your family again – not soon, but you will – and you'll want the little things you brought with you to keep them close and precious in your memories," Javon said. For the umpteenth time that day, Kazari felt tears prick her eyes. "And of course, when things are toughest, memories of your loved ones keep you fighting."

Kazari nodded; it made sense. "Javon, how long is this celebration likely to last?" She felt ungrateful saying it, but her exhaustion was making it difficult to resist the temptation to place her head on the table and close her eyes.

The woman smiled, crinkles appearing around her brown eyes. "You're tired, I gather?"

Kazari nodded.

"It won't be much longer, but this is a celebration – because you, and your fellows, mean that our Order continues – so of course, most importantly, there'll be dessert tonight." She laughed at Kazari's expression. "Dessert only happens on very special occasions. Most nights there's fruit, or you can help yourself to bread and honey, but that's about it. On occasions like this we go all out. Make sure you enjoy it!" She turned to answer a question from her other neighbour, and Kazari decided to concentrate on finishing her meal, hoping that dessert wouldn't be too long. Fatigue was making things a bit wobbly around the edges.

"Overwhelmed?" a voice from across the table said. Kazari nodded and looked up at Sendar's smiling face. In his unrelieved Hunter black, his brown hair looked almost blonde, a contrast to her own black locks. "It's a big day. It was for me last year."

"Last year?" asked Kazari.

"That's right. I've only been part of the Order for a year," he replied. "I bet you're exhausted."

She nodded again, as she heard the sympathy in his voice, but didn't speak in case the words came out the wrong way.

"It's a tough day for a Hunter initiate," Sendar went on, and then lowered his voice. "All the other septs have their own procedures, none of which anyone talks about directly, but I'm pretty certain no-one else has to fight a sucker completely unprepared." He rolled his eyes and went on. "I suspect the most any Growers have to do is identify a plant! Anyway, how's your arm feeling?"

"It's a bit sore," she replied. "Throbbing a little now." Concealed by her long sleeves, none of the other septs had noticed, but the Hunters all knew. They'd been very careful not to jostle her when they'd walked to the dining hall.

"Mine got me across the belly," he replied. "You did pretty well for someone completely untrained."

"Did it show much?" asked Kazari.

He smiled. "About as much as anyone else on their initiation day, I expect. I had no idea what I was doing either."

Kazari sat back in her chair, slightly reassured, and looked around the cheerful dining room. Here and there among the septs she could see her fellow initiates. Most looked tired, but they all looked happy, and truth be told, so was she, even if she was still uncertain about her own future.

A bell rang, and she looked towards the head table where the Abbot was climbing to her feet. The tall woman had her wine glass raised and, next to her, the Prior was tapping on his. Kazari looked at her own glass. She'd never drunk wine before, even well-watered as this was, and she had a sneaking suspicion that some of her wobbles might be due to its influence.

"A toast, brothers and sisters. To our new initiates – may you serve the Lady with truth and honour for all your days. Be welcome among us, now and forever." She raised her glass.

"Now and forever," came the massed voices, and Kazari belatedly reached for her own glass, and hurriedly took a sip.

"Enjoy dessert, and your first official day as part of the Order," the Abbot told the initiates. "For most of you the day will start early tomorrow, so I'll encourage you to eat and then find your way to your beds." She smiled. "My own memories of this day suggest that most of you won't need any urging! Enjoy!" She sat down as servitors moved rapidly down the long tables, depositing sweet cakes dotted with berries, and tall pitchers of cream, on the wooden surfaces. Kazari stared. Cake was something she'd eaten only rarely, and her mouth watered.

"I told you, didn't I?" Javon said, eyes twinkling. "Enjoy it. It might be the last time you see it for a year. Oh, you'll never be hungry, don't worry about that, but cake's only for special occasions." She picked up her spoon and the nearest jug of cream and poured a lavish amount over her own cake. "Food's good here, but there'll be times enough when you'll be on short rations in the field." She passed the pitcher over.

Kazari nodded, and then poured cream on her own cake, picked up her spoon and began to eat. The cake was delicious.

"Good, eh?" Andiss said from her other side.

Mouth full, Kazari nodded.

"Once you've finished, we'll show you our quarters. Don't hurry, and do have seconds if you wish, but I'm sure you're tired."

Relieved, Kazari concentrated on enjoying the sweet goodness of the cake. Whoever had baked it certainly knew what they were about. Finally, she put her spoon neatly into her empty bowl and pushed her chair back slightly, feeling full.

Several minutes later, Javon, the last to finish, pushed her bowl away and then levered herself out of her chair. "Ready for bed, Kazari?"

"Yes!"

The others laughed at her heartfelt tones.

"Follow on then. We'll make our farewells to the Abbot, and then we'll be off."

Kazari dutifully followed the others down the aisle to the Abbot's table. She'd shed her formal robes, and was sitting chatting to the Prior to her right and the Sacristan on her left. Her Hunter Blacks contrasted with the ruby red of the Prior's robes, and the pristine white of the Sacristan.

"By your leave, we'll take Kazari to her quarters Abbot," Andiss said, inclining his head.

"You have my leave. Sleep well, Kazari, I will see you at first light in the training compound. Sendar, you'll take her there. Don't be late." She waggled a finger at him.

"Of course not, Ailani," he replied, but there was a hint of a smile in his reply, and Kazari wondered what he might have done previously that the Abbot felt he needed to be reminded. Her fatigue was growing rapidly, though, and she was simply glad when the Abbot matched Andiss' nod with one of her own.

"Be off," the Abbot said. "Make sure Kazari's in bed very soon; she looks dead on her feet."

Kazari blushed, but nodded and thankfully followed the others out of the dining hall and into the maze of corridors and rooms that made up the Abbey.

"Don't worry about finding your way just yet," Javon said. "For the next couple of weeks, one of us will show you where to go, and when. You'll have other things on your mind first up. There's time enough to learn your way around."

The trek through the Abbey seemed endless, and Kazari had the feeling she was wobbling, rather than walking in straight lines, before the four of them arrived at a door that looked just like all the others they'd passed.

"Here we are," Andiss said as he pushed the door open and Kazari followed the others inside.

The room was lit by several candle lanterns, placed in reflecting niche's in the walls. The light was comfortably warm, showing four neatly made beds, each slightly separated from the others by partitions made of bookcases. There was a set of shelves at the foot of each bed, and the one closest to the door held the few possessions Kazari had brought with her from home.

"There's yours," Sendar said, pointing, "and the door over there leads to our bathroom. Just flip the sign over if you need privacy in there."

"We have our own *bathroom*?"

Javon chuckled. "It's actually easier than having communal ones. It is our responsibility to keep it clean and tidy though, as the newest, you'll be the one doing most of the scrubbing, so don't get *too* excited. I suggest you use it now, and then get straight into bed. You've an early start. Sendar will get you up and going, and you'll see both Andiss and myself later in the day." She smiled at Kazari. "Enjoy your sleep, you're going to need it!"

CHAPTER SEVEN:
MORE BEGINNINGS

Kazari's legs were on fire, and her breath rasped in her throat. The amethyst around her neck bumped her chest as she forced one foot after the other.

"Move it, Kaz!"

She forced her legs to move faster, but it was hard. Sweat tracked down her face, stinging as it dripped in her eyes, and her heart hammered in her chest. Her breath wheezed as she gasped and heaved, struggling to breathe.

"Harder now. Push yourself!"

Near to collapse, she forced herself to move faster, feeling dizzy with the effort, and was rewarded by hearing. "That's it, now keep it up."

Her torturer stood only metres away, and she fixed her eyes on the line inscribed in the dirt and staggered on. "Only a little way now, come on!"

Summoning what felt like the absolute last of her strength, Kazari staggered over the line and nearly collapsed. Nausea surged, and she dry-retched, then wished she hadn't because it interfered with the huge, heaving breaths she needed.

Her legs wobbled and she staggered sideways until a kind hand under her elbow steadied her.

"Much better, Kaz. That's the best you've done. Keep working like that and you'll soon see an improvement in your fitness," Javon said.

Kazari nodded, although she doubted it, and kept on heaving air in and out of her lungs, trying to still both the urge to vomit and the desire to collapse onto the ground beneath her feet.

"Now, let's just get you walking. It'll help, come on."

Legs wobbling, Kazari followed Javon's voice, concentrating on trying to move in some semblance of a straight line.

"That's it," Javon said.

Finally, Kazari was able to straighten up and look where she was walking, as her breathing slowed to normal puffing and she began to walk without feeling as if she was about to fall over. "Was I faster?" She forced the question out between puffs.

"Much faster," Javon told her. "For a shorty, you're doing nicely."

"Thanks. I think."

Hunter training had been hard from the first day. Actually, just becoming a novice Hunter had been hard, thought Kazari, reminding herself of her initiation ceremony. It was physically, mentally, and spiritually demanding. Of course, so was the service of a Hunter, and despite the sucker she'd had to fight on her first day, Kazari hadn't seen another of the creatures since. Hunters patrolled the borders and protected the Lady's people from the gorgones. They kept the byways safe, and the roads clear, and if an invasion of gorgones threatened, they were called upon to repel it.

For that, she'd need to be strong – physically, mentally, and spiritually. She needed to be sure in her faith in the Lady, and strong in her foundations of knowledge and skill. Her bunkmates had been tasked with not only sharing their quarters, but their skills. Javon was her primary physical trainer, while Andiss strove to teach her to guard her mind and her spirit. Sendar was her sparring partner. For over two months now, Kazari had been training day after day, and it still didn't seem to be getting any easier. She was exhausted from the time she crawled out of her bed every morning, until she collapsed into it every evening after she'd bathed and eaten. Some nights she wished she could just avoid the eating and getting clean portions of her day, and move immediately to the sleeping.

Her teachers were patient, calm and encouraging, but some days, Kazari despaired of ever becoming fit enough to be a Hunter, let alone gathering all of the other skills required. Physically, she was short, built for strength rather than speed, and her family's leather-working business hadn't required her to run or lift weights, or to even contemplate fighting anything more than a stubborn piece of knot work.

Finally, feeling her breathing slow to something approaching normal, Kazari slowed her walk and began to stretch her legs.

"What've you got now?" Javon asked.

"I'm meeting Andiss in the glade," she replied. "He said he had a new exercise for me."

"Well, finish your stretches, and then head off. Do you have time to wash first?"

Kazari looked up at the sun, squinting. "I don't think so." The sun had risen further than she'd thought, and if she was going to arrive in the glade at the appointed time she was going to have to run again. She sighed.

"It will get better, you know," Javon smiled. "Give it a few more weeks and the running will become easier."

"Really?"

"Yes, really. We all begin like this." She gestured to Kazari's sweaty face and damp hair. "And then one day it all starts to work."

Kazari nodded, but inside her mind, she was shaking her head despondently. She was thirsty, and now she'd stopped puffing, was beginning to feel slightly chilly.

"You'd better be off if you're going to get to the glade in time."

"Thanks, Javon." Kazari trudged off, feeling discouraged despite her earlier success. She'd had such a sure sense of the Lady during her initiation, but that day seemed so far away now, relegated to her memory by her fatigue and her aching body. Dry mouthed, she detoured slightly so that she could scoop a handful of water from the fountain on the edge of the running track. It was situated at the far end of the Abbey grounds from the glade, and Kazari knew she'd be pushing just to get there in time. She ran her wet hands through her hair, hoping to restore some semblance of order to her shorn locks.

The loss of her hair still left a lingering regret in her heart. She'd been secretly proud of her curls, falling low on her back in spirals that swung and shone as she walked. Her hair had turned heads and drawn admiring glances in her hometown, but now it curled tightly against her scalp, leaving her neck unfamiliarly chilly. It was a tiny thing, but every day it emphasised the changes in Kazari's life.

Realising that she'd be unforgivably late if she didn't get a move on, Kazari forced her legs into a jog, feeling them tremble, and then grow stronger. A few minutes later, she saw the stone archway to the glade come into view. The grey side-pillars were entwined in velvet climber, its deep purple flowers nestling among the dark green foliage like the amethyst at Kazari's neck. Her hand rose involuntarily to the pendant, fingers stroking its smooth planes.

She slowed to a walk and took several deep breaths, composing herself, and then ducked through the archway and into the dimness of the heavily wooded glade. It was always calm in the glade, Kazari thought. Calm and restful, although even here she often felt as if she was struggling to push a huge boulder up a hill. Mindful of Andiss waiting for her, she stepped more quickly as she approached the centre of the glade.

"Kazari," Andiss said, catching one of his throwing knives and tucking it away in its sheath. Kazari's eyes widened even as she dipped her head in greeting. If she wasn't mistaken, her father had made the sheath. Andiss followed her gaze to his wrist, and then smiled. "The sheath? Yes, it's one of your father's. I'm sure you know that your parents supply the Abbey with leather goods?"

"Yes, I do, but seeing one of their pieces . . . " she broke off, slightly embarrassed, because her voice had wobbled a bit. Her parents' tacit disapproval of her choice to declare for the Lady still saddened her. The sadness struck when she least expected it.

"Don't forget the Lady's words, Kaz. 'The one who follows Me, though forsaken by their loved ones, will be repaid a thousandfold on the day of reward.' They'll come around. You'll see. When you stand before them for the first time, garbed as a Hunter, they'll be proud." He seemed certain, but Kazari wasn't as sure. The words her mother had flung at her still stung.

'Some of those who pledge to the Lady die, Kazari – they die, or fall into darkness!' The words echoed in her mind, counter to the calmness of the grove, and she was hard-pressed to avoid tears. She gritted her teeth and breathed out, closing her eyes momentarily to regain control. "I hope so, Andiss, I really hope so."

His eyes regarded her steadily. Their cool green matched the glade, and in them, Kazari saw absolute stillness. She dropped her own brown ones and sighed internally. The glade was where the Hunters meditated. Andiss assured her that it would become easier, but the more baggage she brought to each session, the harder it seemed. Sometimes it seemed as if the glade brought the worst of her to the surface.

"Let's begin, Kaz." Andiss motioned to the grass at the foot of a large tree. It was aeons old and surrounded by granite rocks. "Today you're going to meditate on a particular passage from the Writings. It's from *The Book of Hunters* and it has special significance for us."

"The Book of Hunters? What Book of Hunters?"

"There are special books written for each sept, Kaz. They're only for the Lady's servants, because they teach things specifically for those septs. You're familiar with how the Lady designated the septs?"

She nodded. The septs had been founded before the Gorgone War. The Lady had called each founding leader of each sept in a dream one night, and then provided them with the Writings.

"What isn't common knowledge, except for those who are the Lady's servants, is that each sept leader was given their own Book, additional to the Writings, containing specific instructions and knowledge pertinent to that sept. Ours is *The Book of Hunters.*" He stepped over to a pile of books beside the tree. Andiss frequently brought books to this session, so Kazari hadn't really taken much notice of them. He picked up the top one and handed it to her.

She gasped. The intricately tooled leather binding was set with an amethyst on the spine, and it was by far the most beautiful thing she'd ever held in her hands. "This is yours," Andiss said. "Treasure it and read it daily, for it contains words only for you and your Hunter brethren, and those words must become your most precious possessions. For the moment, I want you to turn to the first chapter, and read the first paragraph aloud."

Kazari opened the cover, feeling the leather speak of home to her. Another pang of homesickness struck, and her hands trembled slightly as she imagined how much her parents would enjoy the quality of the leatherwork on the cover. She turned to the first chapter, admired the illuminations around the first line, and began to read aloud. "'Read here the duties and obligations of the Hunter. Above all, the Hunter will protect. The Hunter's prime responsibility will be to defend the land and the people against the gorgone threat.'" She looked up, but Andiss motioned to her to continue, so she kept reading. "'My Hunters must spend time in contemplation, ensuring that My words are written on their hearts, for only by doing this, will they have the strength to prevail against evil. The character of a Hunter must remain upright and true, unsullied by pettiness, focused on My ideals. My Hunters must remember that in forgiveness lies release, and in integrity lies honour. The Hunter that reads the words of this Book, and enfolds them in their heart, will find favour in My sight, and My gifts will allow them to overcome even the deepest of evils.'"

"These are the words read by each new Hunter at this time," Andiss explained. "What you do with them, determines your path. You are always a Hunter, but our greatest are always those who take the words of the Lady and live them."

"What does it mean, Andiss, when it says, 'in forgiveness lies release, and in integrity lies honour?'" she asked. She understood the words, but the meaning seemed deeper than the words.

"That is for you to puzzle out, Kazari. It's part of the path of a Hunter – reading, meditating, discovering the words of the Lady, and then relying on them when called to do so. The things I've been teaching you, and those that Javon has as well, are all designed to come together when you face the gorgones. That sucker you faced during your initiation was the least of them, and you, like all of us, will require much tuition before you face a greater one. Keep in mind that last sentence, though. A Hunter can overcome – and has done so – the greatest and deepest of all evils."

"But some die, Andiss," she replied, sadly.

"Yes, some do die. But death isn't failure, not when you're a Hunter, Kaz. Death is simply the price some of us will pay in the course of our duties. It's a costly price for those left behind, but it's not the worst thing that can happen to us. For nearly all of us, death is merely a change from this life to a better one in the next." He looked up at her and Kazari thought she saw the shadow of remembered grief touch his face briefly, and she had the feeling that he didn't want to talk about it any further. Clearly, something about a Hunter's death had affected him deeply at some point. "For now, you are to sit, read, and memorise. The words of *The Book of Hunters* must embed themselves in your mind and your heart. Tomorrow, you'll be reciting the first chapter from memory."

Kazari sat in the grass hastily, shivering slightly in her sweat-damp clothing, before composing herself and allowing her thoughts to still enough to begin reading. She was distracted, both by the intrusive thoughts of her family, and her curiosity about her future, and the Hunter whose death still had the power to unsettle Andiss.

"Concentrate, Kazari." His measured tones cut through her thoughts, and guiltily, she stopped that train of thought in its tracks and went back to reading. The Book was fascinating, and as it absorbed her attention, question after question began to emerge in Kazari's mind. The formality of the language was beautiful, and the concepts embedded in the chapters were deep, much deeper than anything she'd ever read before. Where the Writings were written in fairly clear language, easily understood by most, *The Book of Hunters* delved into deep philosophical concepts, and touched on the facets of evil embodied by the gorgones. There was even a succinct description of gorgone hierarchy. She'd barely scratched the surface when Andiss' voice sounded again.

"Time to stop Kazari." She looked up, startled at how fast the time had gone. "It's time for the midday meal."

"It is?"

"It is," he affirmed. "Walk with me, Kaz."

She stood up, feeling stiff from her long sitting, and hobbled a few steps before her stride smoothed out. She had the feeling that Andiss was trying not to smile. "It will get easier," he said.

"So everyone keeps telling me," she replied darkly.

"We all started like this," Andiss said. "Even the Abbot."

"She did?"

"Of course she did. She came from a farm when she was fifteen. She was strong, but she'd never run very far. I was a couple of years ahead of her in training. She hated all the running at first." He smiled in remembrance.

"Well, I completely understand how she felt," Kazari replied, and then she turned her head to Andiss. "Will it take much longer?"

He laughed. "It'll take as long as it takes. Don't worry, in a year's time you'll look back on this conversation and smile."

A year? Kazari wasn't sure she'd survive if it took a year. Still, she had her Book of Hunters now, and she could barely wait to get back into it again. There was a chapter entitled 'Gifts from the Lady to her Hunters' whose opening phrases had hinted that Hunters might have a few skills she hadn't been aware of. "Am I allowed to talk about what's in the Book with anyone?" she asked.

"Just other Hunters. If you have questions, ask either me or Javon, but feel free to discuss it with any other Hunter. We all have questions about its contents. Most of us are still learning things from it."

"Still learning?" Kazari repeated.

"Of course. Would you say you'd learned everything you can from the Writings?"

"Uh . . . no. Of course not."

"Well this is no different. Each time you read it, you'll find something new, something you hadn't considered, and something will pop up one day and you'll look at it from a different angle," he said smiling at her. "*The Book of Hunters* is a lifelong study for us. Don't expect to understand it all on your first read through. Just let yourself read it, think about it, and it'll sink in slowly. The more you memorise the better. Once you're fully trained, you'll realise that."

They walked in silence for a few minutes, and Kazari's legs began to feel a bit more normal.

"You have sparring this afternoon with Sendar?"

"Yes," she replied.

"How are you getting along?"

"He's nice." Kazari smiled. "I think he's being quite gentle with me though."

"Good," Andiss said. "Now, tonight you'll read the section on gifts for me, as well as memorising the first chapter." She wondered how he'd known what she'd intended, and her eyebrows lifted in spite of herself. He went on, grinning. "Every new initiate wants to read that chapter as soon as they see it. I did, the Abbot did – everyone does. It's human nature. You want to know what the Lady might have in store for you. Read it tonight, and tomorrow you'll see a demonstration. Now, you've got just about enough time to go and clean-up before we eat. Off you go. I'll see you at lunch."

He waved her away towards their quarters, and as he walked off towards the priory Kazari gave herself a small shake and did as he'd asked. She could hardly wait to find out what he meant by a demonstration. As her legs wobbled slightly again, she allowed herself a brief wish that she could tuck herself up in her bed with a cup of tea and her Book for the afternoon instead of sparring ineptly with Sendar. Oh well, at least he was nice. She enjoyed spending time with him.

CHAPTER EIGHT: 'GIFTS'

Kazari approached the training hall feeling a slow bubble of excitement building inside her. As Andiss had asked, she'd read the chapter on 'Gifts' in *The Book of Hunters*. She'd raced through it, heart pounding, barely able to contain her excitement. Then she'd read it again, and once again. Then she'd remembered that she needed to memorise the first chapter, and had spent two hours trying to pound it into her brain while the words she'd read about the Lady's Gifts kept bouncing around inside her skull.

Even her meditation session with Andiss had been difficult. He'd forestalled her questions by insisting that she recite what she'd memorised, and then spend the next hour meditating on it. Even then, she'd struggled to concentrate. Finally he'd taken pity on her, or perhaps it had been planned all along, and told her to follow him to the hall.

The doors were shut, and as they drew near, Andiss raised a finger to his lips, and motioned her closer. "What you'll see today is training. Keep quiet and just watch. You can ask any questions you have later. Follow me, and we'll sit where you'll have a good view."

Even more curious now, Kazari followed him closely as he opened the door quietly and entered the hall, the floor of which was now covered with mats. A pair of Hunters stood on each mat, while others sat in the tiered seating around the sides. Andiss climbed up several tiers and then indicated for Kazari to sit next to him.

Clad in their Blacks, it was hard to tell who might be who.

She thought she recognised Sendar standing with his partner though, by his dark skin, height and long limbs. The Abbot strode in, accompanied by an older woman, and each pair drew themselves up in respectful salute. To Kazari's surprise, the Abbot then took a seat not far from herself and Andiss, while the other woman stepped forward.

"Begin on my mark," she said, her voice carrying clearly across the hall. "Prepare yourselves." Each Hunter faced their partner. "And . . . now!"

Nothing happened.

Until Kazari realised that one of the black clad figures had risen off their mat. Literally risen. They were floating higher and higher into the air. She felt her mouth drop open, then the figure wobbled and drifted to the floor while the one who'd faced them toppled to their knees. Mouth still agape, Kazari leaned forward, propping her elbows on her knees, almost craning her neck to see what else might be happening.

One other pair seemed to be staring at each other, almost glaring, but not angrily, more like the intense type of look that showed complete concentration. What the expressions on their faces meant, Kazari had no idea. Another pair appeared to be pushing against each other's hands. Then she realised that their hands weren't touching, but that their body postures suggested that they were exerting great force. Two more pairs were moving in complete unison, looking as if they were doing some kind of complicated dance. Realising that her mouth was still open, Kazari shut it with an audible snap.

"Well done," the old woman said. "We'll try that again. This time, concentrate, but don't tighten your control. Remember Sendar, your gifts come from deep within you, and it may take years for you to develop the control others have."

Kazari turned her head to ask a question of Andiss, but he shook his head and she filed it away to ask later. Filed *them* away. Questions were multiplying like rabbits in her mind. She turned back to watch the Hunters. This time she tried to identify who was who. Slowly she put names to faces and figures. Sendar was the one who'd fallen to his knees. The others were younger Hunters paired with older Hunters, as far as she could tell. Did that mean that she'd be joining them soon? She added that question to all of the others galloping around inside her head.

She ran through what she'd read the night before. The Lady's Gifts had names. She decided to try and identify which was which.

"On my mark, prepare, and ... now!" The woman's voice rang out again, and once again, Kazari focused on Sendar and his partner – was it Javon – as the figure rose into the air. It definitely looked like her. She rose higher this time, and then began to float from side to side, gradually gaining speed, until the woman's voice rang out again.

"And stop. You can put her down now, Sendar." Javon's figure touched down gently, and Sendar staggered slightly, then wiped his face, panting, as if he'd run a long way. Kazari realised that she'd completely forgotten to look at any of the others. "See what I mean? When you concentrate, you use your gifts more surely, and with much less effort. Take a break for a few moments, and then we'll try again."

The lesson went on for some time. Kazari's mind felt as if it might explode with excitement, and awe. Tentatively she matched names to what she was seeing. She was fairly certain that Sendar had the Gift of Ascension, and that those working hand to hand, might well be demonstrating the Gift of Force, while the dancing pairs, as she named them inside her head, probably had the Gift of Anticipation. She had no idea what the two staring at each other were trying to do.

She was torn between watching, and hoping for the session to end, so she could ask Andiss all of the questions that kept popping up in her mind. She was enthralled and impatient all at the same time, sitting there and seeing the impossible right in front of her. She'd never heard even a whisper that Hunters might have such skills. She wondered how they'd managed to keep it quiet. Their reputations were certainly impressive, but this? It was amazing.

As the time passed, she noticed several things that gave her pause.

The fatigue. It became etched into each trainee's face as they practiced their skills. By the fourth repetition, Sendar was grey-faced and trembling. But the exultation. It touched the fatigue with joy, and transformed the black clad figures into bastions of calm. Kazari wondered just how the two things balanced themselves inside one person. She wondered how they'd balance inside herself, and then she began wondering about the other Hunters she could see dotted around the hall, sitting in the tiers. Beside her, sat Andiss. What was his Gift? What was the Abbot's?

Kazari couldn't help glancing at the woman where she sat just a few seats away. The Abbot's face looked satisfied and concerned all at once — and Kazari wondered what was going on that made her expression such a mixture. As she looked, the Abbot turned her head as if she'd sensed Kazari's regard. She smiled as Kazari blushed, and then turned back to watch the trainees again.

Eventually the session finished. The participants looked exhausted, but also jubilant. The Abbot stood up and stretched, as Andiss wriggled his eyebrows at Kazari. "I'm guessing you've got at least a million questions now?"

"At least, Andiss!" she replied. "That was amazing! Will I learn to do that too?" She couldn't keep the longing from her voice.

"Of course. We all do. The difficult thing is to discover your Gift. And if you have more than one — some do."

"They do?" she was breathless.

"Not many, of course, and the secondary Gift is often small, but Sendar is one with two gifts. You were watching him use his secondary Gift today."

"Ascension?" Kazari asked, uncertainly.

"Well done," he replied. "His primary Gift is Anticipation, although he's very strong in both. Let's go down to him and Javon, and we'll answer as many questions as we can."

They walked down the tiers to where Javon stood next to Sendar. He was stretched out on the floor, and Kazari could see he was still sweating heavily. As they arrived, Javon handed him a towel and a cup of water. He sat up, sighed, and drank deeply, and then handed the cup back to Javon. "Thanks." He wiped his face with the towel, and then propped himself on his hands, legs stretched out in front of him.

Kazari didn't know what to say, or where to start asking questions, now that she was confronted with the reality of the hard work that using the Lady's Gifts clearly was. "Come on Kaz, you must be dying to ask something," Sendar said. He smiled through his exhaustion. "I know I was."

She took a seat on the floor and crossed her legs, feeling awkward for just standing there. "Is it hard?" As the question left her mouth, she realised that it was the least of her questions, but it had popped out before she could stop it.

"That's it?" Sendar said incredulously.

Kazari blushed. "No, I've got heaps of questions, but that one ... sort of ... I don't know. My mouth sometimes opens without me thinking about it. But really, *is* it hard? It looked like it was."

Sendar considered for a moment, as he wiped the last of the sweat off his face. "It's hard, but not as hard as figuring out what your Gift is. Actually, my primary Gift comes much more easily – they usually do apparently. This one's just a secondary one, so I have to work harder."

Kazari leaned forward with her hands on her knees. "So how *did* you figure out what your gifts are?" She looked curiously at Javon and Andiss. "Is it different for everyone?"

Javon joined them on the floor, with Andiss lowering himself more slowly to the ground. The hall had emptied, each pair leaving deep in conversation, while the observers had left together, faces intent as they talked, leaving only the four of them sitting together on the soft matting. The two older Hunters looked at each other, and then Andiss motioned to Javon. "You explain."

Javon nodded, folding her long legs beneath her, and began. "There's a number of things, really, and they all have to come together for you to know. Your relationship with the Lady is the most important thing. Most Hunters declare early, just as you have. It seems that she calls us young, for a number of reasons. One of those is that she needs us to know her well, to trust her, and to learn to lean on her. Your Gift is partly a product of that relationship. Another is the physical conditioning – it comes much more easily in the young."

Kazari nodded, wondering. Since her initiation into the Hunter sept, she'd spent more time reading the Writings, meditating and praying, and staggering around in physical pain than she'd ever imagined was possible for one human being. Some days she felt as if the Lady was sitting just behind her, giving her a nudge, while other days, she felt as if she was trying to talk to someone on one of the moons that swept across the sky each night.

She looked at the three of them, not really understanding, but wanting to. Wanting quite desperately to, she realised. "Is it like discovering your sept?" she asked. Maybe she'd just dream and wake up one morning knowing.

Javon shook her head. "No, it's not that easy. That's why we've only introduced you to the idea of gifts now. You've been one of us for two months now. We've watched you work at the purely physical, and Andiss has been working through the beginnings of what you'll need to know to effectively use your Gift once you discover it. This is a tricky stage. Our service is dangerous. Not every Hunter returns from a mission for the Lady. Sometimes we know what's happened, but on those occasions where neither Hunter partner returns, we are left wondering. Wondering whether it was a problem of training, whether the pair fell to the gorgones, or whether they've been captured."

"Captured?" Kazari's voice was incredulous.

Andiss nodded soberly. "Yes, it sounds impossible, particularly for you, a new initiate. But there are times when a Hunter survives an encounter with a gorgone, but is then captured and taken. We have no idea where, and it's not common knowledge outside the Order, but every now and then, we are left wondering. Only a very few in our history have ever made it home after capture, and then, only after a few days in the hands of the gorgones, so we know little of what might happen to them in the long term. In the short term . . . " He shrugged, his face grim, and she heard his unspoken words.

She was aghast. She sat stunned, unable to imagine what horrors might be visited upon one of the Lady's servants in the hands of the gorgone horde. Her mind raced. Why was Andiss telling her this now? And why wasn't it known outside the Order? Was there something else she hadn't been told? "But why?" she asked, trying to put all of her questions into the simple word. "Does no-one go in search of them?"

Andiss closed his eyes briefly, and Kazari saw his mouth tighten before he spoke again. Once again he shared a quick glance with Javon, and then he went on. "As Hunters, we walk closely with the Lady, but we are also relatively few in number. At least one is chosen each intake – but sometimes, like now, it is only one. To retrieve our lost we would need to leave Albatar relatively undefended. It is the lot of a Hunter to know that should she be taken alive, we will not attempt a rescue. Our vow of service is to the Lady and to Albatar. We trust the Lady to keep our brothers and sisters in the palm of her hand." Kazari heard the pain in his voice, but he went on relentlessly. "It is our dream that one day, when the outer world is free of the gorgone curse once again, that we might know what has become of them. Until then, we entrust them to the Lady's care, and remember her words. 'And though My path may lead you into darkness, and your very life become forfeit, I will walk beside you always. Those who lose their lives in My service will walk with Me all the days of eternity.'"

The words fell abruptly into the silence, and Kazari's mind was drawn inexorably to the memory of her mother, quoting those same words. Briefly, guilt enveloped her. It was entirely possible that one day, Kazari's fate might be the one her parents had so dreaded. Then she reminded herself that it might never happen, despite her misgivings. Andiss had said 'occasionally.' She fastened upon that one word, and the guilt subsided.

"By now, you should have developed some enduring habits. When troubled, your mind should turn firstly to the Lady for succour, and then to your fellow Hunters for advice. You should hear the Lady's thoughts in your mind." He forestalled Kazari's exclamation with an upraised hand. "Yes, all of us experience her in that way – not all of the time of course, but intermittently, when we most need to; however, the rest of the septs may not do so. Or at least not in the same way. The Navigators and Intercessors come closest to our relationship with her. There is something built into us that draws us to her, entwines us with her, but also leaves us vulnerable – for want of a better word."

"Vulnerable?" Kazari leaped upon the word. "What do you mean?"

"It appears that we feel more deeply, perhaps. Feel more deeply for others, for our relationships with them, and with the Lady. Actually, perhaps more *intensely* is a better description. It drives us to protect others, but that intensity of feeling can leave us vulnerable when those we love don't live up to our expectations. Or when we feel more for someone than they feel for us." Andiss shrugged. "Wider Albatar does not equate depth of feeling with the Hunter image at all." Then he smiled. "Still waters run deep."

Kazari nodded slowly. She'd never imagined a Hunter as someone who felt deeply, but the idea made sense. *She* felt deeply. And sometimes she'd wondered at her friends' lack of reaction to certain things. On occasion she'd been made to feel like an overly emotional idiot. And then she'd learned to mask her deeper feelings, even at times, from Dari.

Javon nodded and went on. "And that thing is what makes us Hunters. Which is why we wait and allow you to develop your relationship with the Lady further before we compound it all by telling you about the gifts. All Hunters are born with the gifts inbuilt, but that moment, when a Hunter is about to discover their Gift, is the moment that the Hunter must depend most deeply on the Lady. At that time, we experience how closely the Lady walks with her Hunters. We walk on the edge of danger, and she walks that edge beside us." She waved a hand at Sendar, and the young man drew himself up into a cross-legged posture, nodding.

"Remember the sucker, Kaz?"

She nodded.

"It's like that, but this time, you'll face not just one sucker, but four." His eyes shadowed with remembered fear and pain. "You have to be physically strong to be a Hunter, but more than that, you have to be mentally and spiritually strong. It's most likely the hardest thing you'll ever do. And once again, no-one can help you. You will need to overcome them by strength of will, bolstered by the Lady, and by your own prowess."

Kazari's face blanched. "But – but why?"

"Because the sucker preys on your thoughts. Four of them increase the pressure exponentially. They may be small, but they're among the deadliest of gorgones when they're massed. The ability to face physical danger is easily taught in comparison to strength of will, determination, and purpose. Reliance on the Lady comes only from yourself and from the Lady. When the suckers surround you, then you'll be stripped bare, vulnerable, and only your sense of 'you' will bring you through. Denying four suckers will bring you to the brink of your ability to survive, and when you reach that point, your gifts will make themselves evident. *The Book of Hunters* says: 'The Hunter is a vessel of My compassion, love and strength. Only when the Hunter's surrender is complete, am I able to work completely within them.'"

Kazari had read the words, and now they began to make sense. She took a deep breath, feeling it wobble uncertainly through her nostrils, and then realised that her hands were shaking slightly. The excitement of seeing the gifts in action was dampened by the very real danger she'd have to face just to allow her own Gift – or gifts – to be made known to her.

"So, I have to face *four* suckers – alone? Does anyone die doing this?" She was proud that she'd kept her voice steady.

Javon's eyes were grave as she replied. "Sometimes." The words sank like a rock in a pond, and the silence after Javon had spoken was heavy with emotion. Clearly, Javon had seen someone perish.

"H . . . how often?"

"Occasionally. The last time was four years ago." Javon's voice tightened, and Kazari could see the effort she made to keep her words steady. "He was a very promising young Hunter, but he did not prevail in the test."

"What happened?" Kazari was desperate to know, but unhappily certain that the answer might highlight her own vulnerability.

There was a long silence, while the other three just looked at each other. It was mostly Andiss and Javon sharing the looks, but Sendar's face said everything she'd feared to hear.

"Look, just tell me," Kazari said. "I want to avoid the same fate, and knowing what happened might help."

Finally, Andiss nodded, and Javon continued, although the words came slowly, and with difficulty.

"He was well prepared. Like most of us, he'd heard the Lady's call as a child, and then responded at the first opportunity." She looked at Kazari. "We don't discuss the gifts until the initiate is ready. It's different for each of us, that timing. The decision is primarily that of the initiate's trainers, but must be signed off by the Abbot. You've probably noticed that she appears when you least expect her?"

Kazari nodded.

"We waited a little longer with Ziram. His background was particularly troubled, and despite his best efforts, he struggled with many things. Most importantly, we now believe he struggled to forgive."

She paused, and Kazari was surprised to see that Javon's eyes were filled with tears. They shone with them, almost as if her sorrow was so overwhelming that it threatened to overwhelm her completely if the first drop spilled over, but then Javon took a deep breath, and let it out, visibly dropping her shoulders, and went on.

"The Writings tell us many things, but it is often easier to read them than to do them. Ziram's parents had beaten him – and imprisoned him. They didn't want him to choose the Lady, or offer himself in service. They wanted him to work on their farm, so when he stayed true to the path that the Lady had called him to, they decided to beat it out of him."

Kazari couldn't help the exclamation that burst from her lips.

"Kaz, this isn't that unusual. Although our forebears were those who chose the Lady over the temptations of the gorgones, it doesn't mean that all of their descendants have done the same," Andiss said. "Like yourself, at least one-third of the Hunter sept has parents who would have preferred them to stay at home."

"Really? So many?" She was surprised that the number was so high. Among her own initiate group, she'd not met anyone else who'd declared for the Lady against their parents' wishes. Or, she amended to herself, had told her they had. She hadn't been exactly forthcoming with her own story. "But although my Mum and Dad didn't come to the ceremony, they weren't cruel to me."

"They weren't?" Sendar asked. "Didn't their absence hurt you? Didn't you feel abandoned?"

Kazari sat back, deflated. "Of course it hurt me. But Dari's Mum and Dad were there for me as well." She wasn't really being as honest as she could have, though. There had been at least two nights when she cried herself quietly to sleep.

"But your own parents weren't there on the most important day of your life, were they?" pressed Sendar again.

Abashed, and honest at last, Kazari shook her head, feeling tears prick her own eyes, matching those still unshed in Javon's. "N-n-no. They weren't, but I'm sure they'll come around. At least, I hope so." She scrubbed at her face with one hand, and sat up a bit straighter, trying not to sniffle.

"Exactly," Andiss said. "And it still hurts you. It's obvious to all of us."

"Ziram's family did attend his Day of Choosing, sure in the knowledge that he wouldn't attend – they'd locked him up again, after another beating," Javon said. "But they can't have bargained on his determination to do what he needed to. I'm sure you understand. Once you've responded to the Lady's call, there's little that can come between you and that moment of choice. Ziram broke out of the cellar they'd locked him in, hiked cross-country to the square, and then declared. He was so happy to have made it in time, but his parents weren't. There was an enormous scene."

Andiss continued. "When Ziram joined us, he was happy. He applied himself with enthusiasm. He made great strides in the purely physical skills, taking to the training easily. What challenged him most were the skills of the mind and the heart." Kazari raised her eyebrows without thinking and Andiss shook his head. "No, no, it wasn't his devotion to the Lady that was lacking, but his discipline. As you now know from your own training, discipline stalks a Hunter. There's discipline involved in becoming fit and strong, and determination, which drives the discipline. But you have to apply the same thing to your studies and your desire to learn the Lady's way."

Understanding dawned. Kazari had struggled with running – was still struggling, truth be told, but she was determined to run further and further and faster. It was the determination that kept her shoving one foot after another when she'd rather have simply collapsed. "And Ziram struggled with?" She left the question hanging.

"He struggled with understanding the meanings behind some of the Lady's Writings. The application, if you wish," Javon said. "He could duck a spear thrust, fire a bow, and ride a horse without a saddle, but he hated to read, and when you don't practice something it doesn't improve. And without skill in reading, memorising the Lady's words becomes even more difficult. When you don't exercise your mind by thinking and learning, and by struggling with philosophical concepts, making good decisions based on those concepts becomes even more difficult."

"But the Abbot said that the Lady doesn't make mistakes about who she chooses for her Hunters, or for any of her servants," Kazari said puzzled.

"No, she doesn't," Sendar told her, and Kazari looked at him in surprise. "But what we do with that choice is up to us alone. She cannot force us to reach our potential, or to work harder. We choose that ourselves."

"And that is most likely where things went wrong for Ziram," Javon said. "His devotion to the Lady was very real, but his desire to grow up, or become more adult in his faith and his life, was lacking. Despite the opportunities he was given to learn, he tended to choose the simplistic explanation rather than seek out the deeper meanings."

"But why did you let him go ahead with the challenge, then, if you knew that?' Kazari asked.

"Because his answers were never wrong," Andiss replied, heavily, "Just not deep enough, and the distinction is very fine."

"There's a saying that vision is almost always better in hindsight, than it is at the time." Javon sighed. "When he died, we searched for a reason. We felt that he'd been trained as well as any Hunter initiate ever had, but in retrospect, we could see the pattern. The Abbot searched the records of previous failures, and the pattern was clear. You see, Ziram's death was the first in over thirty years, and it took us all unawares. We had become complacent, assuming that our initiates understood why developing maturity is important."

"And you will be the tenth initiate here to face the suckers since Ziram's death, but the first since then whose family resisted her choice," Andiss said starkly.

"And you're afraid for me?"

"Not exactly," replied Javon. "You appear to have a much deeper understanding of the Writings than Ziram did. His parents' early disdain for the Lady probably handicapped him. Despite your family's misgivings, they themselves are still genuine in their beliefs. You can be sure that we've checked."

Indignation struck Kazari. "You *spied* on them?"

"Yes," replied Andiss, simply. "Or more precisely, the Abbot made enquiries. Discreet ones of course, via their local Intercessor. He was able to reassure her on that account. Look, Kazari, Hunters learn to minimise the part that chance plays in an encounter with the gorgones. If the situation permits, we plan, check, and finally act. There are too many occasions when we must react first for a Hunter not to take every advantage."

The retort stung, and Kazari felt her cheeks flame. Her emotions were a mess, a roiling, churning mess of confusion, struck through with tiny jabs of fear. She, like Ziram, would eventually have to face four suckers by herself.

"When will I have to face the suckers?" she asked.

"The rule states that the trial must take place within the first six months of beginning to read *The Book of Hunters*," Javon said. "My own trial came at four months. Andiss' trial came at two. Sendar?"

The young man looked up and met Kazari's eyes. "Mine came the week after I received my Book."

"What?" The word burst from Kazari's mouth.

"The time isn't fixed," replied Andiss. "You'll face the suckers whenever it is that you encounter them. And from today, that might be at any time."

CHAPTER NINE:
THE TRIAL

Kazari lay on her back in her bed, half panicked, and half incredulous. Disbelief warred with terror. She tried to slow her breathing as Andiss had taught her, hoping to still the emotions that surged within her. She knew Javon had said that *The Book of Hunters* was only given when an initiate's trainers felt that he or she was ready to face the sucker trial, and that their training had progressed to a point where the initiate had the appropriate physical and mental skills – but *four* suckers!

She remembered the one at her Hunter initiation. It had been almost beyond her, despite the Lady's assistance. She rolled onto her stomach and opened her lantern shutter to illuminate her *Book of Hunters*. She touched the ornate cover reverently before turning to the relevant chapter, flicking through the pages until she found the right section. 'My Hunters must face their fears in order to liberate their gifts.' She'd read it the night before, but the words had flitted in one side of her head and out the other, replaced rapidly by the excitement of the gifts themselves.

She read on. 'When human strength is exhausted, then will My gifts become known. The Hunter who is free of bitterness can submerge their will in Mine, and open the gateway to their deepest selves.' It seemed relatively clear. Or as clear as any of the Writings ever were. All she had to do was to face four suckers until she was out of options, and then allow the Lady to open 'the gateway' to her deepest self. Whatever that was. She'd asked, but none of the others had been particularly forthcoming. Sendar, closest to her age, had just shaken his head, and said. "You'll know when the moment comes, but then you have to choose."

She closed the Book, staring blindly at one of the bookcases partitioning her portion of the room. Would she be able to submerge her free will in the Lady's when the time came? Would she be dead before she'd managed it? *How* did someone 'submerge their will?' And what was the gateway? And what happened to those who had the inborn Gift but didn't choose the Lady's service? She hadn't asked the others, but the question sat there, ticking away in the back of her head. Finally, Kazari tucked the Book back into the shelf above her head, shuttered her lantern again, and rolled over onto her back. Sleep was slow to come as she imagined all of the things that might go wrong.

Her mind drifted towards her family. Prompted by Ziram's story, she examined her feelings. Did she hold resentment against her parents? What about her brothers? She thought she didn't, but how would she really know? There was regret there – regret that they hadn't agreed with her choice, hadn't been able to distance themselves far enough from their own emotions to farewell her. But compared to Ziram's family ... her own parents hadn't agreed with her decision, hadn't been able to bring themselves to watch her make it, but they hadn't tried to prevent it.

It was the mark of difference between them. She tried to imagine what it would have been like to have your own father try to beat your choice out of you, or imprison you in order to prevent you from doing what you knew you should. She trawled through her own emotions again, sorting and filing, weighing and thinking.

Was she angry? Possibly. But not as she imagined Ziram must have been. She would have been, in his place. Angry and resentful. No, her feelings were more regretful than anything, she decided. But then she thought about the other things they'd talked about – deep thinking, philosophical reflection, and mental discipline. Her trial would begin when the requisite four suckers had been captured by Hunters currently in the field. Once they'd been sourced, Kazari would have only a day to prepare.

In the meantime, she would be training, training and training. She sighed. It wasn't as if she hadn't already been doing that anyway. In some ways she wished they hadn't told her what was about to happen, or not about to happen, she reflected wryly. It was entirely possible that she'd spend six months worrying about the event, not six days, like Sendar. She wriggled under her blankets, noting the soreness of her muscles, and trying to compose herself for sleep. Somehow, she had to teach herself to put the worry behind her.

The next morning, she woke scratchy eyed and tired. Drooping over her breakfast porridge, she was aware of an unusual tension in the room. As usual, she sat at a window table. With her were Charla and Abel. It had been several mornings since the three of them had breakfasted together. New initiates weren't strictly required to stay with their own septs, but over the first few months of early training, the chances to sit together with her new friends had been limited. Despite only knowing Charla and Abel for a short time, Kazari had quickly decided that she liked both of them. She wished they'd had more time to get to know each other properly.

"How's it going?" she asked the other two, as she took another swallow of her porridge.

"I had no idea there was so much to learn," Charla said. "You should see the quantity of stuff I have to memorise every day! And the tests . . . " She took a sip of her tea and then set the cup down with a clunk.

Kazari smiled ruefully. "I can imagine!"

Abel yawned. "They had me up most of the night learning constellations."

"What for?" Charla asked.

"Navigating at night," Abel sighed. "And that was after a full day's hike to the falls and back."

"Ooh," sympathised Kazari. She'd been there herself on a training run. It was uphill most of the way, but the downhill run was even harder. Her legs had felt like jelly by the time she'd arrived back at the Abbey. "They made me run half of it last time."

Abel groaned. "Run? Did you die?"

"At times I wanted to," she replied.

"No wonder you look like you do," Abel said, "If that's what you're doing on a regular basis."

"Thanks," Kazari replied drily.

"Sorry, didn't mean it like *that*!" Abel buried himself in his own porridge, and Kazari realised that he was blushing. "Anyway, I won't be in the Abbey for a while. I have a field test which will last some weeks, apparently."

"Better stock up on breakfast then," Charla said. "Apparently I'll be here for the foreseeable future. Years, probably." She sighed too.

Kazari wondered how she'd cope with being sequestered for years in the same place. She knew that once she'd reached a certain point in her training she'd be assigned to actively patrol with another Hunter. Even before that, like the Navigators, Hunter initiates spent a lot of their time roving. There were similarities between Hunters and Navigators; but Navigators accompanied caravans, and worked in groups, while Hunters actively sought out gorgones within Albatar, and patrolled its borders against intrusions.

"We'll miss you while you're gone, Abel," Charla said.

"Yes," Kazari said. "But I bet you'll have lots of stories when you're back."

"Assuming I survive it," Abel said, gloomily.

"I thought you loved being a Navigator?"

"Love is a tricky term, when you're carrying a huge pack and you're lost."

"Oh."

Kazari applied herself to her breakfast. She had a long session with Andiss in the grove that morning. She felt for *The Book of Hunters*, stowed carefully in her jerkin. Her Hunter garb had proved to be full of all kinds of pockets, sheaths, and places to hook things. She found that she liked it more and more every day. It was comfortable, designed for movement, and very hard wearing.

"We all look so different, now," Charla mused. "You in your blacks, Abel in his greens, and I'm slowly getting used to wearing these." She waved a hand at her robes. They were much more formal than the clothing worn by her friends, but to Kazari's eye, they suited Charla. It was becoming quite easy to imagine Charla in ten years' time, sitting at the right hand of a village Lady or Lord. She knew her friend had many years of learning ahead of her, followed by more years as a scribe in the service of an older Adviser. It was a long road the Lady had chosen for her. No wonder so few were chosen.

No longer than hers, though, although her mouth twisted wryly as she considered that it was entirely possible that her road might suddenly be cut short, should she come up wanting.

"So, anyone know what's going on?" Charla asked.

"What do you mean?" Abel said.

"Haven't you noticed the messengers?" Charla waved a hand at the head table. "That's the second one this morning." The Abbot's head was bent over a piece of parchment on the table. As they watched, the messenger handed another tube to Andiss, who broke the seal and unrolled the contents. He laid it in front of the Abbot after scanning it, drawing her attention to something halfway down the page.

Kazari watched on curiously. It was almost time for the morning readings, but the Abbot pushed her chair back, nodded to Elliam, seated at the second table, and beckoning to the sept leaders left the room. A moment later, Sendar paused at their table.

"Schedule's changed, Kaz. Meet Javon in the training hall. You'll meet with Andiss in the grove this afternoon instead." He nodded at the other two and walked off. Charla watched him appreciatively until Abel dug an elbow into her ribs.

"Charla!"

"Abel!" she mimicked his tone. "Look, it's not as if the Lady forbids us to marry, you know. I can admire."

"And you're what? Fifteen?"

"Nearly sixteen, thank you." She made a face at him.

Kazari smiled, Sendar *was* quite nice to look at, she realised.

She giggled, the first real giggle in months, and the other two looked at her in surprise. "What?" she said.

"You laughed!" Abel said.

"And?"

"Well, you just . . . don't."

Kazari rolled her eyes. "I haven't had time, or a lot of things to laugh about recently. Clearly they're not working you two hard enough if that's all you can think about!"

Charla snickered. "It has been pretty serious hasn't it?"

"Well, the whole thing is pretty serious," Kazari said.

"But the Lady likes us to be happy," Abel said. "She says so in the Writings. And I don't know about *your* septs, but the Navigators do remember to smile at each other on occasion."

"I'd have to have my head out of a book long enough to find something funny," Charla replied, and sighed again.

"It's been fairly intense for me, too," Kazari said, hoping desperately that the others wouldn't want details.

"Elliam said the Hunters can be a bit too serious," Abel said. "But I guess preparing someone to fight gorgones is pretty serious business." He sobered. "Let us know if you ever need to talk, Kaz."

She nodded, uncertain of how much she could share with the others. Perhaps she could ask Sendar. The chime for the morning reading sounded, and Elliam stood, walked to the lectern at the front of the dining hall and opened the copy of the Writings. "From the Writings, 'The Book of Days', Chapter 1."

After lunch, Kazari walked to the grove. Her upcoming trial had played on her mind, and she had found herself imagining all the ways that she could die. It hadn't been fun. She suspected Javon had tried to help by working her until she was exhausted, and her legs were still wobbling as she passed through the archway into the green dimness. Fortunately she'd had enough time to return to her quarters to wash and grab a cloak, so when the clouds began to scud across the sky and the wind to rise, she simply tucked the cloak around her and nestled into its warmth. The winter was almost upon them, she realised. The Abbey was further south than her home, and the weather was consequently cooler. She wondered if this far south there'd be snow. It had fallen only occasionally in her village.

Andiss waited for her, this time garbed in his own cloak.

"Ah good. Dressed warmly, I see. Follow me."

Kazari looked around. The grey sky was darkening by the moment, and it looked like rain. She hoped they'd end up inside as they had on other occasions when the weather had turned. She followed Andiss through the trees, feeling slightly uncomfortable as the sky darkened and the first drops spat from the clouds. Her cloak was waterproof, so she pulled the hood up over her head, squinting through the rain, as Andiss' black cloak became harder and harder to see against the thick foliage.

He ducked around a tree and as she followed him, Kazari realised that the rain was no longer striking her hood. She looked around quizzically, and then realised where she was. They'd exited here on that first momentous night, when she'd become a Hunter. At the time, the Abbot had said they'd make sure she knew where this entry was, but in the pall of exhaustion that had seemed to be her constant companion over the last few months, she'd forgotten about it. She was about to step back inside the Hunters' chambers. She pushed her hood back as Andiss beckoned her forward.

"There is news from the borders that concerns us all. The Abbot awaits us. We're the last to arrive."

Once again, the main chamber was full of Hunters. Kazari thought that perhaps there weren't as many as at her induction, but there were still enough to make the small area feel quite crowded. "Go and stand with Javon and Sendar," Andiss said.

Kazari moved through the throng, nodding to those Hunters who'd participated in her training, until she found Sendar and Javon standing together towards the front of the room. "What's up?" she asked.

"We'll know soon enough," Javon replied. The Abbot waved a hand and the chatter ceased as she stepped forward, Andiss by her side. Two other senior Hunters flanked them.

"We've had word from the borders. There's been incursions at Rethe and Altos. Both incursions have been repelled, however, we've taken casualties. We lost Anathar, and Seros has been seriously wounded." There was a murmur of surprise that washed across the chamber. Kazari turned her head to ask a question, but the Abbot spoke again. "We'll be sending reinforcements to both towns tonight, and also several scouting parties. Anathar sent word as the incursion began. She was concerned about the signs of many gorgones and believed we might be at the beginning of a major wave of incursions. To that end, I'll be sending another eight pairs to the south and eastern borders, and two pairs each to Altos and Rethe. I have word that the other Abbeys will do the same. Report to Andiss shortly for your assignments."

She turned and took a piece of parchment from the Hunter to her left and the chamber quietened again. "Kazari, stand forward."

Dread struck like a hammer in Kazari's chest. Her throat tightened convulsively as she saw the look on the Abbot's face. She knew – knew what was coming.

"You will spend the night here in contemplation. On this hour, tomorrow, you will face your trial." She handed the stiff paper to Kazari, who took it with trembling fingers. "Food and drink have been provided. There is a pallet by the spring and Javon, Andiss, and Sendar will watch with you. Spend time with the Lady and search your Book, but sleep well, for the outcome depends on your ability to survive your trial. We expect that the gifts that the Lady will help you to release will be sorely needed in the days to come."

Kazari's legs quivered. Already tired from the morning's activities, she knew she'd be extremely stiff by tomorrow afternoon. The thought of four suckers terrified her. Failing terrified her. The thought of death terrified her. But she managed to nod, not trusting her voice, and took a step back into the ranks of Hunters around her. Javon pressed her arm warmly, and Sendar moved so that his tallness was closer. It was comforting.

"Those of you who remain in the Abbey – I charge you to witness Kazari's trial tomorrow. Stand with me and watch as the Lady reveals Kazari's gifts."

She prayed briefly, committing all of their endeavours to the Lady, and then dismissed them all to their individual tasks. One by one, the Hunters assigned to the border came up to Kazari. "The Lady be with you. Lean only upon her," each said, and then hugged her gently. Her fellow Hunters could still surprise her. To the larger world, they were stern figures, garbed in legend, skilled in deadly arts, strong and confident. But within their own ranks, they were warm, caring, and sympathetic. Each of them knew the fear Kazari would face the next day. Each had already faced it themselves. Those leaving for the borders would most likely face far worse – and do it far away, possibly alone. Time in company was to be treasured. She found that her eyes were wet once again.

Finally just Andiss, Javon, Sendar, and the Abbot remained. The tall woman came over to Kazari, placing a hand on her shoulder. "We all feel the same way at this point, Kazari. It is natural to be afraid. Tell the Lady – she understands our human weaknesses. Use your time wisely tonight and tomorrow, and make sure you rest. These three will watch over you, and ensure you have everything you require." She squeezed Kazari's shoulder and then strode from the room, straight-backed and strong.

"Well, it's sooner than we'd thought," Javon said, "But you're well able for it, Kaz."

"The messengers brought in two suckers this morning," Andiss said. "But the news from the border is grave. And Anathar – for a gorgone to get the better of her . . . " He shook his head and exchanged a worried look with Javon that wasn't lost on either Kazari or Sendar. "I wonder what's happening in the outer world. It's been a while since we've had a messenger."

Sendar nodded. "Are any of us likely to be sent?" he asked.

"Possibly. Probably not you two – you're not far enough along in your training. You're close, Sendar, but Kaz, you've barely started. It probably depends on Kaz's Gift though, and how well the two of you learn to work together." Andiss frowned slightly. "Speaking of which, Kazari, you need to prepare. Try to ignore the other information and concentrate on tomorrow's trial. I'll see that your friends are notified that you're off on a training trip so that they don't miss you tomorrow morning. Start with *The Book of Hunters*, perhaps, and allow the words to sink in. Memorise what seems right and meditate on the Lady's words. Sendar will take you through some stretching in an hour or two. It's easy to become so wrapped up in the Book that you forget that the fight will be physical too. It's a fine balance. Let us guide you through this time."

Kazari nodded, thankful for their familiar presences. The ordeal before her wasn't just her own. It was part of each and every Hunter. She sat herself on the stone floor and opened her Book.

CHAPTER TEN:
SUCKERS

The twenty-four hours of preparation passed too fast. Kazari felt as if time was racing while her mind crawled. She was focused – more focused than she'd ever been, yet the things she strove to embed within her mind and her body seemed elusive, determined not to be grasped, as though covered in grease. She read *The Book of Hunters* hour after hour, ate as she was bid, attempted to sleep, stretched under Sendar's guidance, and stepped through the training forms with all three of her mentors, just as she had, every day, since her initiation.

The moments counted down, seemingly in time with the sound of the water pouring into the amethyst basin in the chamber, the only measure of the passing hours. Kazari's eyes longed for the light of day, but she was sequestered in the lantern-lit chamber for the entire time. Finally, Andiss stepped over to where she sat cross-legged on the pallet she'd tried to sleep on the night before. "It's almost time, Kazari. Are you ready?"

She looked up at him. He appeared the epitome of a Hunter, well-muscled, and wearing his Hunter garb with an easy competence, amethyst pendant glinting at his neck. "I don't know if anyone can be ready for something like this, Andiss, but if it's time, then I suppose I'd better be." She climbed to her feet and began to check her weaponry. There wasn't much. She'd barely begun on the knife, although she now had had several months of solid hand to hand training. She loosened her belt slightly so that she could move more freely, checked her boot laces, and then practiced sliding her knives from their sheathes.

The sound of the water in the bowl helped her control her skittering thoughts, chaining them into ordered skeins. Even so, as she flicked her arms to settle her jerkin, her heart began to pound. *Lady,* she prayed, *help me. Guide my actions, calm my fears, and help me face the suckers — and help me survive!* That last bit sounded hysterical, even to her. but she figured that the Lady could see how and what she was feeling, so she may as well be honest in her prayers, even if they made her blush as she prayed them. But as cloaked Hunters filed into the chamber, she thrust her hands into her pockets to hide their trembling, and tried to control her rapid breathing. There were fewer Hunters than the night before; some must have left for the borders already.

Four Hunters carried in four sturdy boxes, placing them to one end of the chamber, and she swallowed uneasily as one of them gave a violent rattle. All four seemed to ooze a creeping malaise. The Hunters formed a ring around the room, just as they had on the night of her initiation. This time she was no brand-new initiate, facing the unknown, this time she faced the known, and unfortunately knew exactly how difficult the task ahead would be. Kazari wished she was still ignorant. It might have been easier that way.

Finally, the Abbot arrived, completing the circle. Kazari stood as the Book had prescribed, at the far end of the chamber, flanked by her trainers, with Sendar standing directly at her back. "Are you ready, Kazari?" the Abbot asked.

"I am ready." They were the words specified, but Kazari felt anything but ready. Still, she took several steps forward, poised herself, and signalled her readiness. Waiting longer wouldn't make her any more prepared. Four boxes opened simultaneously, and four suckers appeared. They focused only on Kazari, and in the back of her mind, she wondered why – and how? Surely they sensed the other Hunters standing around them? She put the thought away carefully and began to recite the verses she'd memorised.

"'My Hunters must face their fears in order to liberate their gifts,'" she began. She hoped that facing her fears happened very quickly. Then she began to circle as the suckers attempted to surround her. She crouched slightly, hands before her as the suckers slapped their tentacles on the rocky floor of the room. A wave of hatred swept over her, and Kazari was shaken to her core. Loathsome thoughts whipped at her; images of gore and death spattered themselves across her mind. She raised a bastion of quotes against the thoughts.

"'My Hunters will stand before the defenceless. My Hunter will ground herself with My words.'" She whispered the words even as her hands shook, and the first sucker edged forward from its fellows. It changed its attack, and loneliness swept over her. Fear of rejection tugged at Kazari's soul, and the rejection by her family bit deeply into her mind. The sucker swung a tentacle as her arms dropped involuntarily, and the razor-edged suction cups whistled close to her head. Javon's patient training made Kazari sway out of its way by reflex, and her hand went automatically to her belt for a knife.

The loneliness dredged from her heart by the sucker's attack nearly made her drop it. Despair ground at her, calling blackly to that part of her that wished with all its heart that she was home and in her own familiar bed. The bitterness of rejection seeped into her soul and, as her resolve quivered, she failed to notice that a second sucker had peeled away from the others and circled behind her. *Lady,* she called faintly, as the waves of fear and loneliness assailed her, *Help me!* She thought she felt the amethyst on her chest warm slightly. Even if it hadn't, a tiny part of her held on to the thought that it had.

Her mind firmed slightly against the onslaught, and her knife hand came up as the first sucker made another lunge.

She sliced, and a tentacle parted, and then she buried her knife to the hilt in the thing's exposed belly. Black ichor stained the floor and she leaped back, triumphant.

Hot pain erupted across Kazari's back, and she dived forward reflexively, trying to escape. Fortunately, her leap took her slightly to one side, and as she dived and rolled, she came up behind the other two suckers. She twisted as she came to her feet and forced herself to face the remaining three suckers.

Their minds beat at hers, and she stumbled again, half crippled from the pain in her back, eyes streaming tears, blinding her, while her mind scattered to the four winds. Panting, she tried to lift her arm, holding the gore stained knife in front of her. She could see its point wavering through her tears, and she gritted her teeth, struggling to compose herself, struggling to hang onto her mind and her stance.

She prayed again. *Lady, I hurt. I cannot do this by myself.* And she couldn't – knew it to the depths of her soul and her mind. Two of the suckers separated, and a fresh wave of despair assailed her. She darted her eyes from sucker to sucker. The one in the middle began a slow advance, and the other two sidled in half arcs, trying to sandwich her between them. Kazari shifted her feet, automatically moving from stance to stance as Javon had taught her. After months of practice, she fell into the stances without thinking, unaware of how fluid her movements had become. She didn't hear the murmurs of appreciation from the assembled Hunters, so focused was she on staying alive.

Neither did she hear the indrawn breaths as the experienced eyes around her saw what her opponents were trying to do. For a moment, burdened with pain both physical and mental, Kazari was paralysed with indecision. An image of her mother's face momentarily replaced the suckers before her. The paleness of her mother's skin, and the fear she'd shown when they'd argued, froze Kazari in place, and her feet stopped their fluid movement. The flanking suckers took the advantage she'd offered, and then she was in the middle of a triangle.

If their attack had been vicious before, now it tripled, amplified by their positions around her. Visions of her father, her brothers, her mother. Dari lay limply on the ground while suckers stripped flesh from her body, leaving bloody streaks on her limbs. Kazari's mind shook. How could she possibly survive this? How did *anyone* survive this? And how could the assembled Hunters around her just watch it happening? How could Ziram have died in front of them, while not one Hunter lifted a hand? Why was she here? Why had she taken service with the Lady, only to die here and now, at not even sixteen years of age?

Tears threatened, anger surged, and she almost fell, unaware of the three suckers closing in around her. Their minds beat at hers, and her defences crumbled before them, one by one, laying her entire soul bare. Everything she'd ever hidden crawled out, and the suckers exploited those thoughts. The day she'd stolen a pencil from school – a childhood misdemeanour now magnified under the malign influences of gorgone exploitation. Her innermost thoughts – even those she'd thought only fleetingly, but never acted upon, were fuel for the suckers. They played upon her fears and her real and imagined failings, while slowly sneaking closer and closer.

Almost stripped bare, Kazari staggered, and the suckers began to close in, sensing their victory. The Hunters around Kazari tensed, hands going to knives, legs poised to leap, gifts drawn upon. They knew, even if Kazari didn't, that the moment was upon her.

Kazari almost gave in, almost fell, almost failed, and almost let her arm drop, but then, when there was nothing left, the tiny memory of Jaden's arms tightening around her, warmed her. She raised its memory against the suckers like a flimsy wooden shield against a charging berserker. It gained her a moment, and she opened her eyes, spinning in place, back in her fighting crouch.

LADY! She screamed from the depths of her soul, pouring her anger, hurt and despair, into the cry. And the Lady answered. The amethyst at her neck warmed, and the stone began to glow, brightening exponentially, until it hung like captive lightning at her throat. Almost broken, Kazari had nothing left but her memory of Jaden, and the ashes of her determination. The warmth of the amethyst began to thaw her soul, and her shoulders straightened. More memories came. Early mornings. Her parents' love – it wasn't gone, because she still loved them, and she knew that despite their disapproval, they still loved her. Dari. Abel. Charla. Her bunkmates, giving so selflessly of themselves. Dari's parents. The other Hunters.

The red-hot pain between her shoulder blades flashed to almost nothing, and then Kazari spun, and her gifts were there, scouring the suckers' influence from her, and replacing it with their heady presence.

Somehow, Kazari knew there was more than one gift. She healed. She felt the wound on her back close, tingling as the torn skin became whole. And then she moved, moved as she'd never moved before. She *knew*, knew exactly where each sucker would be. She danced around them, ducking and weaving so quickly that the eyes of the watchers surrounding them struggled to see her move. She was in one place, and then another. To her, it seemed as if the suckers were slow, moving through mud, or deep snow, while she danced on top of it, easily evading their tentacles as they swung them to where she had been.

Kazari felt the power of her gifts, and exulted in them. Stripped bare, her innermost hurts revealed, she had nothing else to draw upon. Those hurts weren't healed – at that moment, she could see that instantaneous relief would be cheating her of the growth she deserved and that perhaps she'd regret that later, but as she moved, and her gifts drove her, she could see that the healing of emotional hurts needed time, maturity, and the counsel of friends. All of that flashed through her mind as she spun, twisted and leaped, and she wondered if she'd think the same thing later on, when she lay thinking in the small hours of the morning.

Finally, the suckers lay dead at her feet, their hatred gone to smears of slime and deflated corpses, and Kazari stopped moving. Exhausted now, she stood trembling, while her gifts continued to flow through her, and the amethyst at her neck blazed, illuminating the chamber in a wash of violet. Almost unable to think, waves of emotion surged through her, full of complicated nuances. Echoes of hurt were soothed by the Lady with the promise of maturity, but the fear engendered by the suckers still sat uneasily in the back of her mind. She had been right. It would take time for them to heal – if they ever did.

As the adrenaline began to leave her system, Kazari let her breath out in a quivering sigh. Around her, the assembled Hunters stood solemnly, just watching. Through her fatigue, she could see their amethyst pendants were also glowing. The Abbot stepped forward and placed her hands on Kazari's shoulders. The warm touch steadied her.

The Abbot smiled at her. "Well done, Kazari. You stood firm when you needed to, and the Lady has made your gifts clear. It is many years since we had a Dancer, and not only a Dancer, but a Healer as well. Your gifts may well save many lives, once you master them."

She took her hands from Kazari's shoulders and turned her gently in a circle, so that all the Hunters in the chamber could see her face. "The revelation of your gifts will leave you exhausted, and it will take some time for you to be able to compose yourself. Sendar, Javon, and Andiss will stay with you this afternoon and answer any questions you might have. From now on, you will meet with me each afternoon for Gift training."

There was a small stir from the gathering, and Kazari had the feeling that perhaps the Abbot's statement was unusual. Still overwhelmed by the emotion and experience, all Kazari could do was nod, speechlessly. She found her hand reaching involuntarily for her amethyst, feeling its warm smoothness under her fingertips. The Abbot stepped back, and then, on an unseen signal, Kazari heard them raise their voices in a solemn hymn – more chant than hymn, she thought – full of rhythm and overlapping parts. The chant helped her regain her equilibrium as slowly her heart began to lose its pounding cadence and her breathing to steady.

Chapter Eleven: Changes

The reason for her tuition at the hands of the Abbot had become clear at Kazari's first training session.

"I'm the only other Dancer in the sept at this point in time," the Abbot had told her.

"Why is that, Ailani?" Kazari asked, puzzled. Andiss had implied that the gifts were usually evenly spread, allowing for a few random variances from year to year.

"The Gift of Dance is very similar to that of Anticipation," the Abbot had replied. "With one very important difference. One truly gifted with Dance, not only anticipates, but it appears that time slows for her as well, allowing her to move more rapidly than is normally humanly possible. You see, those who anticipate, know what an enemy or opponent will do, but only slightly in advance of that move. Then they must rely on their trained reflexes to do the rest. At best, they can choose a direction to move, or counter one movement. Don't discount that, because even that, is much, much more than most people can ever achieve, even when highly trained." She went on, drawing stick figures on a sheet of paper to represent people. "You, and I on the other hand, see what will happen, but we have more time in which to act. Or at least to us it seems as if we have more time, because to everyone else, we look like a blur." Kazari knew that she must have looked confused, because the Abbot began to draw again.

"Look here, Kazari. If an Anticipator was fighting the four suckers, she'd probably have dispatched them one by one, while at the same time anticipating which direction the next one might attack from. What you did, unknowing at the time, was to see it all in slow motion, allowing you to react to each individual movement from each individual sucker, and then position yourself so that you could deal with more than one simultaneously."

Kazari looked at the paper, now covered in arrows, and nodded. "They did look slow. Slow and predictable," she said thoughtfully.

The Abbot flashed a quick grin. "Exactly. And that very predictability is exactly why we use suckers for this test. In a year, you won't even think four are a challenge. Even a Hunter without the Gift of Dance or Anticipation is able to dispatch four of them, because suckers often move in predictable patterns. Those, we can teach. But for this test, with someone relatively untrained, the suckers are easily procured, easily contained, and easily dispatched if required."

"But Ziram still died," Kazari blurted out. "He died, even though anyone in that ring surrounding him could have saved him."

The Abbot sighed. "Yes, that's true, and it still haunts every single one of us who was there. You see, the Hunter taking the test must not simply *feel* as if he or she were in danger, they must actually *be* in danger for their gifts to be made known. Most of us are able to sense when a charade is being enacted, so a pretence of challenge is inadequate for our purposes. And sometimes, even a Dancer isn't fast enough." She looked down, and Kazari realised that the Abbot had gripped both hands to stop them from rising to the amethyst at her neck.

"I'm sorry, Ailani," she replied. "I didn't mean to insinuate . . . "

"You were not wrong to ask, Kazari. Each time we have a death – no matter how few they are – it stays with us. In some ways, it spurs us onward when times are difficult, and for a

Hunter, difficult times will *always* come. It's what we are. For some Hunters, patrolling the borders and putting down the occasional gorgone incursion is all that there ever is, but every now and then, a greater incursion occurs, and we are *all* tested to our limits. We never know when that might be, but we must always be prepared. Four suckers gives you a small taste of what a greater gorgone will be like. Perhaps you will never meet one, but then again, perhaps you will." She shrugged. "It *is* certain that you will meet more suckers. They prey on discord, and where humankind is, there is always discord." She put her pen down, and then stood, pushing her chair back and gesturing to Kazari. "Enough theory. Let's begin. Focus on your gifts, and let's see what you can do." And then she moved, so fast that Kazari's eyes nearly fell out of her head, and was standing on the other side of the training hall before Kazari could shut her gaping mouth.

Many painful hours later, Kazari felt as if she'd been pummelled with a stick. The Abbot hadn't hit her hard, but they'd been playing a kind of dance tag, and she'd been pursuing the Abbot for what seemed like hours – and she hadn't caught her once. The Abbot encouraged her to allow her Gift free rein, but the doing was proving much more difficult than the theory.

And then there were the frequent interruptions to the training session. Messengers came and went multiple times, necessitating interruptions, delays, and moments when Kazari had to sit to one side while the Abbot dealt with whatever required her attention.

As the days passed, she noticed that the interruptions become more frequent, and that the Abbot was growing more concerned every day. She wondered if the unrest on the border was escalating, but despite being in the Abbot's company every day, she still knew no more than anyone else.

Day after day, she rose early, ran with Javon, sparred with Sendar, meditated with Andiss, memorised more of *The Book of Hunters*, and then spent most of the afternoon attempting to perfect her skills as both a Dancer and a Healer. Healing seemed to come naturally, despite the fact that it was a secondary Gift – or at least healing *herself* came naturally. It was at a cost though, leaving her tired and wobbly, feeling as if she'd run twice as far as she did every morning. When she tried to heal others – mostly Hunters with bruises and cuts from training – results were mixed. There were a number of Hunters with the Gift of Healing, but for most of them, it was their primary, or solitary Gift, and they were very skilled.

They healed others from minor wounds readily, and according to the Abbot, with effort, some major wounds as well, given enough time. Daily, a small trickle of Hunters allowed her to try to heal their minor injuries, headaches and colds. She became slightly more proficient at wounds, but more complicated illnesses frustrated and exhausted her, and no matter how hard she tried, or how hard she concentrated, she didn't seem to be improving.

Learning to 'dance', though, was the most exhilarating thing she'd ever done. When she sparred with the Abbot, she could feel and hear and see more acutely than she'd ever considered possible. "Don't slack off in learning your craft though, Kazari. You might have Anticipation, and the time to use it, but if you don't know where or how to strike, it could be all for nothing. You need to practice with Javon and Sendar until you master the knife, the sword, the staff, and the bow – without dancing, and until you can fight a gorgone with nothing but your bare hands and feet," the Abbot reminded her the first time she managed to touch the older woman.

The words were sobering. "Yes, Ailani," she replied, nodding. She was panting, but so was the Abbot she was pleased to see.

"Drink?" the Abbot asked, wiping sweat from her brow.

"Yes please," Kazari said. They left the training hall and walked towards the dining hall. It was cold now. Autumn had come, and was nearly gone, and frequent grey skies heralded the beginning of winter. The Abbot took a deep breath of the cold air and smiled.

"First snows tomorrow, I'd say."

"Really? How can you tell?" Kazari asked, curiously.

"Smell the air – your village is probably too far north for much snow," the Abbot said. "But for those of us from the southlands – we can smell it in the air, feel it on the wind."

Kazari's sweaty face was cooling rapidly, and she dabbed at the now chilly moisture with the back of her sleeve. She sniffed the air experimentally. There was . . . something . . . but she wasn't sure what it was exactly.

"What kind of smell?" she asked.

"It's crisp, with a hint of sharpness," the Abbot replied. She spun as she walked, letting her arms fly out from her sides to Kazari's bemusement, and smiling as if the idea of snow invigorated her. For a moment, she looked as she must have when she'd come to the Abbey, a young woman, full of promise and the joy of the winter season, cares and worries wiped from her face.

"You like snow, Ailani?"

"I love snow." The Abbot smiled. "I grew up even further south than we are now. It was much colder there. In fact, the snow will already be thick on the ground in my village."

As they walked beside the towering granite wall at the southern edge of the Abbey Grounds, Kazari sniffed the air again, hoping to understand what snow smelled like. Once again, she smelled . . . something. It didn't seem to smell the way the Abbot had described it, so she sniffed again, trying to determine what it was. The scent grew stronger as they got closer to the dining hall, somehow overriding the warm woodsmoke wafting from the kitchen chimney, and the savoury smell of soup drafting on the wind.

Sharpness, she mused, but not crispness, rather sharpness and . . . acridity? Was that the word?

"Ailani," she said, "there's a strange smell."

"The snow, isn't it delightful?"

"I'm not sure it's the snow," began Kazari, "I don't think it smells . . . right." The smell escalated sharply, almost painfully, and then a nightmare crawled over the wall and oozed down it, crouching in front of them, its many limbs extending claws and cutting edges, readying itself like a lazy cat stalking a mouse.

"Behind me!" the Abbot shouted. "And sound the alarm. Run, Kazari!" The tall woman slid a knife from her sleeve, even as she drew the longer blade from its sheath at her hip.

Frozen in place, Kazari was struck dumb by the thing in front of her. Scaled and slimed, the monster had left a trail of ooze on the granite. It snapped its teeth and hissed.

"RUN! I said, RUN!"

Finally the Abbot's words galvanised her into action, and Kazari ran.

"Help! Help! Gorgone!" Sensible enough to know she had to sound the alarm, Kazari couldn't help glancing backwards as she ran. The Abbot had dropped into a fighting crouch, more poised than any Hunter she'd yet seen. Both hands held knives, but they looked too small and too fragile to do more than goad the monstrosity that assailed her. The pendant on her chest was glowing – glowing brightly and warmly, cutting through the darkness that seemed to surround the monster crouching in before her.

Kazari shouted again. "Help! Gorgone! The Abbot is being attacked!"

Two Hunters appeared, bared weapons in their hands, and then the Abbey Bell began to ring, in a cadence Kazari had never heard before. Now she'd done as she'd been asked, she turned back to see the Abbot and the other two Hunters warily facing the gorgone. It hissed, and a blast of black fog issued from its mouth, and the air became suddenly cold – no, not cold . . . gloomy. Kazari felt as if the life was slowly being sucked from within her and she shivered, and heard a whimper escape her lips. Then the feeling of gloom turned to dread as she realised what was happening.

The gorgone's radius of influence was much larger than the suckers' had been. All the stories of gorgone incursions rushed to the front of her mind, along with a quote from *The Book of Hunters*. 'When they come, beware them. Even unseen they strangle hope and choke the light that illuminates the soul.' And now, at last, she understood what it meant. A greater gorgone stood before them, and there were only three Hunters to face it.

In the background, Kazari could still hear the bell ringing, despite the creeping fog of despair and dread emanating from the creature. It made her feel sluggish, almost mesmerised, and fearful. She struggled to focus, struggled to form coherent thoughts, painfully aware that her encounter with four suckers was as nothing before the creature that now menaced the Abbey – and it was only one.

The Abbot! Where was she? Her eyes darted from side to side. Surely she'd been facing the gorgone. She could see the other two Hunters, now separated, attempting to flank the creature, but nowhere could she see the Abbot. She couldn't have fled? Part of the rational portion of Kazari's mind said, 'Of course not.' The other part – the bit being siphoned from her by the gorgone said. 'She ran to save herself, leaving you and the others alone. You will surely die in this place.' That part left her feeling cold and abandoned. She struggled to remain in control of her own thoughts, feeling as if she was thinking through thick sludge.

The other two Hunters were still somehow moving. And not just moving but moving normally. They seemed unaffected by the gorgone, and it was clearly annoying the creature. Kazari watched, awestruck, as moving in perfect unison, they darted in, one on either side, and struck at the gorgone. Each struck true, scoring hits with their knives along its flanks, before darting backwards again. And then, from nowhere, the Abbot began to dance. The creature hissed again, grimy fog erupting from within it, and the miasma around it thickened, darkening not only the vicinity, but stifling the furious attempts Kazari was making to break free of its thrall. Leadenly, her foot moved, causing a tiny hope to spark within her, but then she realised that she'd moved towards the creature, not away.

The Abbot's darting attacks had distracted it, but now it swung around, looking directly at Kazari, catching her eyes like a cat stalking a mouse. Terrified, her mind became quivering jelly, and she quailed, certain that no human could overcome such a monster. She stood, paralysed with fear in the cold and the damp, and the dread-filled air.

Then, faintly, as if in the distance, someone's voice tickled Kazari's ears. The words were hard to understand, almost distorted. She lifted her head, trying to understand what whoever it was, was saying. It was barely more than a whisper, a whisper that blended with the hiss emitted by the gorgone, and barely audible. She strained her ears, trying to make out the words, but the darkness seemed to be enclosing her. She lifted a foot uncertainly, not sure where it might take her, hoping it was away, but eerily certain that the gorgone was drawing her to it. And then she remembered. She was a Hunter, or at least one in training. The words of the Lady rose in her mind.

'The Hunter will ground herself with My words.'

With that thought, the darkness seemed to retreat a little, and then the gem at her chest ignited in a burst of purple fire. One step, another, and the gorgone lost its hold on her mind and she was running, not away from it, but towards it – but of her own volition this time. She staggered, caught herself, and felt her Gift rise within her. She danced, forming a kind of duet with the Abbot. They ducked and wove around the beast, flitting through its morass of fear, darting in to strike at it, while all the time it seemed to move in slow motion. Kazari's knife had found its way to her hand, and unhesitatingly she struck at the monster before her.

Despite her speed, she was too slow to stop the gorgone striking at one of the other Hunters. A flick from the creature's ooze-laden tail struck him, and he sailed through the air to strike the wall heavily, and then lay still, limbs spread like the fallen branches of a lightning struck tree. She swung with her knife again as she sped in towards the gorgone, opening a long slice down one side of it. She kept moving, ducking under its head, and then dancing back out of range. The Abbot's blade found its way unerringly to vulnerable spots on the gorgone, while Kazari's untutored strikes did more to irritate than disable, and occasionally she mistimed her movements, impeding the Abbot's precise ones.

More Hunters joined them. Javon soared through the air, and where she passed, the gorgone's strikes were blocked. She seemed to be in just the right place at the right time – every single time – and Kazari couldn't fathom how she was doing what she was doing, or even what her Gift was. The Hunters coalesced into a seamless group, occasionally tripped up by Kazari's inept movements. Even so, the fight was desperate. The gorgone struck back furiously, erupting in clouds of seething darkness, spewing hate and despair into the surrounds, and even the experienced Hunters wobbled slightly. Kazari felt it – felt it deep in her bones and her soul, but then a pure sound cut through the air from behind her, and she spun involuntarily towards it and was almost caught by a swipe from the beast's taloned arm.

Six white-robed Intercessors stood just out of reach of the monster. Singing. It wasn't what she'd expected at all. Three Hunters joined them, placing themselves deliberately in front of the Intercessors, guarding them. Almost incredulously, Kazari recognised two of them as the pair she'd watched staring, motionless, at each other that day when she'd first seen the Lady's Gifts in action. From her studies, she now understood that they were either Suppressors or Projectors.

The Intercessors' sound cut through the darkness in a blast of white, and the Gorgon's shroud of despair lifted like a curtain on a spring day, allowing light and freshness to flood in. And then a claw struck Kazari and pain erupted across her thigh. Distracted by the Intercessors, she'd let her guard drop. She collapsed to the ground, her leg screaming painfully at her. Gritting her teeth, she rolled away from the next swipe from the gorgone, tumbling across the paving stones, to fetch up against the Abbey wall, trapped, and with nowhere else to go. She struggled to focus as she tried to muster her own Gift of Healing.

Around the gorgone, dark clad figures spun and stabbed, while the Intercessors' choir grew in number and volume. And then the arrows began to fall. Not simply wooden arrows, but arrows that blazed brightly, rimmed in aquamarine. Some struck the gorgone, while others appeared to bounce off. The amethyst at Kazari's breast blazed more brightly in response, and she finally felt her thigh begin to heal, and pushed herself to her feet, hopping slightly to begin with, and then as the gorgone took another swipe with one of its many limbs, and she felt the wound close completely, she began to dance again.

At first, she danced slowly, barely ducking in time, before growing faster and faster, until she was buzzing with speed while the gorgone moved as in quicksand. "Kazari! Go to Andiss!" The Abbot's voice galvanised Kazari, and she leaped to run backwards, still limping slightly, looking for Andiss, all the while concerned she was abandoning her fellows. But now, as she danced backwards, she was buoyed by the sound of the Intercessor choir, marvelling at the power of its sound, all the while calling for Andiss. And then realised that her voice might not carry while she was using her Gift. She stilled herself, calming her speed as the Abbot had taught her.

"Andiss!" She looked around wildly, while the other Hunters continued to surround the gorgone.

"Kazari!" She could hear his voice, but not see him. Her eyes lit on Sendar, face creased in concentration. He was sweating heavily, despite the winter air, and she realised that he must be lifting Javon again, while anticipating where best to place her. Then the confusion of black clad figures resolved, and she saw Andiss' muscled form bounding towards her. "Take my hand."

Confused, she held hers out.

"Now, I need you to dance again, but without letting go of my hand. Your Gift is strong, but without guidance, it's ineffective. Do as I say, and together, we can take the pressure off the Abbot. Quickly now."

For a moment, Kazari panicked; how was she to dance with another person? What would happen? *Could* she dance with someone else? How would they keep up? All of those thoughts made her pause indecisively. She opened her mouth to tell Andiss she didn't know what to do, but he gave her hand a small shake. "Just do it, Kaz. Do now, think later. You can do this."

Confidence in her teacher steadied her. If Andiss thought she could do it, surely she could. He was trusting himself to her abilities. Taking a deep breath, Kazari thought a prayer to the Lady, and recited aloud her words again. "'My gifts are for the good of all. Protect My people.'" Then she leaped back into the fray, this time dancing with a partner. Somehow, her Gift encompassed Andiss, but the strain of it was like a leech sucking her blood. The fight rose and fell, along with the song of the Intercessors, and the arrows of the Navigators.

Kazari and Andiss moved as one. Kazari moved as Andiss called, keeping a firm hold on his hand, and every now and then, he'd have her dart towards the gorgone. Each time, he struck it with his long knife, and somehow, his knife struck further than anyone else's, deeper than anyone else's, and the gorgone began to stagger. The fight seemed to go on forever, and moment by moment, Kazari began to feel the strain. She danced harder and faster than she'd ever danced, and for a moment, her concentration wavered slightly, and they stumbled, but Andiss shouted. "Dance, Kazari, the Lady is with you. Dance!" So she rallied herself and kept on dancing, moving as rapidly as she knew how, while her strength siphoned from her limbs at an alarming rate.

"Carefully now," he said, and she could hear the strain in his voice as well. "Keep going, Kaz. We're close to the end now." And they were. The gorgone staggered, seeping ichor, and trailing limbs. The cloud of despair was now completely quenched by the Intercessors' song, and the arrows of the Navigators were striking it more regularly, some sinking to the fletching. "Come around, you monster," she heard Andiss say. "Steady now, Kazari, listen, listen. One more step . . . and in. Strike with me Kaz!" Kazari struck with Andiss, stabbing as hard as she could, following Andiss' direction, and she felt another force strike with her, pushing her knife deeper than she could have managed alone.

Black, stinking ichor burst over her hand, hot and slimy, and then Andiss called. "And again!" And they withdrew and struck again, and again. Each time, that force drove her knife and her hand, until finally, the gorgone crashed to the ground in a twitching pile of tangled limbs. A flight of aquamarine arrows struck as one, and it stilled and shuddered to a puddled mass of reeking flesh.

"Stop, now Kazari. Slow yourself and stop." Andiss' calm words took a moment to penetrate, and Kazari suddenly realised that she'd circled the beast, dragging Andiss with her, while the thing died. "Breathe, Kazari. Breathe, and thank the Lady for her Gift."

Kazari breathed out, letting her mind reach towards the Lady in gratitude, then staggered to a halt. Her limbs shook, and it was hard to draw breath among the stench of death and horror. Her lungs heaved, and she added her own stench of vomit to the filth on the ground. Andiss released her other hand and put an arm around her shoulders. "Well done, Kazari. Come on, walk with me."

CHAPTER TWELVE:
CONCERN

Andiss guided her away from the corpse of the gorgone, talking to her gently and slowly, just as he did to the horses he so loved, and gradually Kazari began to calm down. Still shaking with the aftermath of the fight, she almost stumbled as he led her towards a stone seat. She wobbled the last few steps and collapsed onto the seat, drawing heaving breaths through her mouth. Slowly, her breathing slowed, until she was just panting, much as she had in the early days of running. It was at that stage that she realised that Andiss was sitting next to her, elbows propped on his knees, also breathing heavily.

"A . . . Andiss?" She put a world of questions into his name.

He raised one hand tiredly. "A moment, Kazari." When his breathing had slowed enough, he levered himself upright, and turned to face her. "That hasn't happened for years. In fact, not since I've been a Hunter. You did well tonight, Kaz, very well."

"But . . ."

"Just wait for a moment, and I'll answer all your questions. I need to speak to the Abbot first, and then we'll go and clean-up. Are you hurt?"

For a moment, Kazari wasn't sure, and then her hand went to the back of her trousers, to find the rent where the gorgone's claws had sliced through the material and into her flesh. Her hand encountered the torn edges of the fabric, but the skin on her thigh bore only a slightly raised scar. It was tender though, and she had the feeling that when she stood up, it would still hurt. "Healed, I think, but still sore."

He grunted, nodding. "Thought so. But have the Healers give you the once over. Their skills surpass ours."

She blinked. It hadn't occurred to her that the other septs might receive gifts from the Lady – but why wouldn't they? Surely the *Book of Hunters* wasn't the only sept specific Book. And there'd been those flaming arrows as well. And the songs. Clearly, she didn't know as much about the Order as she'd thought. Or perhaps she'd just been too involved in her own training to look around herself to see what was obvious to anyone with half a brain. She felt slightly stupid.

"How did the gorgone get so close to the Abbey, Andiss?"

His face was grim. "And that, Kaz, is the question, isn't it?" She thought he'd go on, but he didn't, and it was clear from his face that the conversation was over. "See the Healers, Kaz. And then go to Javon and Sendar. Check they're all right and do whatever Javon says. Stand ready for anything. This might not be the only gorgone around."

The thought chilled her to the bone, and as she stood, she drew a shaky breath, looking around at the aftermath of the battle. Andiss moved off towards the Abbot, his normal stride tempered with tiredness, to where the Abbot was standing over the dead creature, with the heads of the other septs gathered around her.

Kazari took a couple of steps, hobbling slightly. Her thigh was as sore as she'd feared, so she limped towards the Healers, her leg complaining with every step. One of the red garbed Healers noticed and hurried towards her. Warm hands enfolded her, and she was ushered towards the Healer group. Around her, she could see several Hunters in the hands of the Healers. One of them was writhing on a makeshift stretcher, and three Healers were grouped around him, hands resting on him, while their rubies glowed brightly.

His moans slowed as they worked, and then he heaved a huge sigh and collapsed into stillness. Horrified, Kazari recognised him as the Hunter who'd been flung into the wall. She thought he'd died, until the Healer guiding her saw her alarm and said. "It's alright. He's just resting – see – you can see him breathing if you look closely. Still, it was a near thing, and he'll be a while in the infirmary."

Guilt struck her. Perhaps if she'd been faster, she could have spared him the injury. Perhaps if she'd been further along in her training, he'd still be unharmed.

"Sit, Hunter. You were injured? You're limping."

Kazari sat as she'd been told, alternately nodding and shaking her head.

"You were hurt?"

"I was, and I healed it, but my thigh – it's still hurting."

"Of course. The Lady's Gifts are good, are they not? Now, we'll need to take a closer look at it, so you'll need to accompany me to the infirmary."

"I have to tell Javon, first, please," Kazari said.

The Healer motioned to another red clothed figure. "Message for Javon the Hunter. I'm taking?" He raised his eyebrows.

"Kazari."

"I'm taking Kazari to the infirmary for a check. She may require further assistance." The other figure nodded, and Kazari had a vague memory of the youngster as one of her fellow initiates. Youngster – *she* was a youngster. "Now, let's get you there, Kazari."

An hour later, feeling much better, Kazari walked slowly back to her quarters in the company of Javon and Sendar. Both were unharmed but clearly fatigued. In fact, Kazari felt a bit of a fraud when she looked at Sendar's grey-faced exhaustion. The Healers had hummed and ha-ed over her leg, probing with gentle fingers while she lay on her stomach gritting her teeth. They'd decided that her injury was relatively minor – she *had* healed it, but the fight with the gorgone had placed too much strain on the newly healed muscle and she'd re-torn it as she danced. Her Healer, Bevon, had then placed his hands on her leg and the pain had vanished. A few moments later, she was walking out with Javon and Sendar, and an admonition to stretch the muscle regularly.

"What now?" she asked as they entered their quarters.

"Getting clean," Sendar said. "You stink, Kaz."

She blushed. "Sorry."

"You go first," he said. "I'll just rest for a moment." He sank back onto his bed, closing his eyes. Kazari looked over at Javon, who nodded and waved Kazari off into the bathroom. Thankfully, she grabbed clean clothing and a towel, and shed her boots. The floor was cool under her bare feet, but she noticed that someone had lit the fire box under the boiler that heated the water from where it flowed from the tank on the roof of the living quarters into their bathroom. Whoever it was, she owed them her thanks. She turned the tap above the bath, and let it fill slowly while she began to sluice the worst of the slime and ichor from her body with the jug, filled and refilled from the tap. Blackness flushed down the drain hole in the stone flagged floor.

Kazari found herself trembling again as she re-lived the fight. Flashes of action and fear flickered through her mind, and she found herself breathing heavily again, and had to force herself to relax. She took her time, scrubbing herself with soap, and pouring dipper after dipper over her head from the tub, trying to remove the worst of the stinking gore from herself before she allowed herself to sink into the hot water with a sigh of relief. The warm water soothed the rest of her aches and relaxed her muscles. She allowed herself ten minutes of soaking, before climbing out of the tub with a sigh. She could have stayed there for hours, but the others needed it at least as much as she did.

She let the filthy water out of the tub, and scrubbed the grimy ring from the sides then rinsed it down and refilled it as she dressed. As she donned her clean outfit, she felt as if she was reclothing herself in her humanity again. The encounter with the gorgone had shaken her more than she'd thought. "Bathroom's free. The tub's full of clean water," she said as she opened the door.

"Can you help me get Sendar in there?" Javon asked. The young man was still lying on his bed. "I'm not sure he'll be able to walk, and we might have to wash him."

Kazari blushed again. Even living as she did, in close proximity to her fellow Hunters, the casual familiarity the other three had with being relatively unclothed in front of each other still made her uncomfortable.

Javon made a face at her. "You'll have to get over this prudity, Kaz. There'll be no time for it in the field. Come on. He's exhausted – more exhausted than either of us." She looked at Kazari appraisingly. "You've come out of it better than he has, surprisingly. Hidden depths, perhaps?" She gave Sendar a gentle shake. "Sen, can you walk?" Sendar mumbled something and tried to roll over. "Sendar! Kaz, stick a chair in the bathroom, will you?" Sendar's eyelids flickered.

Several minutes later, Kazari helped Javon lower Sendar onto the chair. His legs had refused to cooperate, and he seemed to be too tired even to undress himself. Trying not to blush again – completely unsuccessfully – she helped Javon undress him and then begin to sponge him down. Javon was matter of fact and very practiced.

"Y . . . you've done this before?" Kazari asked.

"A few times. In the field, you do what needs to be done. Our job is exhausting at times, and always difficult. It's important that you and your partner – or partners – learn to care for each other in all ways. There's no time to worry about modesty if your partner's injured or exhausted, or you're stuck in a snowdrift – or a desert. You just have to do what needs to be done."

" 'S alright, Kaz. Can't do it myself," Sendar mumbled.

Kazari ran her sponge across Sendar's shoulders. He was well-muscled, despite his length, and she had to stop herself admiring the lean lines of muscle on his shoulders and back. She blushed again, and distracted herself by pouring another dipper over him and rinsing off the grime and sweat. She tried to view the exercise clinically, through the lens of the fight, but it just made her focus on what she should have done, rather than what she had done, so in the end she just made herself look for more dirt, and wash it off when she found it, while trying to keep Sendar awake by talking of nothing in particular, and anything but the gorgone.

Once they were done, they helped him back out to his cubicle where Javon viewed Sendar's bed, with distaste. "We'll put him in mine for the moment," she announced. "I'll clean his up after I've had a bath."

They rolled him onto Javon's bed and pulled a blanket up over him. Sendar closed his eyes with a sigh and immediately dropped into an exhausted slumber. "Back shortly," Javon said, and vanished into the bathroom.

Kazari looked at Sendar. He was soundly asleep, and his eyelashes seemed very dark against the brown skin of his face. She wondered how long he'd sleep. And then she thought about what he'd done, pairing with Javon as he had, throwing her around in the air, while she blocked the gorgone's strikes to protect her fellow Hunters. She thought back to her own part in the fight. The terror she'd felt when the gorgone had tried to drag her towards it resurfaced, and she found herself clutching her amethyst and chanting "Lady, Lady, Lady," under her breath. "Lady, how did I survive?" she whispered finally. *Only by her grace*, came the answer from her own mind. She shook her head. *Oh Lady, how do I learn to use my gifts properly in time?* The thought startled her. In time? In time for what?

Andiss' words replayed themselves in her mind. "That hasn't happened for years . . . " They echoed darkly in her thoughts. Not for years. A gorgone at the Abbey. An incursion on the borders. The messengers. Just what was happening? Was there a serious threat to Albatar?

Her reverie was interrupted by Javon's return. The woman was still rubbing her hair dry, and its short lengths stuck up in all directions. She ran her hands through it, smoothing it into some semblance of order.

"Javon, what's happening?" Kazari demanded.

The older woman sighed. "Help me make Sendar's bed and we'll talk." Javon pulled the grubby sheets off Sendar's bed as Kazari sourced another pair from the chest at the foot, trying to contain her queries. Javon went on as she tossed the dirty linen to one side. "At the moment we don't really know. There've been signs the gorgones have been preparing for something. The border incursions, the rumours of unrest in the outer world, and now this. They're all pointing to something, but what that is. . . " She sat down on her bed with a sigh. "How tired are you, Kaz?"

Kazari made a face. "I think the word is exhausted, but I don't know if I can calm down enough to sleep. And there's so much I don't know, Javon. Like how did Andiss know that I could take him with me?"

Javon's face stilled, and she was silent for a few moments. Finally she looked up at Kazari. "He didn't."

"He didn't?"

"It was a possibility, no more. The Abbot told us that the potential was there a few weeks ago, but that she hadn't tested it. Some of us can do it. Expand our gifts to encompass someone else. It's not common, but your Gift of Dance is strong, and it would have been tested shortly. Andiss and the Abbot clearly judged it worth the risk."

Kazari was silent, allowing the implications to sink in. "But what if it hadn't worked?"

"It did work," Javon said. "And it shortened the battle. It's a valuable Gift, Kazari, and with the gorgones on the move, it will be needed sooner rather than later."

"But Javon, I'm not ready. I know that. If Andiss hadn't been directing, I'd have been nearly useless, and even then, Deris was hurt." She curled her legs and sat cross-legged on her bed, feeling tears threaten.

"Deris was not your fault, Kaz. It happens in battle – nothing really ever goes to plan – even if you have time to *make* a plan." Javon's face was serious, and she caught and held Kazari's eyes so that the girl could see that she was genuine. "Don't beat yourself up over it. There was nothing you could have done. I saw Deris get injured, just as we arrived. Even a Dancer as good as the Abbot couldn't have stopped it happening. Just remember that you are one person and that you can only ever do your best. For someone not fully trained, you did well, Kazari, very well." She ran a comb through her hair while Kazari pondered her words.

"Javon, what exactly is your Gift?" Kazari asked finally as Javon finished making the bed and sat down with a sigh of relief.

The other woman laughed. "You mean you didn't recognise what I was doing, Kaz? Surely we've trained you better than that!"

Kazari flushed slightly, and ran the battle through her mind again, trying to remain objective. "F-force?" she stammered. "But. . ."

Javon nodded. "I have a secondary gift – Suppression. What you saw were Sendar's gifts moving me safely, while I Suppressed and blocked the beast with Force at the same time. With Sendar Anticipating and throwing me around, I was able to use my own gifts with impunity. It's something we've been working on together."

"And Andiss?" she asked, curiously.

"His primary Gift is one that's rarely seen. It's called Vigour. It enhances his strikes, and those of anyone nearby, or in contact with him. His secondary one is Healing, just like yours."

"I thought you said that more than one Gift is unusual?"

Javon nodded. "It is, usually, but nearly all of the initiates in the last three years have had secondaries."

Kazari unfolded her legs and wriggled closer to the edge of her bed. "But what would have happened if I hadn't been able to include Andiss in my Dance? Or if he hadn't been able to share *his* Gift with me?"

"As I said, Andiss and the Abbot judged it worth the risk. And it did work – don't worry about the what-ifs now. Besides, the Abbot has 'a feel' for these things, or perhaps the Lady imparts the information to her. Whatever it is, she's pretty accurate, so the risk was minimal."

Kazari tucked her feet up again. Her mind raced as she thought about what she'd seen and experienced that afternoon. It was clear that there was much more happening in Albatar than she'd been aware of in her tiny village. She had a feeling that there might well be even more.

CHAPTER THIRTEEN: SCENTS

Kazari woke with a start. Javon was shaking her shoulder gently. "Kazari, wake up, you've been called to attend the Abbot. She wants to see you now."

Kazari groaned as her body complained.

"Come on, Kaz. Get yourself together. The messenger's waiting for you outside."

Kazari struggled to her feet, yawning. She hadn't meant to fall asleep, but exhaustion had overtaken her. As she yawned her way to the bathroom to tidy up, her aches began to subside a little. By the time she'd straightened her clothing and made sure that her hair wasn't sticking up in all directions, she was walking comfortably. She wondered if her Gift of Healing was the reason, or whether it was just because she was moving.

It was cold outside. Her breath smoked in the night air, and despite her thick cloak, the chill seemed to penetrate to her bones. She followed the messenger in silence, wondering what the Abbot wanted with her. It wasn't as if she had the experience to comment on the tactics used during the fight.

She looked upwards, but the sky was dark, and the first snowflakes began to drift down as they walked through the door of the priory. Kazari hadn't been in the Abbot's private quarters before.

The priory itself was enormous, to allow it to also house the Abbot's staff and the heads of the other septs, as well as their assistants. What surprised her was the relative simplicity of the building. It was sturdy, with high ceilings, and was clearly ancient. The histories said that it had been the first Abbey, when Albatar had been founded. Indeed, as they entered, Kazari could see the entrance to the Abbot's private chapel next to the flight of stairs that led upwards to the other levels. With a sense of awe, she read the inscription in the stone. *'For the Glory of the Lady, and the Salvation of Albatar'*.

"Two flights up, third door on the left," her guide said. It was one of the initiates from the Adviser's sept, and Kazari wished it had been Charla instead of the solemn young man who had paced so silently in front of her. Perhaps Charla might have been able to give her a few hints about what might be required of her. He gestured with one hand towards the stairs, clearly urging her on, and she nodded silently and began to ascend as requested. The stairs were sturdy wood, polished to a high gloss, and flanked by stone walls on either side. The staircase itself zigzagged back and forth as she climbed, and then exited the stairwell onto a wooden hallway with a long indigo carpet runner. She counted the doors as she walked, and then paused and knocked hesitantly.

"Enter."

She pushed the door open, to find herself in a large room lit by a multitude of lamps. A fire crackled on a hearth on the opposite wall, bathing the room in warmth, and Kazari swung her cloak off her shoulders, folding it over one arm.

"Kazari, please, join us," the Abbot said, rising from her seat. The sept leaders and their seconds sat around a large table to one side of the fire, the remains of a meal on one end, while maps and papers were strewn across its polished surface at the other. To her discomfort, every head turned as she walked towards them.

Uncomfortably, Kazari took the chair the Abbot offered her, trying not to make too much noise as she draped her cloak on it and pulled it in towards the table.

"Thank you for coming so promptly. You must be tired. Tea?"

Kazari nodded uncertainly as the Abbot poured her a mug of hot tea and pushed a plate with a wedge of cheese and a sliced apple on it towards her. Her stomach rumbled, and she blushed. "Javon sent word that you hadn't eaten," the Abbot smiled.

"What can I do for you, my lady Abbess?" Kazari asked, uncertain of the degree of formality required.

"Ailani," the Abbot corrected with a gentle smile. "There are a few questions we need to ask you about today's encounter."

Kazari couldn't imagine what she might have to offer to the conversation, but she nodded quickly. "Yes, Ailani, whatever you need."

The Abbot tapped her pencil on the table, a small frown creasing her forehead. Her long fingers were muscular and strong. For the first time, Kazari noticed the fine tracery of scars across her knuckles gleaming faintly in the lamplight. They married with the deadly grace she'd seen when the Abbot had faced the gorgone alone, badges of experience and hard won skill.

"Do you remember the conversation we were having just before the gorgone came over the wall?"

"Yes, Ailani."

"We talked about the snow, and how it smelled, and then you said something. Can you remember what it was?" The Abbot's eyes were intent.

"You'd been explaining how to smell if snow was coming, and describing what it smelled like, so I sniffed – to see if I could smell it too."

"Go on," the Abbot said. "What did you smell?"

"At first I thought it was the snow, but it wasn't like you'd described, and so I told you it didn't smell . . . right?" Kazari said slowly, wondering what the point of the conversation was.

"I thought that's what you'd said," replied the Abbot. She turned to Andiss next to her. "Read the list of gifts again."

The muscular Hunter looked tired, Kazari thought, but he lifted his *Book of Hunters* and read. "'The gifts of the Lady to her Hunters are many. They are the Gift of Ascension, the Gift of Force, the Gift of Anticipation, the Gift of Health, the Gift of Dance, the Gift of Suppression, the Gift of Projection, the Gift of Vigour, and for only a few, the Gift of Sensing. By these will My Hunters prevail.'" He placed a bookmark in the pages, lowered his Book and looked up. "Is that what you think it is, Ailani?"

The Abbot turned to the others around the room. "What do you think? Are there records within your septs that might point more clearly to this Gift?"

Elliam leaned back from the table and narrowed his blue eyes thoughtfully. "It could be. It could be. The Navigators have records of Hunters who could detect gorgones when they were close by. In a few of our earliest records it was described as smelling, or, possibly, feeling? The words were unclear, the pages damaged by age, when I last read them. Hesta, does your sept record anything similar?" He turned to the woman to his left. She wore Intercessor's robes and was nodding her head thoughtfully.

"Yes, similar. Once again, the wording is old and unclear. It is possible that you are correct, Ailani. The question is, how do we test it?"

Kazari sat quietly. The others seemed to have forgotten she was sitting there. She sipped her tea, and nibbled at the apple slices and cheese, enjoying the contrasting flavours, while the others talked around her. She wasn't certain what they were talking about. She'd read the list of gifts herself, when Andiss had provided her with her copy of *The Book of Hunters*, uncertain then, of what each Gift might entail. Of course, some had now been explained, usually with a demonstration. To the best of her knowledge, she'd now seen Ascension, Health, Dance, Anticipation, Force, Suppression, Vigour, and possibly Projection. But the Lady's own words said that Sensing was only for the very few. She'd not thought to ask about it in the excitement of learning to use her own gift of Dance.

She returned her attention to the apple, while trying to listen in surreptitiously to the conversation.

"So you think that Kazari might have sensed the gorgone in advance of its entry to the Abbey?" Hesta asked the Abbot. "Do you think you might be placing too much reliance on a random conversation? It's pretty circumstantial."

"The point is, Hesta, that she commented that whatever she was smelling was not right."

"Not 'right' is hardly evidence," the Intercessor replied. "You were discussing the smell of snow, and Kazari comes from an area with little snow. She might just have misunderstood."

"Perhaps we should ask Kazari?" Elliam's dry voice cut across the conversation, and Kazari blushed, a piece of apple halfway to her mouth, as all eyes turned towards her again.

The old Navigator smiled faintly.

"What exactly *did* you smell?" he asked.

"It . . . it was different to what Ailani was describing," Kazari stammered. "She said the smell of snow was 'crisp' with a hint of 'sharpness.' This smell was sharp, but the only other word I can use to describe it is 'acrid.'"

"Acrid? That's a word not commonly used by initiates of your age," Hesta said.

Suddenly self-conscious, and a little defensive, Kazari replied. "We use it to describe some of the leather dyes at home. I do know what it means." She went on hurriedly. "And this smell cut through all the other normal smells, as if it was blotting them out."

"Might just have a keen sense of smell – the things stink," the Healer's leader said. Kazari didn't know his name.

"But she was actively looking for something at the time," Elliam said. "Perhaps it triggered the Gift."

"That is, if it's actually a Gift," replied a green garbed man. *Gregor?* Kazari thought, trying to remember his name.

"I think it *is* the Gift," the Abbot said, finally, "but clearly, we need to test it. Then we'll know for certain."

There was a sudden silence, and then they were all looking at Kazari. She squirmed in her seat and put the last slice of cheese down. Hestia's face was concerned, Kazari thought. Elliam's was thoughtful, while Verephon, his sept leader, frowned, and she wondered if she'd done anything wrong.

"Ailani," Andiss said, and Kazari could hear the caution in his voice. "If you want to test this possible Gift, it will be dangerous, and Kazari is nowhere near fully trained."

"I know." It was the first time that Kazari had ever heard that tone of voice from the Abbot. "But today's incursion tells us that the troubles we're experiencing on the borders are much more than simple unrest. Perhaps there is a reason that the Lady has provided this Gift at this time."

Hestia looked concerned. "Ailani, it is certain that more initiates with multiple giftings have joined us recently – each sept says the same thing, and all the Abbeys are reporting that they too see more and more multiple gifted initiates. We also know that there are more initiates every year, and that their gifts are more wide ranging than ever – but Sensing? We don't even really know how to recognise it, or even how it works! And to place one of our newest into a position where she will have no choice but to face another gorgone – that is madness!"

Kazari saw Andiss and the Abbot exchange a long look. He nodded to her. Once. Very deliberately. Decisively the Abbot turned to face the table. "Kazari has already faced down five suckers."

"She's what?" Verephon exclaimed.

"Each sept has its own ceremonies. Our initiates face a sucker the night of their pledge. They do it alone, untrained, and with only a knife. Later, they face four at once. It is in this manner that their gifts are made known." A babble of sound rose around the table, and Kazari could see more than one mouth agape. The Abbot raised a hand and her voice thundered out, authority in every syllable. "And this is something that does not leave this room. I will have your promise that you will tell no-one of this. A Hunter must come unknowing to her first trial. This is the Lady's will for our sept. It is her way of allowing her Hunters to prove themselves while they are yet untrained and helpless. Kazari is young, and her training is incomplete, yet she is not unaware of the dangers we would ask her to face." The Abbot turned to Kazari again. "Do you remember smelling anything during your trial?"

Kazari considered the question for a few moments, and looked at her plate. and then shook her head. "Truthfully, Ailani, everything happened so fast I didn't really think about what was going on." She was tempted to add 'and for a few moments there I thought I might die' but decided not to, however, from the hint of amusement in the Abbot's eyes, she suspected that the head of her sept had heard her unspoken words.

"You understand that I believe that you have the Gift of Sensing in addition to your other gifts. Are you willing to be tested?"

Kazari's heart beat faster. She knew exactly what the Abbot meant. Exactly how the testing would be undertaken, she wasn't certain, but she knew that it wouldn't involve just suckers. How could it? What if she did have the Gift, and different gorgones 'smelled' different? And how close to a gorgone would she have to be in order to 'smell' it?

She knew both Andiss and the Abbot were aware of exactly what they were asking. She also knew, without a doubt, that some of the others didn't. She drew a ragged breath. "With the Lady's help, I will do it. I hope." She found her hand clutching her amethyst. It warmed slightly at her touch, and she knew that she'd made the right choice, but it didn't stop her feeling as if she'd just jumped feet-first into quicksand. Her mother's fear-filled face flashed before her, and guilt flared briefly, but she suppressed it and turned her face resolutely towards her future. For once she was glad that her family had no idea what was happening to her.

Chapter Fourteen: Travel

"**M**ount up," Andiss said.

Kazari climbed obediently into Stumpy's saddle, avoiding his continued efforts to nuzzle her for treats. She'd continued weekly riding lessons during her months of training, and she was much more comfortable with her own skills in the saddle now, still it was nice to know she was riding a horse who had been trained to stay with his group, and one who'd been trained to stand in the face of gorgones. Andiss had imparted that small fact to her as they'd saddled up. She didn't know if it made her feel better or worse about the upcoming journey.

She ran a hand down Stumpy's neck, surprised to find it was fluffier than normal. It seemed horses grew a winter coat to keep themselves warm. Very sensible, she thought, and shivered slightly, despite the layers of clothing she was wearing, as an icy breeze stirred her cloak. She could feel Stumpy's warmth beneath her, and patted his brown neck in gratitude.

"Let's go," Andiss said. It was an anticlimactic kind of departure, Kazari thought as she signalled Stumpy to move. Two nights ago she'd been in the Abbot's quarters discussing whether she might be able to 'sense' gorgones and now she was on her way to 'somewhere', to see if she really could detect them. In some ways, it was a pity that there were no suckers nearby, let alone any of the greater gorgones. If there were, they wouldn't have to head off for the southern border regions, and further into the cold. She sighed, and her breath made a plume of steam in front of her.

As they rode out of the Abbey gates the sun was just rising over the Priory. It was a blue-sky day, but the ground was covered in a layer of snow, and their horses left clear hoof prints behind them. By her side, Sendar rode muffled in his cloak. He'd slept without moving until midmorning the day after the gorgone attack, and when he'd awoken, he'd been stiff and sore. He'd continued to recover slowly, but he still looked tired, she thought.

"Are you feeling alright, Kaz?" he asked, riding slightly closer as they followed Javon and Andiss down the road.

Kazari wondered how to answer his question. Was she all right with hunting gorgones? She examined her feelings and came up with 'sort of' – it was what she was meant to do as a Hunter, but she wasn't really one yet, just a part-trained, short, stocky initiate.

She sighed. "Sort of. Look, I know we need to find out if I can sense gorgones, but I wish there was a simpler way of doing it. A safer way, actually."

Sendar nodded and they rode in silence for a while again.

Kazari concentrated on her position in the saddle, the feel of Stumpy underneath her, and took the chance to look around at the countryside. The last time she'd ridden this road it had been in the other direction. It had been spring, and she'd been on her way to become an initiate. She thought back to that girl – the one who'd thought she'd be one of the Judicars, or a Grower. Her lips twisted wryly. The Lady hadn't exactly given her any hints she'd end up a Hunter.

That thread of thought led inevitably to her family. It was a long time since she'd seen them, and she wondered if they'd forgiven her yet. She wished she knew how her brothers were, and how Dari was. She also wished she could send a message to her family, but she hadn't heard from them at all, although she'd had regular letters from Dari, and sent some in return. Her own letters to her parents had remained unanswered, so she'd eventually given up sending them. Still, she wished she could tell them that she was fine. Well, that she was *currently* fine. The future was looking somewhat uncertain.

From the discussion in the Abbot's meeting room, it was clear that something serious was happening. While gorgone incursions were a fact of life in Albatar, they were usually isolated events, only occurring once or twice a year. Lesser gorgones, like suckers, were relatively common – attracted by the pettiness and insecurity that was part of being human, even in this realm, with its love of the Lady part of everyday life. Kazari had learned that dealing with suckers was the bread and butter work of the Hunters. Dealing with greater gorgones happened occasionally. They were drawn to greater conflicts, or perhaps were the result of greater conflicts – where a murder had taken place, or where a village lord had decided to annex the property of a neighbouring lord unlawfully.

Sometimes they came in from outside, usually as a result of unrest in the outer world. But every now and then, a massive incursion took place. The last had been over a hundred years ago, and was now part of Albatar's history. There were tales from that time though; of Hunters who'd stood against greater gorgones, and Navigators who'd taken entire villages to safety. In the Abbey, she'd been taught about Intercessors, Healers, and Advisers who'd placed themselves in danger to protect their people. Of the Growers and Judicars who had kept the people of Albatar fed and safe and calm, when crops had been overrun by gorgones and their accompanying armies.

It had been so long though, that the people of Albatar had been lulled into believing it was unlikely to happen again. The Abbot believed otherwise.

"It is possible we're in the early stages of a large invasion," she'd told them the night before their departure.

"Kazari, if you can sense gorgones, and particularly if you can sense them from a distance, you might well become one of our most valuable assets in this fight." To Andiss and Javon she'd said. "Keep them safe. And stay safe yourselves. I suspect the incursions we've had are only warnings. There will be much worse to come. The Navigators are preparing several groups to go beyond the borders and bring back word from the outer world. Our information is outdated, and we need to know what is happening that might cause a greater gorgone to assault the Abbey itself. It must have known it wouldn't succeed. That, in itself, is the most puzzling thing. There was no real reason for it – certainly not unaccompanied." Then she'd turned to include them all in her admonition. "Keep your eyes open. If you see anything – anything at all outside the usual – report it. Go with the Lady, and my thanks, and return home as soon as you're sure one way or the other."

Kazari mused on the Abbot's words as they rode. She thought and prayed, and beseeched the Lady to make it clear whether she possessed the Gift of Sensing. And then she prayed that others might have it too – that she might not be set apart by her differences. She realised that in the Order, she'd been finding friends and purpose even more than she had in her village. She saw Charla and Abel less than she liked, but she now realised that Sendar, Javon and Andiss were also friends. They'd spent hour after hour teaching her, and she'd become very fond of them all. Sendar was only a year ahead of her, and still exploring his own gifts and skills, and he understood when she struggled, and understood when she was tired from running, or sparring, or trying to use her gifts.

Sendar, Charla and Abel were slowly filling the hole in her heart left by her family and her farewell to all that had been familiar. One day she'd see her family again, and one day she'd see Dari, but for now, she had new friends who were also companions and teachers, and who warmed her with their presence and their patience. Despite the chilly morning, Kazari felt cosy inside herself – comforted in a way she hadn't been for months.

For several days they travelled due south, and then began to angle towards the south-eastern border area, along a road that began as a wide, well paved highway. They skirted several larger towns, and for the first time in her life, Kazari saw one of Albatar's cities in the distance. She was awed by the sheer size of it, even as far away as it was. But as they travelled further south, the villages began to shrink, and the path began to narrow until it was little more than a goat track that meandered through rising country before beginning to climb steeply. A week into their trip, Javon signalled a halt and dismounted. She dropped to one knee beside a small pile of rocks, and then fished around in it with her gloved hands, before standing up with a rolled piece of oiled silk in her hands. It was tied with a purple cord.

She cracked the wax seal and undid the cord, then beckoned to the others. "Dismount you two. You need to learn about this." She took them over to the pile of rocks. "Look here – see the rock pile? Note the arrangement – it's a standard marker left by another Hunter. Always check them if you see them. One you've read the message inside, you can add to it, replace it, or take it, depending on what it is. This one's a note to say that two of the pairs sent by the Abbot were here a week ago. They're following rumours of gorgones and unrest at Suborden."

Kazari looked at the pile of rocks. It was a conical cairn, much like the trail markers, which indeed she'd mistaken it for, but with a tiny difference. Half way up the cairn, a group of horizontal stones stuck out at the four points of the compass. They were not large, but just big enough to be obvious to someone looking for them. Javon had removed the western one to reveal a hollow inside. She committed the arrangement to memory, and then climbed onto Stumpy's back. He snorted gently, and she patted him. The track ahead narrowed again.

"Will we follow them to Suborden?" Sendar asked.

Javon looked at Andiss and raised an eyebrow.

Andiss nodded. "Where there's unrest, there's likely to be gorgones. Kazari, keep yourself alert from now on. Let us know if you 'smell' anything unusual. Or feel anything unusual for that matter."

"Yes Andiss."

"And be wary all of you. The snow's likely to get deeper the higher we go. This track's not the best either. Kaz, Sendar, you need to trust your horses. They were bred in this region, and they're better at hill climbing than we are."

The track steepened rapidly and Kazari's legs soon began to ache from keeping her weight forward as Stumpy negotiated the track. His gait was confident, despite the drops that fell away on either side. Kazari wasn't nearly as confident, wishing she could close her eyes and wish herself away. She was cold, too. Camping in the snow hadn't been nearly as pleasant as she'd fantasised, despite the excellent equipment available to the Hunters sept.

As they wound their way further and further into the mountains, Kazari tried to experiment with Sensing, sniffing to smell the air, and looking for gorgones. The problem was, she had no idea what she was trying to do. She'd been handed a sheaf of paper with all the information the Abbey had been able to dig up about her supposed Gift. It wasn't much. The last Hunter with her Gift had been dead nearly a hundred years. He'd died of old age, forty years after the last major gorgone incursion. He'd been instrumental in detecting gorgones near the western border of Albatar, and had led sortie after sortie against the gorgones, both greater and lesser.

The histories were quite clear about his activities as a Hunter, but were much less clear about how his Gift worked. The commentaries simply stated that: 'Janish sensed the gorgones around the entry to the pass. Navigators and Hunters were able to contain them, and then remove them from Albatar', or 'On that day, Janish detected four greater gorgones prowling the outer reaches of Rethe'

The records never went into *how* Janish had detected them. It appeared, from scattered fragments, that he'd been able to do it from some kind of distance as well, but again, there were no records that suggested what that distance was. It was very frustrating.

Every few minutes, Kazari made herself draw a deep breath, trying to replicate whatever it was that she might have done when the gorgone came over the Abbey wall. She felt stupid after the first half day – sniffing the air like an idiot with no result. It didn't help that she could hear the unspoken questions from her companions when she did it, or that the cold air made her nose run and she was convinced that the tip was going to freeze off any second. By the time they paused on the crest of a rise to eat the midday meal, her nose felt soggy and red, and she was feeling annoyed, embarrassed, and as if she was just stumbling blindly. Which of course she was.

"I don't even know what I'm trying to do," she complained as she dismounted. She gave Stumpy a pat and led him over to where some old grass poked through the snow. He pawed the snow away, dropped his head and began to nibble. Kazari perched herself on a log, feeling the chill bite through her trousers, and took the flatbread Andiss handed to her. She took a bite and stared morosely into the distance.

Javon rested a hand on her shoulder, but didn't say anything to her, while Andiss just grunted and bit into his own flat bread. The view from the rise was spectacular – snow-capped mountain ahead, while below the fertile lands of Albatar, now snow covered, spread out before them.

Kazari looked at the view, and despite its beauty, found herself dwelling on the what-ifs. What if there was a major gorgone invasion about to occur? What if she didn't have the Gift of Sensing? What if she did, and could never understand how to use it? Her anxiety began to spiral round and round inside her mind. She clutched at her pendant, but the amethyst didn't warm to her touch. *Lady, what should I do? How do I do what I need to do?* The entreaties went around and around inside her head, but she felt as if they went no farther than the bones of her skull.

Objectively, she believed that the words of the Lady were true, but emotionally, she felt further away from her presence than she ever had before. Kazari finished the final bite of her flatbread and walked over to Stumpy to remove the water bottle from her saddle. The water was icy, stinging her lips and making her teeth ache, but warned by Javon about the issues of altitude sickness and dehydration, she forced herself to continue sipping. She could feel the beginnings of a headache tightening the skin around her temples, when a spatter of cold snow slapped her in the back of her head.

She spun around, suddenly frightened that they'd been assailed by some gorgone she hadn't smelled or sensed, to see Sendar looking slightly embarrassed.

"Oops," Sendar said, shamefacedly, "That was meant to be a snowball."

Confused, she looked at his hands. They were empty, and there were no flakes of snow on his gloves. Then she realised what he'd meant. "You used *Ascension* to throw snow at me?" she said, incredulously. "One of the Lady's *Gifts*?"

He shrugged. "Well, I've got to keep practicing, or I'll never get stronger, and Javon suggested moving snow around might help, because it's not completely solid. What she didn't realise was that because it's not solid, I have to compact it first, and that's really hard . . . " He broke off. "What?"

"But – it's a *Gift*, Sendar!"

Kazari was aghast at the whole irreverence of it all. Weren't the gifts meant to be holy, or something?

Sendar laughed. "Kaz, it's a skill, just like knife fighting, or wrestling, or shooting arrows, or anything really."

"But it's from *the Lady!*" she insisted.

"And the Lady doesn't want us to enjoy ourselves? Or practice?" he asked, lifting an eyebrow at her.

She stuttered for a moment, but then his logic won through. The Lady was known to encourage her followers to find joy in life. And some of the stories in the Writings were rather humorous.

Eventually Kazari shrugged helplessly. "You'll have to do better than that if you thought *that* was a snowball!" she said.

Sendar joined her at the horses, and took his own water bottle from his saddle. "You know it's all right, Kaz, don't you?"

"What's all right?" she asked, replacing the cap on her bottle and tying it back onto her saddle.

"You not knowing what to do, or how to do it. No-one expects you to magic it out of thin air." He sipped again, then replacing his bottle, ran his hand down his horse's legs, lifting its feet one by one to check for balled snow. "Kaz, it's been a hundred years since the last time a Hunter was given the Gift of Sensing." He removed a snowball hammer from a pocket and tapped away at the snow balled in one hoof.

"It's just . . . Sendar, have you ever not known what to do?" she asked frustrated, as she followed Sendar's lead and began to check Stumpy's hooves.

"Of course! Just because we're Hunters, it doesn't mean we all know what to do all the time. Or at least I hope not, since I'm still making heaps of mistakes, and most days the best I can hope for is a slight improvement over what I managed to do the day before."

"It's just that . . . I suppose I thought that once I was at the Abbey, things would become simpler . . . . easier."

"I thought when I entered the Abbey that I'd never be so exhausted from work that it hurt to sleep, or that I'd never have another sleepless night worrying about stuff ."

Despite her frustration, Kazari laughed. "Oh dear." The day suddenly looked brighter.

"Yes, oh dear."

They finished checking their horses over, and a few minutes later were back in the saddle, climbing higher into the mountains. Kazari kept trying to detect gorgones, still without any idea of what she was doing, until eventually they reached a fork in the path and, to Kazari's dismay, they headed up the steeper, narrower way. Even if she detected a gorgone, or, the Lady forbid, a gorgone detected them, the idea of fighting one on a goat track on the side of a mountain horrified her.

Fortunately, neither thing happened, and as the winter sun touched the horizon, a small village came into view, smoke from its fires drifting into the air, and the warm lights in their windows welcoming them. The path finally began to level out. The village was perched on the shoulder of a mountain – almost the only flat spot Kazari had seen since they'd started upwards. Snow lay thickly on the steeply gabled roofs, and the village was picturesque and tidy. Every now and then, an overload would slide down, splattering onto the ground below the eaves.

The clank of goat bells came faintly on the air, and from somewhere nearby, the rich smell of soup, or possibly stew, wafted in their direction. Kazari's stomach grumbled so loudly that Stumpy turned his head and looked at her. Sendar snorted softly and she blushed, wishing her stomach had kept its thoughts to itself. They followed Andiss through the village, leaving the savoury smells behind to Kazari's regret, and continued on towards the town's chapel, perched on a small knoll, just before the path began to climb upwards again.

Like every chapel in Albatar, this one had the local incumbent's living quarters nearby, along with barracks for any of the Lady's servants who might be visiting or passing through. Dismounting stiffly before the long stone building, Kazari looked around at the neatly kept grounds. Despite the snow, the chapel grounds were as precisely laid out as the Abbey's. The arrangement reminded Kazari of the Priory. The barracks were backed by a stable, she guessed, judging by the smell of horse on the breeze. Andiss handed her his horse's reins and rang the bell beside the door.

A few moments later, the incumbent Intercessor opened the door. "More Hunters?" she asked. "We have four here already. Not to worry, of course, but we'll be a little cramped." Her voice carried clearly on the evening air, and Kazari could see she was surprised.

"Cramped is fine," replied Andiss. "We'll assist the Hunters already here, and then be out of your hair. I have a message for you from the Abbot." He passed a note to the Intercessor.

"My thanks to the Abbot for thinking of me," she continued more formally. "And the Lady's blessings be upon you. Welcome to her house in Suborden. There is shelter for your horses in the stable around the back, and one room left in the barracks. There are four bunks, and it has its own fire. The bathroom facilities are shared, I'm afraid. Dinner will be ready within the hour."

"Our thanks, Intercessor. After a week of living rough, your barracks will be more than adequate. I have spices and herbs for you from the Abbey Growers, and Elliam has sent new maps to add to your collection."

"Many thanks, Hunter. Those things will be very welcome. I am Androvar. And you are Andiss of course – I recognised you from my time in the Abbey. Your companions?"

"Javon, Sendar, and Kazari. These two are currently under instruction." He waved a casual hand at Kazari and Sendar as Androvar smiled a welcome. "We'll unpack, clean-up, and be with you within the hour."

The barracks were a welcome change from a bedroll and a bush. As Kazari unpacked her gear and readied herself for dinner, a knock sounded on the door. "Andiss?" a voice called.

"Mikel. Welcome, or should I say, well met?" Andiss said as he let the other Hunter inside the room. "Since you're already here."

"It's good you've come," Mikel replied. "Something's not right here."

"Gorgones?"

"Possibly. We haven't seen any, or even seen any sign of them, but the village is ... " He frowned. "There's something wrong here. Not Androvar," he hastened to add. "She was the one who sent the alert. But there is something not right." He sighed and perched himself on the end of Sendar's bunk. "Welcome, Javon, Sendar – and Kazari?" He looked up quickly at Andiss, raising an eyebrow. "You've brought our newest initiate?"

CHAPTER FIFTEEN: ENCOUNTERS

Mikel's eyebrows lifted until they seemed they were about to defy gravity and fly away, as Andiss explained why they'd come to Suborden. "So, you've brought Kazari here in case we find gorgones? To see if she can sense any of them?" He made a face. "Seems dangerous to me."

Javon sighed. "It is dangerous, but if the Abbot's right, and this is just the beginning of a major incursion, then we need to know if she can do it. And sooner rather than later."

"Does the Intercessor know?" Mikel asked. He pulled one of his knives from its sheath, and a whetstone from a pouch, and began to sharpen the knife. The sound was oddly soothing to Kazari, even if Mikel kept looking at her as if she was some kind of fascinating new bug. She looked away and fiddled with her own knife, absently sliding it in and out of its sheath, and then tucked her hands under her legs when she realised what she was doing.

"It was in the Abbot's note," Andiss told him.

"She's a good sort," Mikel replied. "And the people here truly like her, which makes whatever's going on around here even stranger. I just wish we could put a name to it."

Kazari looked around at the village as they walked from the barracks to the priory. Even in the snowy night she could see it was prosperous, well-kept, and beautiful, despite its remoteness. The whiteness of the snow on the roofs glowed luminescent under the moons, and warm light shone from every house. Even the sky above was pristine, the stars glittering like jewels against the blackness. She drew a deep breath through her nose, but there was nothing unusual on the wind. Nothing at all like the acridity she'd smelled before the gorgone had crawled over the wall.

Over dinner, the talk turned serious again. "You have Kellis and Sherd scouting further towards the border?" Andiss asked.

"Yes," Mikel replied, "Androvar, would you allow us the use of your maps, please? Thank you." He pushed his soup bowl to one side as he spread a map out on the table. "We've been here, here, and over here, and the others have been in this area. So far, there's been nothing, so we thought we'd come back and spend another few days with Androvar, while the others patrol the border this side of the range. We're still trying to put our finger on what's going on here. I thought a couple of days with Androvar might shed some light." He tapped the map, and then outlined the border with a fingertip. Sendar leaned in towards the map, frowning.

"That's very rough ground."

"That's part of the problem," Mikel replied, sitting back again.

"Androvar, you've talked to the people?" Andiss asked.

"Of course I have. For the most part, they're lovely people – devout, practical, hardworking." She spread her hands. "But there's something I can't put my finger on. I've been here for six years. And for the last six months or so, something's been changing the tone of things. No-one says the wrong thing, or does the wrong thing, but the exuberance has gone, and there are undercurrents I can't explain. In addition, the Lady has sent me warning in my dreams." She touched the diamond pendant sparkling at her breast.

Kazari looked at Androvar curiously. Intercessors spent hours in prayer and meditation, seeking the Lady's will for her people. Some found their way as incumbents, guiding the people of Albatar, while others stayed in the Abbey. It was clear that some had gifts she'd never expected, and she wondered what else Androvar might be able to accomplish. Posted this close to the border, she suspected that Androvar had unexpected depths. The Abbot was a clever woman, and a Hunter. She would never have sent anyone without skill to the border, and having seen an Intercessor choir in action, Kazari now knew that there were more hidden depths to the Intercessor sept than she'd expected. She'd recently found herself musing on what else the other septs might have up their sleeves.

It had become clear to her that although the Lady's Hunters were the point of her spear, they were not the only weapons she wielded against the gorgones. Now Kazari had had time to think about it, she realised that *all* of the Lady's servants were part of her battle against the forces of evil, not just her Hunters. They were, however, the forefront of her defence – or perhaps her attack.

"Kazari!" The voice penetrated her musings, and Kazari realised that Androvar had been trying to gain her attention.

"Sorry, I was thinking."

"Thinking about what?" Androvar asked.

She looked down, slightly embarrassed. "About how the Order is much more than I originally thought. And about how the Lady gives gifts to all her servants, not just her Hunters." She blushed. She felt a movement by her side, and she had the feeling that Javon was smiling slightly.

"Then you've made the first steps along the path of wisdom, Kazari. It takes some of her servants a lot longer to come to that conclusion."

Androvar looked at Andiss and Javon. "What I wanted to know was whether you'd do the rounds with me tomorrow. Get a feel for the village. Perhaps Sendar might come along as well, while the rest of you look around further afield. The people might speak more freely in front of the youngsters. With your permission?"

Andiss nodded. "Javon and I will use the morning to become familiar with the village environs. What we're looking for are suckers, hopefully, because what you've described sounds very much like their influence. If we can capture one, then we can discover whether Kazari can sense them. It will allow us to perform tests in a controlled environment, and that way we kill two birds with one stone. Do you have a basement, Androvar?"

"There's the cellar, I suppose. I mostly use it to store root vegetables. I think there's enough room to confine a sucker, if you can – did you say capture?" She blinked, clearly surprised.

Andiss nodded. "Suckers, despite their propensity to cause discord and unrest, are the easiest gorgones to confine." He looked at Javon, who nodded. "We use them to train our initiates."

Androvar's eyebrows nearly vanished into her hairline. "I see. Thank you for entrusting me with this knowledge – you can be sure I'll keep it close." She gave a wry smile. "I used to dream of being a Hunter. In my first few months as an initiate Intercessor, I'd beg the Lady to change my path. I grew out of wanting to be a Hunter quite quickly, though, and into realising that the path she'd chosen for me was right. And tonight you've confirmed it. Training on suckers?" She shook her head. "Nope."

The following morning dawned grey, and tiny snowflakes were sifting from the sky as Kazari and Sendar joined Androvar on her rounds. She began the day as they had begun every day in the Abbey – with a reading from the Writings, then, surprisingly, she'd sung in a clear voice to welcome the day. Her voice was pure and shining, and Kazari felt echoes of something more than just music in its perfect tones. Androvar smiled at Kazari when she'd finished, and Kazari knew that she'd given them a hint of one of her gifts. Then they'd moved to the chapel, leaving crisp footprints in the dusting of new snow, to help Androvar to tidy the sanctuary and light the chapel fire. The Lady's chapels were open to all, available for anyone who wanted to spend time in prayer and contemplation, and in cooler climes, the incumbents made sure that her people were well cared for.

As they accompanied Androvar on her rounds, Kazari began to understand what both Androvar and Mikel had said. On the surface, Suborden was content, and again Kazari saw overt evidence of comfortable wealth. Each dwelling or small shop was warm, well lit, and comfortable. Hot drinks were pressed upon Androvar, Sendar and Kazari as Androvar explained that the youngsters were on a field trip as part of their training. Which was true, really, when Kazari thought about it – she just wasn't providing the villagers with all the information she had. At one dwelling, Androvar left a book; at another, she enquired after a sick child; while in a small warehouse, she spent time examining the hands of an oldster. The oldster's hands were worn by years of spinning the soft mountain wool into the warm blankets and fabrics that were laid out for sale when traders came through the village in spring and summer.

The comfortable air was a thinly held illusion, Kazari realised as they left the warehouse. As Androvar had examined the gnarled hands with gentle fingers, Kazari had become uncomfortably aware of eyes watching her. In the shadows behind the spinning wheels, she caught a hint of movement, and the glimpse of an indistinct figure. At first she'd thought it had been her imagination, but then she'd heard the conversation falter – not stop, but hitch briefly – and then resume, but the tone had changed. The oldster seemed in a hurry for Androvar to finish examining her hands, and the final few minutes were uncomfortable.

There was a flurry of hurried looks between those in the warehouse, and Androvar's attempts to show Kazari and

Sendar the beautiful woollen creations were cut short as they were ushered towards the door with murmurs of "I hear the Mayor's expecting you, Androvar." And "We don't want to make you late, Intercessor."

Sendar nudged her on the way to the next house. Suborden's leadership was provided by a mayor, as it wasn't large enough to have its own lord. His house sat at the edge of the village, notable for its size rather than anything else, much like in her own home village of Athos. The gabled roof was the same design as all the others in the village, as was the general construction, yet it sprawled rather more than any of the others, with several meandering wings covering the ground. Kazari wondered how many people it housed. The house was warm, and the floors were gleaming wood that reflected the lamps set in niches in the stone walls.

Androvar had decided to share some of the spices they'd brought with them from the Abbey. The three of them were welcomed by the Mayor and his wife, and Androvar made a little ceremony out of presenting the spices, once again trotting out the field training story. Of course, all the villagers must have realised that it was highly unusual to have six Hunters and two trainees in such a tiny town, but no-one was impolite enough to mention it, although they must have been wondering. As they sat down to drink tea, and eat small biscuits with the Mayor's family, Kazari noticed that all four of the children were eyeing her and Sendar curiously, and with something like awe.

As she looked at the teacup and saucer balanced on her lap, she realised that compared to the girl who'd entered the Abbey all those months ago, she was a very different person. Still short and stocky, she was now much more muscular than she had been, and she was garbed identically to Sendar. Their comfortable, form fitting clothing was designed for easy movement, and the amethysts hanging from their leather cords said 'Hunter' all too clearly. She'd also become so accustomed to wearing an assortment of knives on her person that she sometimes forgot that it wasn't normal garb for everyone else.

As she sat there, making small talk, she remembered the one time she'd seen a Hunter in her own village. She'd been awed, a little frightened, and fascinated at the same time, and to her everlasting embarrassment, she'd snuck around behind him, just to see what he'd do. In retrospect, she suspected he'd pretended not to notice her, just to bolster her own sense of achievement. It was the kind of thing she'd expect of a Hunter now.

She smiled at the children, hoping to put them at ease. Three dropped their eyes, while the oldest, a girl who Kazari thought was probably close to her own choice, smiled hesitantly back. The girl couldn't have been much younger than herself, she reflected.

Kazari took a sip of her tea as Sendar elbowed her in the ribs, and turned her attention back to the conversation. The Mayor thanked both Androvar and the Abbey for the spices, and his wife bustled around making sure everyone had a hot drink and a biscuit. They talked of inconsequential things, pleasantries and trivia. It had been such a long time since Kazari had needed to make small talk that she had to dredge up the proper responses from her memory, and stammered over them.

So much of what she'd experienced over the last few months had changed her life so dramatically that she'd had little time for small talk or chatter. And then there'd been the recent life and death experiences. The conversation stalled when Androvar asked after the Mayor's elderly mother. His wife covered the hesitation with another round of biscuits, and then Androvar deftly turned the conversation in a different direction. Kazari caught a flicker of movement from the children, and turned her head to see the eldest, Clorri, looking down uncomfortably. Kazari tried to catch her eye, but she kept her face carefully averted.

House after house it was the same. Unseen eyes. Awkward pauses. Truncated responses and unspoken sentences. The missing words hung heavy in the air, and their absences began to emphasise the feelings of unrest that stirred in Kazari's mind. For the elderly, they fetched water, chopped wood and cleaned, and for the young they provided news, a listening ear or a piece of advice. It would have been a fascinating insight into the life of a village incumbent, had it not been for the nagging sense that something was dreadfully wrong. That sense grew stronger and stronger with each visit.

"I see you picked up on the issues?" Androvar said as they returned to her home for the midday meal.

Sendar and Kazari nodded.

"The question is, what's the root cause? There's something going on — and whatever it is, they all know about it — even the children — but they're trying to pretend that nothing's wrong," Sendar said. "Have you asked anyone?"

Androvar nodded. "Of course — both directly and indirectly. The answer is always that 'everything's fine.' That it's a good season for the wool, and that it's going to be a hard winter." She sighed and placed a jug of water on the table, and they ate in silence.

The remainder of a long day later and Kazari's sense of unease had escalated even more. It was an itch inside her mind, and a feeling of eyes everywhere. She wondered if she was just being paranoid, but as they walked back to the chapel through the now thickly falling snow, she stopped suddenly, and her sense of alarm flared.

She sniffed; had she really smelled what she thought she had? Nothing. Slowly, she turned, senses alert, eyes searching. A quiver began deep inside her. She sniffed again. Still nothing. Androvar and Sendar were looking at her with wide eyes. She turned again, wondering, but there was nothing. She began walking again, shaking her head at the other two.

"Thought I'd smelled something, but I think I was wrong. There's nothing now."

They continued walking, leaving deep tracks in the snow now. It had fallen on and off throughout the day, first in flurries, and then as the day wore on, in larger flakes. There was little wind, and the silence was eerie. Kazari couldn't help sniffing intermittently, wondering if she had or hadn't smelled something.

Androvar took them in a wide circle around the perimeter of the village. Kazari's shorter legs were finding the deepening snow challenging, and she had to concentrate to make sure she didn't slip on a patch of ice. As they passed the Mayor's residence, she was distracted by the lit windows. It looked warm inside, and the smell of woodsmoke hung heavily in the still air. The open curtains showed the family briefly at the table, before a hand drew them closed. As they walked past, Kazari thought she saw movement at an upstairs window, and almost missed her step, sliding on the ice.

Sendar's strong hand caught her under the elbow before she could fall. "Careful, Kaz."

She nodded her thanks, and looked up at the window again. "Can you see anyone up there?" she asked, pointing with her flick of her head.

He shook his, and they continued on, but Kazari couldn't shake the feeling of eyes. She wondered why someone in the house wouldn't be eating at the table, and shivered involuntarily, and then dismissed the image as a simple fancy. The snowfall became thicker, making it harder to see.

"Link hands," Androvar called. "We're not far from the chapel now, but you can get lost very easily in this."

Kazari took Sendar's proffered hand, and placed her other one in Androvar's mittened one. The cold began to intensify, and the snow came more thickly at every step. Kazari was grateful for the Intercessor's guidance, and sense of direction in the poor visibility. She concentrated on placing her feet in Androvar's footsteps, drawing Sendar along after her. The feeling of unseen eyes remained with her, though, making her shoulder blades itch. And then she smelled it again. Not strong, but just a hint. It wasn't quite the same odour she'd smelled before the gorgone had scaled the Abbey wall, but it was close. She sniffed, and felt Sendar's hand stiffen in hers.

She stopped, pulling Androvar to a halt. "I can definitely smell something."

"Kazari, if we don't keep moving, we'll lose all visibility," Androvar said, urgently.

"It's like I smelled it at the Abbey," she replied, "but only faint, and not all the time."

Androvar pulled at her hand. "Kaz, we need to move." The Intercessor's tone was urgent, and she waved at the falling snow with her other hand.

"But I might miss it, Androvar. It's why I'm here. I'm sure I can sense something." Concern now drove her. The smell was faint, but it was definitely there, and the thought of a gorgone among the people of Suborden chilled her to her core. If it was a sucker, perhaps they had a chance, but if it was something larger, the three of them didn't have the skill, or more importantly, given what she'd seen today, the will to face one.

Sendar's hand was firm in hers, and she took strength from it. The feeling of eyes was intensifying, along with the smell. "It's getting closer." She dropped both of the hands, spinning in place in the snow, wishing she could see more clearly. Even the Mayor's house, behind them, was indistinct, despite its lighted windows. In front of them, she could barely see the outline of the chapel. She sniffed, and then took a deeper breath. *Lady, how do I do this?* She asked, desperately certain that somewhere, a gorgone was stalking them.

Androvar grabbed her hand again, and gave a tug. "Kazari, if we don't move, we might die out here in the snow, even this close to the chapel. Yes, a gorgone is dangerous, but so is the snow. Trust me, I know."

The smell vanished. Kazari hesitated for another moment, drawing a deep breath, trying to smell, or feel, or whatever it was that she was doing to detect the gorgone she was now certain was nearby. She had no idea. But Androvar was right, the middle of a worsening snowstorm was not the place. She held her hand out to Sendar again, and then gave in to Androvar's increasingly urgent tugs.

The snow closed in around them like a smothering blanket, and then she had no choice but to trust that Androvar knew what she was doing and where she was going.

Chapter Sixteen: It Begins

Kazari slept fitfully. Her dreams were full of eyes. Eyes that peered from the darkness and stalked her through landscapes that held hiding places around every corner. She woke unrested, and with her eyes stinging from tiredness. She dragged herself out of bed weary and worried, and feeling inadequate. As Androvar read from the Writings to the Hunters grouped around her breakfast table, Kazari found herself unable to concentrate. The others had returned to the chapel before she, Sendar, and Androvar had, so they'd arrived to a cheery warmth and hot food, but this only underlined the unease she had felt.

Despite her warnings that she was certain a gorgone was in the area, Andiss had decided that today would be a repeat of yesterday, and that Kazari and Sendar would assist Androvar in the village while the others patrolled the approaches. He'd insisted that it was important to get to the bottom of the unrest in the village, and that if he and Javon, along with Mikel and his partner patrolled the area surrounding the village, while Kazari and Sendar accompanied Androvar, they had everything covered.

As Androvar sang to conclude the reading, Kazari realised she hadn't heard a word. She apologised to the Lady, mentally castigating herself, and reminding herself that the Lady had specifically said: *The Hunter will ground herself with My words* and that she had absolutely no hope of doing that if she didn't concentrate when those words were being read to her. The slight guilt she felt added to her unease, and as she swung her cloak around her shoulders, she sighed heavily.

"Bad night's sleep," Sendar asked.

"Yes," she replied shortly. "Sorry," she apologised. "It's just . . ."

He elbowed her, and she looked up, surprised.

"We're all worried Kaz. But we have to be methodical about this."

She nodded silently, and then went outside into the snowy morning. It was sunny and blue, and the snow was very deep. It made getting around slow and arduous, and after the first few minutes of ploughing through it, Kazari was secretly glad she wasn't out with Andiss and Javon. She could only imagine what the snow was like on the slopes around the village. Trudging after Sendar, behind his long legs, she couldn't help but envy him. Fortunately, she was able to follow in his wake for most of the trek to the chapel, rather than breaking the trail herself. Her short legs were strong, but she rather thought she might have vanished in some of the deeper drifts.

After a little while, she noticed that the snow seemed more compacted than it had been, and as she squinted in the bright light, she was certain she'd seen snow moving in a wave away from Sendar's boot as he stepped. She leaned forward and poked him gently, and he turned his head back towards her with a wink and a quick grin. Briefly, she considered throwing a snowball at him, but it didn't seem like an appropriately dignified response while they were in the company of an Intercessor.

The day went much like the previous one. Visiting, helping, and chatting, but once again the feeling of eyes followed Kazari everywhere. By midmorning, she found herself searching every dark corner, in every room, almost obsessively seeking the owners of the unseen eyes and trying not to sniff too obviously every time she entered a dwelling – although she realised that expecting to find a gorgone sitting at a kitchen table was ridiculous. When Androvar asked her to pop back to the chapel for another medicine bag after checking the oldster's aching hands again, she walked out of the tiny warehouse into the freezing air with a sigh of relief. The warehouse's dimly lit depths had her itching between her shoulder blades and wondering just what was going on in the village.

It was hard work walking back to Androvar's quarters by herself, even using the path they'd forged through the snow earlier that morning. Sections of the trampled down snow had melted slightly in the sun, and then refrozen when they moved into shadow as the day had worn on. Several times, Kazari slipped and slid on the slick surfaces, once almost toppling into a deep drift. She managed to regain her balance, and then walked more carefully each time she saw the trodden down snow glinting ominously.

It took her some minutes to locate what Androvar needed. The chapel itself was a warm haven, free of the unseen watcher, and although she knew she needed to get the bag back to the Intercessor, Kazari found herself lingering there, breathing deeply, and allowing the tension to drain from her neck and shoulders. She hadn't realised just how tense she'd become. It was a wonder she hadn't begun to start at every unknown sound.

She paused and kneeled briefly at the front of the little chapel, near the arc of brilliant gems that symbolised the Lady and her septs. *Lady, please reveal the watchers, and guide our paths,* she prayed, and then walked through the sanctuary, watching the play of light through the windows, feeling the medicine bag swing from her shoulder and bump her hip at each stride.

A quiet rustle flicked her head around, and she sniffed, seeking danger. But then a very human shape stepped hesitantly out of the shadows. The young girl from the Mayor's house had been sitting quietly to one side of the chapel, hidden from view. With a shock, Kazari realised that her face was swollen and bruised, and that her lip was cut. She dropped the medicine bag and hurried over.

"What happened to you?" she demanded, placing a hand on the girl's shoulder. "Did you fall on the ice?"

The girl flinched backwards, crumpling under Kazari's touch as if it had stung her. Fresh tears traced shining trails across the swelling, and the girl sank to her knees, face in her hands.

"Clorri?" Kazari thought that was her name. "Clorri? Tell me, what happened to you."

Clorri shook her head, shoulders shaking, and Kazari kneeled beside her. She tried to place a gentle arm around the other girl's shoulders, but again Clorri flinched away as if Kazari's touch had hurt.

"Please tell me. Has someone hurt you?" The girl choked back a sob, and belatedly Kazari added, "You're safe here. I won't let anyone near you if you don't want them. Now, can you tell me what happened? Or would you like me to get Androvar?" The girl shook her head mutely as more tears dripped from her face.

Kazari didn't know what to do. Androvar needed her bag, but Clorri didn't want to move, and Kazari was certain that she shouldn't leave the girl alone. Not until there was someone else to watch over her, and they knew what had happened.

"Clorri, please tell me what's happened to you," she pleaded. "Come, let's go closer to the fire, you're cold." She laid a hand tentatively on one of Clorri's hands, wary of the fear in the girl's eyes, and drew her to her feet. Clorri limped as she took her first step, and Kazari exclaimed and ducked under the girl's arm to support her. Grimacing, Clorri allowed the contact, but by the way she was trembling, Kazari began to wonder what exactly she was hiding under her clothing. "Come," she repeated, and helped Clorri over to one of the seats closest to the fire. And now, let me look."

She eased out from under the girl's arm and gently indicated her shirt.

Clorri shook her head violently, and then winced, but Kazari held her eyes with her own.

"Clorri, you're hurt, that's obvious, but you're safe here. Just let me look, and then we'll see what I can do."

The girl's face crumpled again, and then she nodded once. Cautiously Kazari stood and helped her remove her thick outer jacket. Underneath, Clorri wore a close fitting fine wool garment. It was delicately soft, and probably amazingly warm, and Kazari would have envied her the fine shirt, had she not seen the dried blood that marred its weave. Gently she began to lift the fabric. Clorri hissed in pain, gritting her teeth, and turning her head away as Kazari raised the shirt. It was stuck to the girl's back with old blood – not new blood, but old. Blood that had been shed at least twenty-four hours before, judging by its colour and the vigour with which it adhered to the fine fabric. By Kazari's estimation, the blood must have been shed just after their visit with the spices.

"Someone beat you," Kazari said flatly. "Who?"

Clorri refused to answer, shaking her head.

Kazari tried again. "Clorri, please, just tell me. The Lady gives sanctuary to you. She will protect you – and so will I, but you have to tell me what happened so we can stop it happening again."

Clorri sobbed – deep gasping sobs that seemed dredged from her soul. It was as if there was a battle going on inside her. A raging battle of some kind between her desire to explain, and her desperation not to. The girl's back was a mass of old and new bruising, bleeding, and cuts. She'd obviously been beaten more than once. Even worse, to Kazari's eyes it appeared as if she'd been beaten regularly, and almost systematically. Kazari gently lowered the fine wool, covering the mess of Clorri's back. She was at a loss, so she crouched beside the girl again, and gently placed an arm around her shoulders, trying to remember where the worst of the bruising was, and trying hard to convey that human touch could be used for healing, and not only horror.

She wished her ability to heal others was more developed, but she knew she didn't dare try healing the girl without assistance from Andiss.

Clorri's sobs stilled slowly, and Kazari took the opportunity to touch her hand gently again. She was encouraged when this time, Clorri looked up and didn't pull away. "Clorri?" The other girl dropped her eyes, breathing out raggedly, and then sniffed and looked back at Kazari.

"M . . . m . . . my grandmother."

"What?" It wasn't what she'd expected to hear.

"My grandmother," Clorri repeated. "She's changed – lots of them have changed." She shook her head slowly. "They've all changed."

"What do you mean?" Kazari demanded. "Who changed and why?"

Clorri's tear stained face threatened to crumple again, so Kazari repeated her words more quietly. The girl looked away.

"I shouldn't have told. I shouldn't have come here! They'll know! They'll come and find me!" Her voice rose on every sentence, until she was almost shrieking.

"You're safe here," Kazari repeated over and over, wondering what she could do to calm the almost hysterical girl. It was obvious that the girl knew what was going on, and had been driven to seek sanctuary with the Lady's servants, but Kazari felt completely out of her depth. She had no experience to draw upon, and no idea of what to do but to keep repeating: "This is the Lady's place. Her sanctuary. You are safe." She looked around, wishing there was another of the Lady's servants to help her, but there wasn't. She was alone, with a frantic, and abused girl, completely out of her depth. *Lady, what do I do?* She implored. *Please, send someone to us!*

Perhaps she could signal someone, she thought, as Clorri's shrieks assaulted her ears. But how? The windows were thick stained glass, not clear panes. The door to the chapel was closed – unlocked but closed to keep the warmth inside. The chapel itself had no bells or gongs, just the raised platform for the incumbent to speak from, and rows of wooden pews. The double walls, with their cavity filled with straw to keep the warmth in, would muffle any shouts.

"Clorri, calm down. I won't let her come for you. I won't let anyone take you." Kazari's pleas seemed to fall on deaf ears, but she was slightly encouraged by the fact that Clorri was no longer pulling away from her. "You're safe, remember? Safe."

Slowly, the words seemed to penetrate Clorri's mind, until once again, she was drawing huge heaving breaths, and no longer shouting. Finally, Kazari judged that she might be able to leave her long enough to duck out and signal someone from the village to send Androvar to her. Surely the Intercessor would know what to do and how to cope? She certainly didn't, and it was clear that the information they so desperately needed was within Clorri, but that the girl was in no shape to be questioned.

She eased her arm gently from Clorri's shoulders, and let go of her hand with what she hoped was a reassuring pat. "I'm just going to find Androvar, Clorri."

"Don't leave me!" Clorri grabbed her arm. She was stronger than she looked.

"I'm not leaving – just going to signal, to send her a message."

"Y . . . you won't go?"

"Only as far as the door. You sit here, I'll be back in a second," Kazari promised.

Clorri let her arm go reluctantly, and Kazari pushed herself to her feet. At the door of the chapel she looked back at Clorri, who had huddled into herself, looking somehow smaller. Worried, Kazari ducked around the back wall and opened the door. Freezing air rushed in and slapped her cheeks, and her breath steamed as she exclaimed involuntarily. The bright blue sky had clouded over again, and the chill had deepened. The village was silent. Not a soul was in sight as she turned her head and craned her neck.

The sky seemed ominous, and the clouds looked heavy, weighted down with snow. She wondered if another snowstorm was imminent. Androvar hadn't mentioned anything.

Mindful of her promise, Kazari didn't step through the door. Clorri was an emotional and physical wreck, and Kazari suspected that should she leave the chapel without her, she would run, and their hunt for the cause of the unrest in the village would be stymied again. Apart from the fact that Clorri was an abused individual who deserved to feel safe, she was now their best clue as to what was going on within the village. The frigid air was very still, but faintly, Kazari could hear the sound of someone crunching their way through the snow. Hope rose – perhaps it might be one of the Hunters, returned early from their reconnaissance around the village.

It wasn't. Instead, the Mayor's stocky figure ploughed through the snow towards the chapel. Kazari ducked back inside, hoping he hadn't seen her, just as a waft of acridity assailed her nostrils. Her heart seemed to turn over in her chest. The stench cleared, and for a moment she had the faint thought that she'd been mistaken, but then another wave of the stink rolled over her. It was sickening, and harsh in its intensity. It wasn't quite like the smell at the Abbey, but it was strong enough to make her gag. Gorgones! Somewhere close, she was sure. She no longer wondered if she had the Gift of Sensing; she was sure she did, but she knew she couldn't yet interpret what it was that she was sensing.

She was torn. The Mayor was vulnerable to gorgones, like any undefended human being, but Clorri needed her too. She looked around, hoping to see Androvar, or Sendar's tall form – or any of the Hunters. She was alone, and encumbered with an abused and hysterical girl.

"Kazari?" the voice sounded through the open door from inside the chapel, and she ducked back around the wall, holding a finger to her lips.

"Shhhhhh, your father's on his way here. Stay quiet," she hissed. Clorri shrank back towards the fire, scrambling off the chair, and tucking herself away next to the wood box. Fresh tears started down her cheeks, but Kazari could see that the girl was holding her hands over her own mouth to muffle any sound, while her body shook uncontrollably. Pity for her plight gripped Kazari's heart. Pity, and compassion, followed by anger.

"Stay there," whispered Kazari. "I'll see him off." She grabbed the medicine bag she'd discarded earlier, and ducked around the divider again, then slipped through the doorway. She was just in time. Making a show of closing the chapel door, Kazari straightened up and almost walked into the Mayor. "Sorry," she apologised.

"Clorri's here." His voice was flat.

Mentally apologising to the Lady, Kazari replied. "Clorri?"

"My daughter. We . . . we had a fight this morning, and she stormed out. I've been looking for her for hours. This is the last place." The Mayor cocked his head at Kazari, and her mind raced. What should she say? the Lady's Writings encouraged all her people to speak the truth, and not lie. But if she spoke the truth, the Mayor would want to go inside the chapel.

"Your daughter, sir?" she asked, hoping to buy a little more time.

"You met her yesterday," he said impatiently. "The oldest one." He moved to walk around Kazari, but she sidestepped and blocked his path.

"Excuse me?"

The stench intensified along with the anger on his face, and Kazari was hard put not to gag. "I'm sorry sir, but the chapel is currently closed."

"Don't be stupid, child. The chapel is never closed." Child? He'd called her a *child*. Red rage rose inside Kazari and flared brightly, but she kept a tight rein on her temper, despite the images of Clorri's injuries that kept trying to overwhelm her control. She stayed where she was, lips compressed in a thin line.

"I said, the chapel is never closed," he repeated.

"It is right now," she replied, trying to keep her voice steady, when all she wanted to do was to rage at him and to do to him what had been done to his daughter. The Mayor took a step sideways, clearly intending to move around Kazari, so she moved to block him. As she did she breathed a prayer to the Lady that someone would come soon. Surely Sendar and Androvar would be wondering what was keeping her. To delay would be her best strategy, yet the acridity on the wind shivered warnings down her spine, and she couldn't resist glancing around, looking for the gorgone she knew must be close by – but how close she had no idea.

She tried to think back to the previous episode – how long had it been between sensing the gorgone and seeing it? Her memories were confused; once the gorgone had appeared, everything had moved so fast. The fight itself was a montage of images that seemed to merge into each other, and Kazari was a bit hazy on whether she remembered smelling the gorgone during it.

Once again, the Mayor attempted to sidestep her. Without conscious thought, she mirrored his movement and blocked him again. Frustrated, he raised a hand, and Kazari steeled herself. His eyes were hard, cold, and angry.

"Do you really think it wise to lay a hand on the Lady's servant?" It was Androvar.

The Mayor's head whipped around, and he dropped his hand. Relief flooded through Kazari's body. Unnoticed during the altercation, Sendar and Androvar had approached through the snow, and now stood only a few metres away. Hands on her hips, Androvar's voice rang with unmistakable authority. The Mayor turned to face her, fists clenched by his sides.

"She told me that the chapel was closed. She is lying. The chapel is never closed," he said shortly. "And my daughter is missing, Androvar. We've been searching for hours."

"Clorri's missing?" Androvar said, and Kazari saw the question in her eyes.

Kazari wondered how she could make Androvar understand that the Mayor shouldn't be allowed inside the chapel. Sendar was looking at her, puzzled, and she willed him to change his expression, hoping that the Mayor might not notice him. Androvar continued smoothly, "And the chapel *is* closed today. We're scrubbing it this afternoon – it's not often I have enough help, so I'm making the most of it."

The Mayor paused for a moment, but then rallied. "You only had to ask, Androvar – we'd have helped."

"Thank you, Mayor, however, there are some things only the Lady's servants may do," she replied graciously, and as far as Kazari knew, completely untruthfully, but from the glance she flicked towards Kazari, it was obvious that she'd realised that Clorri was inside, and that for some reason Kazari didn't want him to go in. She heaved an internal sigh of relief for the woman's intuition. For a moment Kazari thought they'd won, but then the Mayor's face hardened, and she could visibly see him reorganising his thoughts.

"But Clorri – I need to find her. I've looked everywhere except the chapel. You must let me look. There'll be a storm later." He turned towards Kazari and the door again. She tensed, ready to fend him off if required, but then the stench of gorgone intensified, and she crouched instinctively, looking around.

"Androvar, Sendar. Something's coming!"

Sendar spun, and his long knife appeared like magic in his hand. Androvar shot a look at Kazari.

"Are you certain?"

"Yes." And she was. Completely certain now. The stench was growing stronger by the second, and as Kazari's eyes hunted from side to side, searching for whatever gorgone was about to assail them, she almost missed the Mayor's lunge towards the chapel's door. As it was, she was forced to leap diagonally backwards in order to place herself in front of it.

"Move out of my way, girl!" he snarled, raising a fist towards Kazari. This time, she was ready, falling smoothly into a Hunters's stance, hands relaxed but ready, desperate to have the confrontation over with, so that she could get on with the more important task – finding whatever gorgone was coming before it reached them.

"Mayor!" Androvar's voice was cutting, but this time the man didn't listen or stop. His fist swung towards Kazari, and she blocked it with a forearm, ducked, slipped under his arm and used her hip to throw the man. He flopped heavily into the snow, a stunned expression on his face, as she immobilised him deftly. Those long hours of sparring had paid off.

Chapter Seventeen: Gorgone Revelation

The smell of gorgone strengthened as the Mayor writhed in Kazari's grasp. Well taught by Andiss and Javon, she was undisturbed by his struggles. She tightened her grip slightly, moved her weight fractionally, and he grunted in pain as she looked up into Androvar's startled eyes. "Gorgones," she said urgently. "They're coming."

Behind Androvar, she could see Sendar casting around, moving with a Hunter's smooth gait. Fortunately, the urgency of her warning wasn't lost on Androvar. The Intercessor nodded, and then reached for the medicine bag Kazari had dropped when she'd tackled the Mayor. She removed a small vial, checked the wind direction and carefully uncapped it, and then dripped the clear fluid onto a sponge.

She held it under the Mayor's furious nose. He took a deep breath, probably intending to shout for help, Kazari thought, but instead his eyes rolled back, and his body went limp under her hands.

"You can let him go now. He's out for several hours with that much," Androvar said, as Kazari looked a question at her. Each time she thought she had the Intercessor figured out, the woman revealed new depths. Kazari released the Mayor's arm and cautiously removed her body weight. He remained limp, body half covered in snow.

"Quick, Androvar – can you take him? Sendar and I need to be able to watch. I don't know how much time we have before the gorgone arrives. Clorri's inside – she's been badly beaten." The Intercessor's face creased in concern, and as she looked down at the Mayor, Kazari realised that Androvar was struggling to decide what to do with him. "Put him in the chapel if he's out for hours. We can sort him out later. Just warn Clorri." she suggested. "It's warm enough in there. Can you drag him by yourself?"

"I think so. You go – see what you and Sendar can find. Leave them to me."

"Thanks," Kazari said, and went to help Sendar.

"Can you tell which way, Kaz?" he asked.

She sniffed, drawing the smell of the gorgone deep within her, despite its stench, pondering. It nauseated her. Last time, she hadn't known what was happening. This time, she was determined to discover the depths of her new gift.

"I hope so. With the Lady's help, that is. *Lady, lead me.*" It was the first time she'd prayed out loud to the Lady in Sendar's company. She'd kept her personal devotions quiet, feeling that she didn't need to make a song and dance out of her piety, stupid though that had seemed in an Abbey full of fellow servants.

"*Walk with us, Lady, as we hunt your enemies,*" he replied, startling her. The clouds had now completely covered the sky again, and the ambient light was dimming by the minute. The snow seemed colder, and the stench greater. Whatever it was, it wasn't very far, Kazari thought. It was almost as if she could reach out and touch it. Then she felt it – not just smelled it, but felt it. The familiar feel of a sucker's emotional draw clouded the air, and the glint of many eyes cut the dimness. It wasn't only one gorgone, it was a whole creche of suckers.

"Be ready," she warned Sendar, "there's more than one, and I think they're suckers." Then Kazari drew two of her knives. She and Sendar crouched, back to back as they'd been taught, slowly turning to survey the eyes as the suckers drew closer and closer. She tried to count them as the stench became almost unbearable, but there were too many, and they were weaving and gliding all around them, suckers and tentacles and eyes on stalks flailing.

Lady help us! She prayed again, as the assault on her mind began. The suckers circled, and her mind spun in spirals. The measured beat of Sendar's booted feet, and the warmth of his back were the only things that kept her mind from plummeting into the morass of despair and self-doubt that the suckers preyed upon.

She'd fought four by herself, and survived. So had Sendar. But there appeared to be no end to the numbers of suckers about to assail them in the cold afternoon light. Where could they all have come from, she wondered? And how was it that they'd left so little sign for the experienced Hunters to find? She prayed again. *Help me Lady! Help us both – and help us to protect those who need our protection!* Images of Clorri's bruises steeled her resolve. There was a young woman who'd already suffered more than she should have. But even as she readied herself as well as she knew how, Kazari could see more suckers arriving. How would they hold them off by themselves? And where were the other villagers? Where was the local militia? Every village had those who helped maintain the law, and dealt with local misdemeanours. Where was *anyone* for that matter? The underlying strangeness in Suborden began to take on a more ominous tone.

She felt Sendar's back tense as the suckers tightened their ring, and Kazari realised that the creatures weren't attacking immediately, but seemed to be waiting for something. The smell in her nostrils was intense, and she found herself trying to breathe through her mouth. It made no difference at all. However she was doing it, it really wasn't her nose doing the sensing. Another wave of despair flooded outwards from the oncoming suckers, but Kazari heard Sendar reciting from *The Book of Hunters.* "*Against fear, I give love, against despair, I give hope, against evil, I give purity of heart, against hatred, I give compassion.*" His voice grew stronger on every word, and Kazari tried desperately to mimic him. It was very hard.

The fear of loss threatened to overwhelm her. Thoughts of the villagers and their terror were replaced with thoughts of her own family. Somewhere, she imagined that she heard a voice among the images and sensations projected by the suckers. It was soft, faint to her ears, but it was there. *You think you can overcome me?* it whispered. Kazari felt her face blanche. It wasn't enough that she could *smell* gorgones, but now she was imagining that she could hear them? Perhaps she *was* going mad.

"Kaz, be ready." Sender's voice jerked her away from her wonderings.

"R . . . ready," she replied, gritting her teeth. She wished she'd had time to shed her cloak. It was interfering with the smooth flow of her movements. "*Walk with us Lady,*" she said, speaking the words out aloud for the first time. "*Love for fear, hope for despair, purity for evil, compassion for hatred.*" She used it as a mantra. As something to beat back the flood of the gorgones' projection. No wonder the village was struggling if this number of gorgones were in the vicinity. She resisted the urge to clutch her amethyst, and instead kept reciting the words of the Lady. And then the first rank sprang.

She danced. Ducking, weaving, spinning up and over and around, somehow maintaining her connection to Sendar as he struck with both knives, and thrust gorgones into the air and through the snow if they approached near enough for him to lift them with his Gift. His Anticipation and Kazari's Dance allowed them to deal death to more suckers than Kazari would once have believed possible. It was both like and unlike the fight with the greater gorgone at the Abbey. Like in that she wasn't alone, but unlike in that this time, she felt as if she was actually fighting properly.

Sweat stung, and then froze, as the fight wore on. The suckers seemed endless. Gore, and then blood, spattered the pristine whiteness. Kazari was bleeding from a dozen slices from suckers. Even a Dancer it seemed, could only cope with so many opponents, and her endurance and strength were not infinite. Even if every strike went true, and every duck was perfect, it would still be impossible to survive the sheer numbers flooding in on them. She could hear Sendar's harsh panting at her back, and feel his exhaustion through her own bones.

'I see your family. I hear their fears. And I will come for them. And you will not save them, because this day, you die." That half-imagined voice cut through the fog of sucker sendings like a knife to Kazari's brain, and she faltered, allowing a sucker tentacle to slap her face. The teeth on the cups cut into her cheek and she cried out in pain. Sender's knife whipped backwards and severed it, but she was half blinded by the blood and the fear. No! Not her family! Anger strengthened her limbs and she fought back with renewed vigour. And then she heard Sendar's voice.

"No! No! No!" There was such pain in it that she half turned, caught dancing between another two suckers. She allowed her blows to follow through even as her head turned, and saw three suckers using his distraction to close the distance between him and them. One flung a knife-edged limb towards his unprotected back, while he stood, helpless and staring. *Lady!* She begged soundlessly. Her Dancer's senses knew, but she did it anyway. She threw herself under the limb and raised an arm, its leather bracer no shield against the toughened sharpness of the sucker, knowing that if she didn't, Sendar would die and they were both lost.

As the limb descended, agonising in its slowness in her dance state, she shouted. "Move Sendar!" She felt the beginnings of his movement, but it wasn't going to be fast enough. She braced herself, bringing up her other knife so that the two of them crossed directly underneath the sucker's knife edge. It struck, and even though Kazari had braced herself, she knew she wasn't going to be able to stop it completely. Her arms quivered, her thighs ached, and her stomach muscles screamed as she tried to keep her arms in position and stop the sucker's strike. Slowly her knives were forced apart so that only their tips were keeping the sucker's blade from her body. They strained, one against the other for an eternity. And then even Kazari's Gift showed her no way out of the situation.

The suckers were thick around them, too many for her to duck, too many for Sendar to throw, too many for them to prevail. Gasping and panting, Kazari prepared herself for death, calculating how many of the suckers she could take with her. The slowness of their motions enabled her to plot her path of destruction, while the last of her life's blood would continue to pump from the thigh wound she was unable to avoid. She'd heard that death would be fast with a deep thigh wound. She just hoped the pain wouldn't incapacitate her too much before she could cut a swathe through the suckers in the time she had left.

Lady, she thought, *be with my family.*

And then she heaved with all her might, trying for one last moment to prevent the gorgone slicing through her leg. It almost worked, and then her knives were forced apart, and the gorgone's blade plummeted towards her leg. It sliced through leather and then skin, and then the gorgone was flung away from her with a force that seemed to have come from nowhere. Blood dripped hotly from her leg, but the already planned movements had her dancing away from the puddle into her predetermined course of destruction. Knives and arms flailing in patterns barely sensed, Kazari danced on, unable to believe she was still alive. Alive, but not unharmed, as the hot pain in her leg throbbed and burned as she moved.

And then Kazari's healing power swept through it, and the throbbing and burning reduced to a background ache. Suddenly there were no more suckers left to kill. Kazari stood in a bloodstained daze, arms trembling and legs wobbling. Her thigh ached, and her cheek burned, and the trickle of blood from the face wound pooled on her collar. She wondered dimly why it wasn't healing like her thigh had. "Sendar, Kazari – we came as soon as we could." It was Andiss. He was breathing heavily, and not unscathed either, she realised. His normally immaculate clothing was covered with gore and spattered with blood. By his side, Javon was crouched, turning over the corpse of a sucker with one gloved hand.

Mikel was jogging the perimeter, with his partner, Jern, both with knives in hands, while Sherd and Kellis stood with drawn bows, both looking as if they were on a knife edge of alert. Kazari sniffed. The stench – except the natural one of destroyed sucker corpse – had gone, and the chill breeze was fresh and clean. She inhaled deeply, savouring the freshness, as Sendar limped up to her and wrapped an arm around her shoulders. "Thank you," he said. His face was drawn and tired, and he too, was filthy with a mixture of ichor and blood.

"I think we're even, Sendar. Thank *you*," she managed. "And I think they're all gone, Andiss. At least, I can't smell any at the moment."

"So much for our controlled experiment," Javon said dryly. "I've never seen so many suckers in one spot. We got here in the nick of time." She let her gaze wander over the carnage in front of them. "The Abbot needs to know what's going on here."

"Androvar?" asked Kazari. "Did she get the Mayor inside in time? And is Clorri alright?"

"Who's Clorri?" asked Andiss.

Kazari shared a look with Sendar. "It's complicated. Very complicated. But I think we might know more of what's going on if we talk to the Mayor. That is, if he's conscious yet."

Andiss raised his eyebrows, but then turned away and waved at the other Hunters. "Kaz says it's clear for the moment, but there's more to this than meets the eye. We'll need to take turns on the watch while we get to the bottom of it. Kellis, Sherd – are you up to the first watch?" Kazari was surprised how quickly Andiss was willing to trust her Gift.

Both women relaxed their stances, lowering their bows as Kellis nodded. "We'll keep watch for now, and get the clean-up happening." She looked at Sherd, who loped off into the village. "We'll need a Hunter's conference afterwards."

Andiss raised a hand in agreement and then motioned to the others to follow him into the chapel. Inside, the warmth enfolded Kazari like a blanket, and she felt her muscles relax, soothing her many aches and pains even more. Androvar hurried forward, beckoning them towards the fire. Clorri was still huddled by it, and the Mayor was lying unconscious on a pew. Kazari saw Javon's eyebrows rise into her hairline as she came close enough to see the Mayor's somnolent body. "It looks as if you have a bit of explaining to do, you two," she said.

CHAPTER EIGHTEEN: WEAKNESS

Clorri, you'll be safe in the residence," Androvar said, gently ushering the girl to her feet. She slipped an arm around the girl's waist, and helped her to her feet, turning her head to the others. "I'll just get Clorri settled, and then I'll be back with hot drinks." She and Clorri vanished, and Kazari limped tiredly over to the fire to settle herself in one of the chairs nearby with a sigh. It felt slightly irreverent to be sitting, covered in dirt and grime, in the Lady's place of worship, but her history lessons had told her that the Lady's chapels were always a place of safety when gorgones threatened the peace of Albatar. There were many stories of last stands made against the darkness in the light of the Lady's chapels – both in Albatar and in the wider world, where the Lady's sway was not nearly as strong.

She fumbled her way to her feet again and removed her cloak. Rents and tatters showed how close many of the suckers had come to her. The hem was soaked in a revolting mixture of wet snow, blood and ichor, and she folded it inside the rest of the cloak to keep the disgusting mess off the floor. Closer inspection showed that her outer garments were also somewhat the worse for wear. She wiped her knives on the folds of her cloak, and began to inspect them for damage as the others drew closer to the warmth. By her side, she could see Sendar inspecting a long rent in his trousers. They were flecked with blood, and he eased his leg slightly as he stretched it.

"Let me take a look at that, Sendar, and your face too, Kaz," Andiss said. He ran his hand over Sendar's leg, and

Kazari could see the angry redness of the wound change to a better colour, and then start to close. It didn't close completely though, despite Andiss' frown and subsequent hand pass. Finally, he looked up at Javon with a questioning eye. She shook her head and he turned his attention to Kazari's cheek. It stung hotly, as he ran cool, gentle fingertips across it. She could feel the heat reducing as he worked, but it didn't heal completely, much as Sendar's leg hadn't. He tried again, but then, silently rocked back onto his heels, deep in thought. "Two wounds that won't heal properly. Kazari – did any of your battle wounds heal spontaneously?"

Kazari looked back at him, suddenly frightened. "Some, Andiss, but my leg isn't completely healed, and this one doesn't feel as if it will."

Andiss frowned again, deep in thought.

"Do you know why, Andiss?" she asked worriedly.

"I'm not sure. We'll need to go over what happened during the fight in depth I think, but for now, we need to know what's going on here. Who's Clorri and why is she here? And what on *earth* did you do to the Mayor?"

Kazari made a face. "Well, Androvar was the one who actually knocked the Mayor out," she began.

"After you took him down," Sendar interjected.

"You took the Mayor down?" Javon exclaimed.

"Um … yes, I did," Kazari replied, blushing. In retrospect it seemed rather hot headed. But she had been angry, she realised – very angry about Clorri, and very angry that the Mayor wanted his own daughter to go back to the place the beatings had occurred. Although the girl had said that her grandmother was the one who'd hit her, Kazari was certain that the Mayor was complicit in the beatings. "He was trying to get inside the chapel."

Andiss and Javon exchanged confused looks. "Kaz, I think you'd better start from the beginning," Javon said.

"From the very beginning, and make sure you don't leave anything out. Sendar, if there's things you need to add, just butt in."

Kazari began from the beginning as requested. Explaining took some time. At one point Andiss interrupted. "You said Clorri said her grandmother 'changed'?"

"She said lots of them 'changed,'" Kazari replied. "But we never got around to discussing what that meant, because her father arrived, just as I was going to call Androvar and Sendar."

"Changed," Javon mused. "I wonder what that means, exactly."

"I don't think you're going to like the answer," Androvar replied grimly. She was carrying a tray of steaming cups, and her face was set in lines of dismay. She handed the mugs around, and Kazari took a sip thankfully. She was thirsty, and the brew was hot and satisfying, full of sweetness and spice. "Clorri's story is almost unbelievable – and if I hadn't seen her injuries with my own eyes, I don't think I'd have believed her." She pulled up a chair and sat down, slightly hunched over, with her hands wrapped around her own mug. Her eyes rested on the fire as she sipped and went on. "About six months ago, I first noticed something was amiss. I've been here for six years. I know these people. On the whole, they're good people, hardworking and prosperous, for all that this village is so remote." She sipped from her mug again, slowly, and Kazari saw that her hands were clenched tightly around its patterned pottery. "A group of travelling traders came through – over the mountains from the border they said. They were looking for wool as most traders do. I remember thinking that it had been some time since the last group from that direction. They didn't seem any different to the normal ones, but from what Clorri's told me, they were." She fell silent, still staring into the flames.

"But the Lady?" Andiss queried. "She didn't provide warning?"

Androvar looked at him. "She did. But not clearly. Each morning in my devotions while the traders were here, I felt a sense of unease – of disquiet. I was troubled in my soul, but there appeared to be no reason for it. It's often like that for Intercessors. Of course, the Lady could speak directly into our minds and hearts, but we know that more often she asks us to look more deeply into the people around us – so that we remember to see them as people, with driving forces caused by everything around them, and not simply as favoured or not favoured – down that path lies self-righteousness and legalism, and often harshness and judgement. She reminds us to be a people of love."

"And?" Andiss prompted.

The Intercessor sighed heavily, fingers clenching and unclenching unconsciously on her mug. "Nothing. I looked and found absolutely *nothing*. Not one thing had changed, the people were still all doing their normal things, the stock was growing well, and nothing had changed outwardly at all. It was only over the months, as my sense of unease grew, that I began to notice that something was not quite right – the conversations that took tangents, the rooms I was shepherded past, and the slow reduction in those seeking counsel from an Intercessor. That was when I notified the Abbot, and then of course you Hunters began to arrive, and I was even more certain that something was very wrong."

Kazari wondered what she meant, but Androvar went on.

"You see, when something occurs slowly, over a long period of time, it's very hard to know what's changed, and whether you're imagining it, or as an incumbent, whether you're the one making it all happen. The arrival of Kellis and Sherd, and Mikel and Jern, along with the information from the Abbot, reassured me that I wasn't."

Kazari found herself nodding. When she'd first arrived in the Abbey, everything had been new and different. Over the months of her training, she'd become accustomed to many things, not the least the readings every morning, the casual discussion of the Lady, and Her inclusion in every part of Abbey life, which she now saw as a normal part of her day.

Androvar continued. "The biggest issue now, is what Clorri's told me. Her injuries . . . if any of you have the Gift of Healing, I would be very grateful for you to use it on her. Her back! How someone could do that to a child!" She grimaced angrily. "Her mind, though – well that will take some time, and it is the care of the mind that the Lady entrusts to her Intercessors, so I will do what I can."

"I would be pleased to assist," Andiss replied. "And Kazari will help me. Clorri trusts her, I suspect."

Androvar nodded.

"But what did she tell you that has you so concerned?"

Androvar appeared to struggle with herself for a moment, and Kazari wondered what it could be that had her so worried. Then the Intercessor put her mug down and folded her hands in her lap, clearly composing herself. "Clorri said that her grandmother 'changed.'"

Javon nodded. "Kazari told us that, but she didn't know what the girl meant."

Androvar sighed heavily. "The traders brought things with them. Things long outlawed in Albatar. Things that can do unspeakable damage to the soul – things that entice the unwary. Those things were too much for some of our villagers. They took them, used them, and in doing so, were changed." She shrugged. "They appear as baubles, mostly, or jewellery. But each one of them has been made by those who worship the greater gorgones. They are infused with the hatred, and the malignancy that dwells within such people. People who willingly use such things cannot remain unchanged. It starts with tiny things, usually, but those little things feed the seed of destruction set within them." She looked suddenly sad, and Kazari wondered why.

"You're talking about malmetal charms, aren't you?" Andiss asked slowly, and Kazari's heart sank. Malmetal was the stuff of legends. Evil legends. Legends that spoke of men and women who became monsters under the influence of malmetal. By her side, she felt Sendar stiffen.

Androvar nodded. "Yes."

There was silence in the chapel as they digested the import of what Androvar had told them, and then Javon stirred herself and sat erect in her chair. "How many?" The words dropped heavily into the void.

"I'm not certain," she replied. "Clorri's grandmother for one, and at least one person in the weaver's warehouse. Who, I'm not sure. But I had the impression that there were more than just a few. I think it's going to take some time to get to the bottom of it all, and I'll need your help. According to the records, the influence of malmetal charms is insidious and wide ranging. Where there is greed, hatred, or envy, they find fertile ground in which to plant their poison."

"Of course," Andiss replied. "And we'll need to find out just why, and how, so many suckers came to be in this area as well. How, in fact, so many managed to get past our patrols." Once again, he and Javon exchanged meaningful glances, and Kazari wondered what it was that they knew that she and Sendar didn't. Of course she was only a trainee, but it still rankled there were some things she wasn't privy to – yet.

The chapel door opened and closed, and the other four Hunters appeared, filing in, brushing snow off their clothing, and shedding their cloaks in the warmth of the chapel. "Clean-up's done, and the villagers are warned off," Mikel said. "You acquitted yourselves well, Sendar, Kazari." He nodded at the two trainees, and Kazari felt herself blush faintly, and then her stomach rumbled loudly and completely inappropriately. She blushed again, embarrassed, and hastily buried her face in her mug. Fortunately, the last of the drink Androvar had made quieted the rumbles, at least briefly. She hoped her stomach wouldn't embarrass her again.

"Androvar, this is your village, perhaps you could make a list of those you think *might* have been corrupted by the malmetal charms, and we'll begin by reviewing what Kazari and Sendar learned during the fight. There's a few unanswered questions yet," Andiss said. He stood and gestured to the other Hunters. "Kazari, we'll need you to show us where you were when you first sensed the gorgones. And we'll need both of you to talk us through what happened when you encountered the Mayor. Speaking of whom, Androvar – how long until he wakes up?"

"My goodness!" exclaimed Androvar, "I'd forgotten him!" She squinted at the light slanting through the windows. "About another two hours, I'd say. Will you help me move him to the residence? I've a lockable room there. With a bed. Although I'm not sure he deserves that."

Mikel and Jern carried the unconscious form between them, after Androvar signalled that there were no villagers nearby, and the others returned to the filthy churned up circle in the snow. There was no stench of gorgone in the air, just the cold, clean freshness of new snow, but the darkening clouds spoke a warning of more snow to come. As they drew near, Kazari looked towards the village. She was certain she'd seen a curtain move in the nearest house. She supposed she'd have been peering outside too, if her village had just experienced an incursion of gorgones, but it made her uncomfortable, itchy from the watching eyes. She realised sadly that not one person from the village had come to help her and Sendar. It was impossible that their fight could have gone unnoticed. Perhaps the corruption went deeper than any of them imagined. She shivered, but not from the cold.

Andiss had them step through the altercation with the Mayor, first Kazari alone, and then Sendar as well, speaking through the conversation as they remembered it. Kazari stumbled over some bits, realising that her memory was unclear about some things said in the heat of the moment, and that the fight had already blurred into a series of unconnected flashbacks. Suddenly, stepping through the fight, there in the muddy circle surrounded by pristine whiteness, Kazari remembered the voice. Had she heard it? Or had it been her imagination, magnified by the suckers surrounding her?

Hesitantly, she turned in a circle, retracing her footsteps as much as she could remember them. At her back, Sendar also worked through his movements. She'd danced, he'd anticipated, he'd thrown, and together they'd killed many gorgones. He'd saved her – and then she remembered. The voice had sounded in her head, and she'd frozen, only to be saved from a much worse injury than a tentacle slice by Sendar. "There was a voice," she said, hoping she didn't sound stupid.

"What? You heard it too?" Sendar demanded.

She spun to look at him, face stinging in remembered pain – not completely remembered, she realised, as her hand touched the tentacle wound. It was throbbing.

"It wasn't just me?" she asked. "I thought it was my family it was threatening." Relief rolled off her in waves. Perhaps the voice had meant Sendar's family, and hers would be safe, and then she blushed once again, shaking her head in embarrassment, and shame. It was an unworthy thought. *Forgive me, Lady.*

"Your family?" Sendar looked confused. "No, it threatened the Abbey! It said that we would die, and the Abbey would fall!"

"Hang on," she replied, and her heart sank again. "What I heard was 'I see your family. I hear their fears. And I will come for them. And you will not save them, because this day, you die.'"

Sendar shook his head. "I heard, 'You think you defeat us? The Abbey will fall to me. And you, and she, will die here today'."

Kazari raised confused eyes to Sendar. He was looking at her, stricken, and she didn't know what to say. Where had the voice come from, and who had it been? How had they heard it? And why had they heard different things?

She touched her cheek again. "That was when I got this." She saw his hand drop to the rent in his trousers, where the wound was still vividly red on his skin, its edges not quite closed.

"And me, this. And if you hadn't saved me just then, I'd have died. I froze." He said it bluntly, looking directly at Andiss and Javon.

"So did I," replied Kazari. "You saved me too." She turned to face Andiss and Javon apprehensively. She couldn't imagine either of them freezing in battle. "I'm sorry, I froze in the middle of the fight when the voice sounded in my head. Perhaps if I hadn't, we wouldn't have needed rescuing."

Once again, Javon and Andiss exchanged looks, and then Andiss stepped forward, placing his right hand on Kazari's shoulder and his left on Sendar's. "Hesitation when you're a trainee is to be expected. Hesitation when a strange voice sounds inside your mind, and threatens you, is only to be expected. Any Hunter would have hesitated at that point. Neither of you froze completely – the evidence speaks for itself – you are both still alive, and relatively unharmed."

Kazari was confused, looking from Andiss to Javon, trying to make sense of what Andiss was saying. He didn't seem to be unhappy with either of them.

Javon joined Andiss. "No, we're not mad at either of you. You faced down more suckers than any trainees ever, and for that matter, most fully trained Hunters. The Lady has given both of you great gifts, and together you're already a formidable force. Fully trained, the two of you will stand among the most skilled."

Kazari felt Sendar fumble for her hand and squeeze it. Slightly awkwardly, she squeezed it back. His hand was warm, and seemed to radiate its warmth right up her arm and into her body, and she was slightly disappointed when he gently let it go. She blushed, and hoped that Javon and Andiss thought the blush was for the words of praise. Still, her hand tingled with remembered warmth.

"As far as the voice goes – well, we don't really know, but stories and records tell us that some of the greater gorgones can speak their thoughts directly into human minds, either via an intermediary, like a sucker under their sphere of influence, or directly. We think it's most likely to be the latter, as you've confirmed that there are no gorgones within reach of your Sensing Gift, Kazari. But those wounds that won't heal? There are old stories that suggest that the influence of a greater gorgone can have long lasting effects."

Suddenly worried, Kazari opened her mouth to ask a question. Sendar beat her to it.

"Are we contaminated?"

They weren't the words Kazari would have used, but they conveyed her worries.

"The Lady has her hand upon you," Andiss said. "She walks closely with her Hunters, because her Hunters must meet the gorgone threat in person. That greater gorgone believes the two of you are a threat, but it warned you by speaking, and now you're on guard against its wiles. Make sure you have the Lady's words embedded deep in your hearts, and if you feel uncertain, talk to either Javon or myself. Or Androvar while we're here. *Everyone* is tested when they encounter greater gorgones. That one has taken an interest in you, and that alone signifies its fear. Always remember that they lie, and that what this one has said is a fabrication, designed to strike deeply into your innermost being. Its words are not truth, even though what they say seems as if it might be, so be easy – your family will be safe, Kazari, and Sendar, the Abbey holds many of the Lady's servants. The gorgones hold no sway there."

He stepped back again, and then waved them on. "We'll see if we can discover where these suckers came from. Follow Javon and learn from her tracking skills."

Still unsettled, and with her mind whirling, Kazari nodded and followed Javon, as she realised that although the gorgones might hold no sway at the Abbey, it didn't stop them climbing its walls.

CHAPTER NINETEEN: HUNTING THE 'CHANGED'

The snow poured thickly from the now-leaden sky, and Kazari stumbled back towards the faintly seen lights of the village. They hadn't gone far on the suckers' trail before the clouds had thickened and snow had begun to fall. At first it had been light, tiny flakes drifting downwards, and Javon had ploughed onwards through the snow, intent on the trail. But the plummeting flakes had fallen faster and faster, and then the flakes had become bigger, until now it was difficult to see even a few metres ahead. Javon had finally given up and turned them back towards the village.

Already tired from the fight, Kazari's short legs began to struggle with the snow depth. Even walking in everyone else's footprints was becoming difficult. Still, she forced herself to keep trudging. Her cheeks were numb, and she pulled her scarf more closely around her face, trying to protect them, then thrust her hands deeply into the pockets inside her cloak. The thought of Androvar's warm brew drew her onwards, and for a moment she believed she could almost smell its warm spiciness.

The figures ahead of her seemed to be further away than they had been only moments before, and she realised that she'd stopped moving, caught up in her thoughts of hot drinks and warm fires. Slightly panicked, she began moving again, trying to make sure she didn't lose sight of the others in the snow. Her breath came more quickly as she forced herself faster, heart beating rapidly at the thought of being stranded alone in the whiteout. She put her head down and forced her tired legs to push her along, battling the cold with each step, and cannoned abruptly into Sendar, sending them both tumbling into one of the deeper drifts.

With her hands stuck in the pockets of her grubby cloak, Kazari floundered, and the cloak wrapped itself tightly around her, until she felt as if she was trapped in a cocoon, with her face buried in Sendar's back. "Kaz, can you get off? I'm stuck," he said thickly, and she realised that he was struggling to push his face out of the fresh snow. She wriggled, trying to free herself, first gently and then more vigorously. "Ouch!"

"Sorry!" She rolled off Sendar, and finally her hands came free, and she sat up in the snow, and tried to brush herself down, while Sendar rolled over and pushed himself out of the drift. His hands batted at his hood, and then a shower of snow added itself to the flakes falling around them. "Sorry," she mumbled again, feeling herself blush, despite the freezing air.

"Come on, Kaz, we'd better get moving." He held out a gloved hand, and pulled her to her feet. "Where are the others?"

They looked around. Now surrounded by a curtain of thickly falling snow, Kazari couldn't see Javon and Andiss. Neither could she see the village lights, or even be certain which way the tracks she'd been following went. She stepped closer to Sendar, suddenly nervous. The snow continued to fall. "Andiss? Javon?" she called, but the snow swallowed her words.

Sendar tried calling, but his voice sounded flat against the curtain of falling snow.

"We'd better move, Sendar." Kazari tugged at his sleeve, shivering. She could feel a damp patch on her chest, where snow had worked its way inside her layers of clothing and melted from her body heat. It was chilling quickly.

"Which way?" he asked. Kazari looked back and forth. The drift where they'd fallen was being quickly filled by the snow, and their tracks were now only faint outlines in the all-encompassing whiteness.

"That way, I think," she replied, pointing. "We'd better join hands, just in case." She held hers out, and he took it in his gloved one, and once again, she felt slightly warmed. Hands joined, they began to trudge after the tracks left by Javon and Andiss, but it was only a few minutes until they petered out, filled in by the thick snowfall. They paused, and Kazari felt the first stirrings of fear begin to rise within her as she realised just how cold she was. She looked around, hoping to see even a faint light through the snow, but all she could see was whiteness.

They were lost.

"Andiss!" she called, only to have her voice absorbed once again by the whiteness. "Javon!" Nothing. Sendar's hand squeezed hers more tightly. He called again, and then both of them together, but there was no reply. "What do we do?" she asked.

Sendar looked at the swirling snow, blanketing everything it fell on. "I think we should just keep on moving. We were heading in the right direction, and the village wasn't far. When I could still see the lights, it looked as if it was only ten minutes away. I'll try and push some of the snow out of the way for you." He tugged at her hand and they set off.

He took the lead with his long legs, forcing his way through the snow, and every now and then, Kazari saw the falling snowflakes fluff outwards from him, but even with Sendar's trail breaking, Kazari found that her short legs struggled. Moment by moment, she began to tire, until she felt as if there was nothing left in the world but whiteness and cold. *Lady, help us!* she begged. But it seemed as if even her prayers were captured by the blizzard, and the amethyst at her neck remained cool.

Step after step she followed Sendar. Almost blindly at times, caught up in her world of white. Once again, his sudden stop took her by surprise. "Smell that?" Cold deeper than the snow struck her. Did he mean a gorgone? Of course not. Sense reasserted itself somewhere inside her brain, and she realised she could smell woodsmoke. Somewhere close by was a fire.

"Smoke!" She sniffed deeply, drawing the freezing air into her lungs, trying to figure out which direction it was coming from. The air seemed to add to her coldness, and she shivered convulsively. "That way?" she asked, pointing with the hand not clutched in Sendar's.

"I think so. Come on." They trudged off again, and this time, Kazari noticed that his limp had grown more pronounced. His wound – the one from the fight earlier hadn't healed properly. And now he was cold – chilled to the core by the unexpected blizzard, with a rent in his trousers, and his skin covered only by a thick bandage. He'd stopped pushing the snow with his Gift, she realised. Ashamed she'd let him do most of the trail breaking, Kazari pushed herself harder.

"Let me break the trail," she found herself saying as she forged ahead, suddenly energised by the need to spare Sendar further pain. For a few minutes the extra work warmed her up, but the snow became deeper and deeper, and the need to take deep breaths as she tried to determine where the woodsmoke was coming from began to leech the warmth from her again. Finally, she was simply stumbling along, dragging Sendar after her, desperately following the trail with her nose, just trying to keep moving, rather than give in to the impulse to rest.

The temptation to stop, to lie down and sleep in the snow became almost overwhelming, but she gritted her teeth and forced one leg after the other, until at last, she caught a glimpse of light shining warmly through the snow. She tugged at Sendar's hand. "Look!" He hobbled forward and nearly fell, and she ducked under his arm. "Come on, we're almost there."

Together they staggered towards the light. Every now and then the snow parted briefly – just enough to reassure Kazari that they were on the right path – before closing in again. And each time, Sendar's breathing became more ragged. It seemed forever until they reached it, the dark bulk of a house looming in their vision at last. Kazari and Sendar staggered to the door and Kazari pounded on it, supporting the other Hunter, as her own legs trembled and threatened to collapse.

When the door opened, she stumbled through it in a flurry of snowflakes and freezing air, dragging Sendar with her. They toppled to the floor in a tangle of limbs, and as the warmth from the house flowed over them, Kazari dropped her head to the floor, grateful to be safe at last. Hands pulled at them, dragging them forward across the threshold, and the door closed behind them, locking the warmth inside the house and the freezing air out. Kazari slowly pushed herself to a sitting position in a soggy puddle of slowly melting snow, feeling as if her limbs were made of lead, and then hurriedly checked her companion.

Sendar was shivering, rubbing his leg and barely able to sit upright. Warm hands urged them up, and Kazari allowed herself to be drawn further into the house, taking the cup thrust into her hands and sipping the warm liquid gratefully. Her hands were shaking so much that she was unable to stop it vibrating against her teeth. Slowly, the chills began to ease, and her muscles began to relax. The hands at her back directed her into a chair, and she sat down with a sigh of relief, finally looking around, feeling dazed and exhausted, and desperate not to let go of the hot cup in her hands.

Then she recognised where they were.

It was the Mayor's house, and they were perched on chairs in the reception room they'd been entertained in only two days before, and his wife and children were watching the two of them with wide eyes.

"Have you found Clorri?" Calinda, the Mayor's wife, asked.

With still shaking hands and her worry over Sendar's leg, Kazari was hard-pressed to know how to answer. Should she lie? Or should she tell the truth — that Clorri was safe with Androvar?

"I beg your pardon?" she asked to give herself time to think, and shot a look at Sendar, hoping he might have some idea how to proceed. Like any mother, Calinda must be worried that her missing daughter was lost in the snowstorm. But how complicit was she in that same daughter's abuse?

"Clorri?" Sendar asked. "Your daughter?"

The woman's eyes sparked with hints of anger, and Kazari saw the three younger children move apprehensively, sidling a little further away from their mother. Perhaps that was her answer. She decided to hedge her reply. "We were on our way back to the residence when the storm began, perhaps there will be news after the storm is over?"

"Liars!" snapped another voice, and Kazari looked up, startled. From the darkness of the stairwell, the sound of someone descending step by step echoed coldly through the warmth of the house. There seemed to be something wrong with the sound, though. It wasn't the sound of boots, striking the wooden treads one by one, but a sliding kind of thud, a step, and then another sliding thud, in a limping cadence.

"Who's that?" Kazari asked. There seemed to be something wrong with her too. Her voice was thick, and her tongue wasn't behaving properly. She blinked her eyes, trying to clear her vision, as the room swam in and out of focus. "S, S, Senddd . . . " Her mouth wouldn't work properly. The slide-thud was coming closer. She could hear it. Hear the heaviness of it, and there was a smell . . . dizzily she fought to stay upright. What was wrong with her. "Ssss . . . " she forced out. There was no reply, and as the cup slid from her suddenly nerveless hands, she saw Sendar's body topple from the chair next to her.

His eyes blinked rapidly, and he seemed to be trying to speak, but she was unable to reply, and her nostrils seemed full of a growing stench. From a great distance, Kazari felt her own body topple from the chair, feeling, yet not feeling, her face plough into the woollen rug on the floorboards. The slide and thud reached the bottom of the stairs, and Kazari lay sprawled on the floor of the house, as her vision slowly faded to black. The last thing she saw was a heavy boot, accompanied by . . . a hoof? Her last thought, scrambled though it was, was that whatever drug Calinda had put in the hot drink, it certainly provided some bizarre hallucinations.

***

When Kazari woke, it was dark. Dark, dank, and chilly. She wasn't frozen like she would have been had she still been lost in the storm, but she was cold. She shifted uncomfortably and discovered she was lying on some kind of stone flooring, unable to move freely. She groaned, as the mother of all headaches slammed into her skull.

"Kaz?" Another voice sounded in the darkness. "Kaz?"

"Sendar?"

"Are you alright?"

Kazari groaned again. "I have a hideous headache. And I can't move." She panicked for a moment, before working out that the reason she couldn't move were the ropes around her wrists and ankles. Whoever had tied them hadn't been concerned about her circulation, she realised, as she wriggled around. She struggled in the darkness for a moment, and then inched her way up what she assumed was a wall into a sitting position. "Where are we?" She wished her head would stop pounding long enough for her to think properly. She also wished that her hands were free enough to hold it up.

"I think it might be the cellar in the Mayor's house?" Sendar sounded uncertain. "You must have drunk more of the drug than I did, I've been awake for a while. The headache will eventually go."

"It'd better."

Kazari sighed, and rested her aching head back against the cool stone wall behind her, trying to take stock of their situation. Her face was still throbbing, but it had been eclipsed by the pounding in her head. Her hands seemed partially numb, and someone had taken her gloves and cloak leaving her clad only in her Hunter's garb. She tried to wriggle her hands around to her hips, hoping that the knives in her belt were still there, but the sheaths at her waist were too light, and she already knew they were empty.

Suddenly nauseated, Kazari stopped wriggling, trying not to dry retch, fighting against the heaving spasms that threatened to make her vomit. Finally, panting, she was able to swallow against the sharpness in her mouth and throat, and then she closed her eyes, feeling drained. The darkness, of wherever they were, was unrelenting, and eyes open or closed made no difference to how much she could see, but the simple act of closing her eyes made her feel slightly better. The headache began to abate, until a few moments later, there was only a dull ache in her temples.

"Where are you Sendar?" she asked, suddenly wanting to know that he wasn't too far away.

"To your right I think," he replied. "I'm leaning against a wall."

"Me too, hang on, I'll try to wriggle over to you." And by pushing her feet against the floor and leaning against the wall, Kazari was able to lever herself to the right, until she contacted something soft and warm. Sendar. "Oops, sorry." She overbalanced and toppled sideways, unable to save herself with her bound hands.

There was a sudden grunt from Sendar, and from the warmth under her face, she realised that she was probably lying with her face on his injured leg. She wriggled back upright again. "Sorry," she said again. "Is your leg alright?" She kept her hip in contact with his, though, reluctant to leave the company of another human being in the darkness.

"I think so. It's hard to tell. Still sore, but not much different to before."

"I was worried you were going to end up frostbitten," she replied, feeling a bit stupid, talking about not much in the darkness. "Do you think the others are looking for us?"

His voice was tired. "Probably depends on the storm. I don't know how long we were out."

"Can you move enough to see if we can undo these ropes?" Kazari felt Sendar's hip move, and tried to turn herself so that they were back to back. Even sitting he was a lot taller than she was. Her own hands were partially numb, and felt clumsy, as she tried to explore the knots on his bonds. "My hands are numb; can you feel any better than I can?"

Warm fingers tickled her wrists. "The knots are very tight." She could feel his fingers working away at the ropes on her wrists, but her numb fingers felt as if they were only half there. "Stop wriggling your fingers, Kaz. They keep getting in the way."

"Sorry." She stilled the urge to move her hands, but it was almost uncontrollable. It was as if her mind wanted to feel her fingers so desperately that it kept forcing her to seek out some kind of sensation. Still, she was a Hunter, and Hunters were disciplined, so she resisted the urge and kept her hands still. Sender's warm touch was the only pleasant thing in the darkness, so she concentrated on it. Feeling his warm hands brush against her numb fingers kept wanting to send her into twitches, but she focused on the strength of his back instead, feeling some security in its muscled warmth. And then found her mind wandering towards the day when she and Javon had needed to care for him after the fight at the Abbey.

She blushed, suddenly glad of the darkness that hid such trivial thoughts from the casual observer.

"Sit still Kaz."

She realised that in her embarrassment, she'd wriggled. "Sorry," she said again, contritely. Then, to distract herself. *Lady, help us, please!*

The amethyst at her neck seemed to warm, just briefly, and she was suddenly much less alone. She and Sendar had got themselves into this predicament, but they weren't in it alone. Sender's hands seemed to be tugging fruitlessly at the ropes around her wrists, and her hands, in their partial numbness, had begun to burn at the wrists. She wondered how much pressure it might take to completely cut off the circulation and damage her permanently. Perhaps her innate ability to heal was all that had kept her hands alive so far. She almost panicked again, but then she remembered the Lady, and her fellow Hunters, and took a deep breath, and tried to keep still.

And then the slide thump noise began, coming nearer and nearer until Kazari knew that whatever was making the noise was not far away. The faint smell of gorgone came again, and then began to strengthen. The sound of a key in a door lock echoed through the darkness, and then the room was flooded in light so bright that Kazari's eyes teared and closed involuntarily. But not before she'd seen the creature holding the light. She felt Sendar's hands stop tugging at her wrists, while the image remained burned into her retinas.

What had once been an old woman, held a brightly burning lantern. "Liars," she cackled, limping forward. One hoofed foot thudded against the floor, and a spiked tail slid behind her. One arm, and one eye were still human, along with one side of her face, but the other? Skin had been replaced by scales, and the whole side of the face drooped below a pupil with a vertical slit. A gleaming chain hung around the woman's neck, reflecting reddish gold on the scales. The left arm had been replaced by a tentacle covered in fine barbs, and with a jolt, Kazari realised just who, or what, had inflicted the injuries on Clorri.

CHAPTER TWENTY: TUNNELS

Liars," repeated what had once been human, but was now ... what? "Dirty, little, liars. You know where the girl is, and you know where my son is too. Servants of Her – Servants of Filth!" She limped forward, trailing the tail, hoofed foot stomping heavily on the stone flooring.

Kazari's eyes finally stopped tearing, and she sat, stunned at what remained of the woman, and nearly fell as Sendar twisted himself around to sit beside her. In the sudden light, she could see the rent in his trousers had torn even more, and that his leg wound was now a puckered purple – someone had removed the bandage. Her own face seemed to be throbbing more than it had before. And the smell – she could still smell gorgone. Not strongly, but enough to tell her that what faced her was not wholly human, even if it had been once.

"What happened to you?" she asked, trying to keep her voice steady.

"What happened to me?" cackled the woman. "Better to ask what has happened to you! My Master will be very pleased, and I will be well rewarded. You are precisely what he likes – young, tender, and barely touched by the Witch."

"The witch?" Sendar asked.

"*You* call her Lady," the old woman spat. She stomped forward. "Cretins. Pathetic worms that you are. Deceived by her pretty gems, and holding all of us in your sway." She spat, and even her spittle was discoloured, staining the granite where it struck, algal green. "But before I turn you over to him, you will talk, and tell me exactly why you're here. And exactly where my granddaughter is. She was almost ready to join the change before *you* came to our village."

The tentacled arm flicked out, and a line of hot fire joined the throb on Kazari's face. She jerked backwards, away from it, falling onto the flagstones beneath her and cracking her skull on them. Her renewed headache joined the line of fire.

"Stop it!" Sendar yelled. And then he was lying on the stone floor beside her, writhing against the tentacle that pinned his injured leg to the floor. Kazari struggled to a sitting position again, wishing that Sendar had managed to undo the ropes restraining her. She twisted her wrists, but all she was able to do was to increase the pain already spiking through them. She felt the new cut on her face begin to close, and sighed in relief as the stinging began to subside, and prepared herself to wriggle forward. Perhaps she could use her bound legs to sweep the old woman's limbs from beneath her.

"Hold where you are!" The voice stopped her in her tracks, and Kazari realised that the woman wasn't the only one in the stone room with them. Blinded by the lantern light, she'd not seen the others enter. But now, the old woman – Clorri's grandmother – was flanked by others. Once human, all of them were now caricatures – hybrids maybe? Or what? Half remembered images from the bestiaries she'd studied rolled across Kazari's mind – these human beings appeared to be well on the way to becoming gorgones. But was that even possible? Nothing she'd ever heard had suggested that it was.

Whip like tentacles were common. Half melted human faces topped scaled and furred bodies. Legs were hoofed, clawed, and even multiplied in some cases. One of the creatures – the 'changed', thought Kazari – slithered forward on a snake's body, flickering a forked tongue from all too human lips. It spoke again. "Do not move, Hunter younglings. We have questions, many questions, and you will provide the answers." It circled them, gliding on the stone floor with a dry slithering sound, as it rocked its head from side to side. The creature had clearly once been a woman. Long hair still hung from the skull in flowing locks of rich red, but the whole head had flattened until the only things left recognisably human were the luscious lips from which that forked tongue issued.

Kazari's blood ran cold. There was menace shrouding the snake like a cloak, and it seemed to roll through the stone flagged room like a bank of fog. She held herself very still, and saw Sendar's body shudder with the effort of trying to remain motionless. The old woman's tentacle lay across the purpled lesion on his leg, and she could see it moving, sliding back and forth, sawing its barbs into his thigh. Fresh blood trickled from the rent in his trousers and dripped onto the grey granite floor.

The snake woman motioned, and four more creatures swarmed forward. Arms and tentacles lifted Kazari, and sliced her shirt and layered vests from her torso, and then she was left shivering in the cold, clad only in her breast band and trousers. The old woman hissed and snarled, beast-like, and the snake woman left off her circling to stand with her, looking at Kazari. Sendar lay pinned to the ground by two of the others. The old woman removed her tentacle from his wound, and stumped forward to look into his face. "Answer me, or she pays the price."

Kazari shook her head frantically. "Don't, Sendar. Don't tell them anything!"

"Where is my son?" hissed the woman. Kazari shook her head, willing Sendar not to speak. She saw him close his eyes and breathe deeply, and then he, too, shook his head. The snake woman gestured, and Kazari's minders spun her about, forcing her to her knees, holding her on either side. She clenched her teeth as she heard the old woman step forward, her hoofed foot thudding onto the ground not far away. Without warning, a ribbon of fire erupted across her back. The pain was shocking in its intensity, and Kazari heard a grunt force its way past her clenched teeth. The pain didn't stop after the blow, and she could imagine what the woman was doing, slowly dragging the embedded barbs back and forth across her back. She sobbed, a deep, animal sob of pain. Finally, after what seemed forever, the fire retreated, and her back began to throb wetly.

Trickles of what could only be blood ran down her ribs, and then the wound began to heal.

The old woman cackled. "What sport! She heals! Wonderful – our entertainment will be long, and fulfilling!" There was a murmur from the assembled 'changed'. It was hungry, ravenous, and anticipatory.

"Young Hunter, I will ask you again. Where is my son, and where is my granddaughter?" Kazari heard the dry sound of slithering as the snake woman slid around in front of her.

"Just a touch this time, I think. Hunters," and her voice was scathing, "They believe they can endure anything, with the help of the Witch, but we know the truth. When they're alone, they will never speak, and we are left only pain for our own pleasure. But when another is close by? They protect. It is a thing deep within them. He will break, should you find the right pressures." She stared deeply into Kazari's eyes, and the stench of gorgone rose more strongly in the room. Could they be transforming even as they spoke? Or was there something more deadly coming closer. The remembered pain made it hard for her to think.

"Sendar, no." She forced the words out through lips that didn't want to speak, that didn't want to feel the pain of the old woman's tentacle again.

"Bring him nearer – make sure he can see her face." The snake woman's words were caressing, almost gentle, and

Kazari wanted to vomit. The scent of gorgone strengthened again, and she swore she'd just seen the woman's snout elongate slightly. Those luscious lips smiled; their rich flesh caressed by the snake's tongue. Nausea rolled through Kazari's body.

Sendar's head slid into view, and Kazari shook her head again. She could see the pain in his eyes – both his own – and hers. Then she took a deep breath and forced herself to breathe out. The old woman struck again. "Tell me, or it continues." Multiple strikes, multiple lines of fire across her back. Sendar's eyes, staring desperately into hers, full of tears that spilled and ran down the sides of his face. Her own tears, and his pain, the wound in his leg sawed slowly open before her eyes, but still they hung on. It went on, and on, and on, for what seemed like eternity.

And every moment, the stench of gorgone heightened. The snake woman's snout became a snake's in truth. The old woman stomped on two hoofed feet, and the crowd of tentacled monsters lost limbs and grew eyes on stalks, until the tiny room became a prison full of nightmares and pain. Yet still Kazari healed, and still the monsters salivated and hooted, and then scrabbled for Kazari's drops of blood as they sprayed from her back. She held on grimly, willing Sendar to do the same. Surely the others would be looking for them by now.

At last the pain ended, the changed retreated, and the light left the chamber, but not before the snake woman hissed into Kazari's ear. "This is just the beginning for *you*. A Hunter who heals is sport for many days. One day you will speak, but by then, it will be too late. Our Master awaits you. Until then, speak or not, you will aid our transformation. We will find the man and the girl, once our Master comes in truth, and even the Witch's servants will not be able to keep them from him." She circled them once more, and left the chamber. The door clanged shut behind her, leaving Kazari and Sendar in darkness.

Cold, battered, and exhausted, Kazari lay slumped on the floor, and then wriggled her legs underneath herself and began to inch towards where she knew Sendar lay similarly exhausted. The difference between them was that her injuries were healing themselves, while his were not. "Sendar?" she croaked, through a voice made hoarse by screaming – wordlessly for the most part – when she'd willed herself not to speak. She was exhausted from blood loss and repeated healings.

"Kaz?" Sendar's voice wavered, and she found herself tearing up. She wormed her way over to him, slipping in the sticky pool of blood near his leg, feeling it soak into her trousers, and coat her arm.

She rested her head on his chest, shivering, clad only in her underwear and trousers as she was. "You're cold," he whispered.

"Your leg?" She felt him move, almost drawing away, but she inched closer, desperate for his comfort and to provide comfort in return.

"Bleeding still, I think. I can't move it very well." Cold coursed through her. What if he'd been injured so badly he was unable to walk? Or wouldn't recover fully, even with healing?

"If I help you, can you sit up enough to try the knots again?" she asked.

"I – I don't know," he replied, but as Kazari forced herself into a sitting position, her tied legs curled to one side, he managed to lever himself up, slowly and painfully, judging by the indrawn breaths she could hear in the darkness. Once again they sat back to back. The numbness in Kazari's hands had grown even more, and she wondered how long her Gift of Healing could cope, as its resources dwindled further and further under torture. Would she lose her hands entirely, or would her body divert its ability to heal into preserving her hands?

Sendar's hands continued to work at the knots, but she could feel that he was reluctant to lean his back against hers.

"You're not hurting me, you know," she said quietly. "My back's healed."

She felt his hands pause in their attempts to undo the knots. A moment later he allowed himself to lean back on her with a small sigh of relief, and she realised that leaning away from her had been causing him even more pain.

"We mustn't give in, Sendar," she went on, as he resumed picking at her rope. "The others will be looking for us by now. The storm has to be over."

"How will they know where to look, though?" he asked, his voice sounding discouraged in the darkness. "I mean, they might think we wandered out of the village, and there are only six of them to look."

She shrugged, and made a face to herself in the darkness. "Maybe the Lady will guide them."

His hands stilled, before they resumed their tugging. "Maybe." But he didn't sound convinced. "The Lady more often helps those who help themselves." He sounded depressed, angry, and sad, all at once.

"Well then we'll have to help ourselves, won't we?" The words seemed to fall into the darkness, but Sendar's hands kept on picking at her wrists.

What seemed like hours later, Kazari was awoken by a sharp tingle in her hands. She roused herself guiltily.

"Kaz, I think I've loosened the knot."

The first sharp tingle was followed by burning pins and needles that throbbed and made her hands feel as if they were three times their normal size.

"Ouch! Yes, the blood's coming back into my hands," she replied. Her hands reached the point where they felt if she were to move them, something dreadful might happen, but she forced herself to clench her fists anyway. The pain was excruciating, but then all of a sudden, she could feel more with her fingers, and she thought that the loops around her wrists were loose enough to slide down her hands.

"Hang on, I think you've freed me." The rope slid off, and she dragged her arms in front of her, feeling as if her shoulders might snap after being held in one position for so long. She rubbed her wrists, feeling indentations ridged with corrugations from the twists in the rope that stung and burned. Bending forward, she fumbled at the ropes on her ankles, then decided to ignore them in favour of freeing Sendar. With her hands in front of her, it was much easier.

The knots were tight, but with sensation in her fingers and her hands before her, even in the darkness, it was much easier than fumbling behind her back with numb hands. A few moments later, she was able to attend to both their ankles while Sendar rubbed his own wrists. "Let me see what I can do for your leg, Sendar," she said, closing her eyes and fumbling her hands up his leg in the darkness. She held her hands gently on the flesh as Andiss had shown her, feeling as if she were stumbling around blindly without a clue. She could feel the deep slice in his leg with her hands, the wet stickiness of the blood still oozing from it, and the warmth of the swelling around it, but not quite how to make it close completely.

Still, she concentrated, did what she could, and at least the bleeding stopped. She felt around in the dark for her clothing, salvaged what she could of her shirt and vests, and harvested the most badly torn vest to wrap around Sendar's leg by touch. Then she felt her way to the door by working her way around the room. She was still exhausted, and her legs trembled. The combination of drugging, pain, and fighting, had taken their toll, not to mention the constant healing. She could only imagine how Sendar felt.

The door seemed immovable. The lock was solid, and the key missing, but when she felt around the door hinges, she realised that they were an older kind – the hinges themselves were slotted into matching plates and fastened by a simple peg – on this side of the door.

"Sendar, we might be able to lever the peg out of the hinges!"

She heard him move, and then the limping sound of him shuffling slowly around the wall towards her. He almost fell as he stumbled into her. "Sorry, Kaz," he whispered.

She took his hands and guided them to the lower hinges. "See?"

"Have you got anything that I can use to give them a bit of a tap? The top one's a bit stuck, but I think the others will move pretty easily." She hadn't been able to feel the top hinge. She was too short. She ran her hands over what remained of her belongings. Perhaps her knife sheath? No, it would bend too easily. She undid her belt and handed it to him, trusting that her hips would hold her pants up.

"Use the buckle?"

The tapping sounded enormously loud in the darkness, and Sendar stopped almost as soon as he started. Then she heard him start again, but this time the tapping was muted. He must have doubled the leather over the buckle. There was a sliding sound, followed by two more, and then he handed her two of the three long screws that had been sitting in the hinges, keeping one for himself. Of course, small, but useful makeshift weapons. She tucked one into the top of her boot.

"Help me lean on the door, Kaz."

She added her weight to the door and felt the lock bend. Hopefully it would give under their combined weights.

"Stop for a sec. Let's try and bend it inwards, then we can slide past."

They heaved backwards, and the tongue of the lock slid right out of its hole, and they both fell over with the door on top of them. It seemed to make an enormous noise. Kazari eased the door off them and scrambled to her feet as the faint light from outside finally allowed her to see. She pulled Sendar up, slipping a shoulder underneath him to support his weight when his leg buckled. Now upright, she awkwardly slung her belt around her waist again.

"Come on, quickly. If there's a guard, there's no way they could avoid hearing that." She peered cautiously around the door jamb. A half-shuttered lantern hung further down the hallway. Perhaps they weren't underneath the Mayor's house as she'd thought. The passage seemed to go a long distance in either direction. She sniffed, and the air smelled fresher to her left, so they stumbled off that way. When they reached the next lantern, Kazari unhooked it and took it with them, carefully shuttering it, in case it betrayed them. Its warmth in her hand buoyed her slightly.

Sendar's leg was clearly causing him difficulty, and he struggled to walk. He leaned heavily upon her, and she was hard-pressed to keep them both moving. The passage seemed endless, but eventually Kazari thought that the air was beginning to grow colder, and then the tunnel lightened, and it was the brightness of natural light, not that of lanterns. They hurried onward, and then, after rounding a bend, burst into cold, fresh air at last. It was almost daylight – of what day, Kazari had no idea – and they were perched on a rock ledge above a glacier fed river, its waters tumbling and splashing far below.

CHAPTER TWENTY-ONE:
ESCAPE

The wind outside was icy. Water tumbled and surged far below, the whiteness of its foam standing out brightly in the early morning dimness, as Kazari and Sendar stood on the ledge. Looking up, Kazari could see the top of the cliff, a dizzying distance above them. She wondered what the purpose of a tunnel ending on a ledge was, but as she looked over the edge, she could see what looked like whitened tree branches sticking out of the water, caught in a conglomeration of rocks, and with a small thrill of fear recognised them as bones. Who, or what, had died there she didn't know, but there were many of them. The river was even further away than the top of the cliff, and she wondered whose bones they had been, that now decorated the glacial spillway far below? Androvar hadn't mentioned missing villagers.

"Looks like we'll need to climb. Can you manage?" she asked Sendar, and looked down at his leg. Her torn vest wrapped around his leg showed seepage, and he had been limping heavily, leaning on her for support.

"I don't know, Kaz. I'm barely walking." She looked around the tunnel, hoping for a rope, or something, anything that might help them. There was nothing. The end of the tunnel widened, so that they were able to stand to one side, making them invisible from inside, but apart from a few old boxes and some scrubby tussock grass, the exit was completely barren. "I think you might have to go up alone and then go and get help." He shivered, and Kazari was aware that the wind was icy. The rocky cliff face looked frightening, covered in snow, ice and sparse vegetation. She looked at Sendar with concerned eyes, worried that even if she did manage to get to the top, he'd freeze to death before she could return.

"I'll be back as soon as I can," she replied, squashing all of her doubts about climbing, in the face of Sendar's injury. "I, um, haven't ever climbed anything before – any advice?"

He looked at her, a glimmer of a smile breaking through the greyness of pain and fatigue. "Kaz, you don't have to climb. I'll lift you." Relief washed through her. Of course – he had the Gift of Ascension. He'd lift her up and over the cliff edge.

"Oh yes. Of course," she replied, feeling stupid.

"Ready?" he asked. "I'll position myself so that I can see, but you need to be ready for anything. I'm not sure how much shove I've got left."

His pale face looked exhausted in the darkness, and for a moment, Kazari imagined him boosting her up and then dropping her. Her stomach flipped over, and she had to focus on the feel of his warm hand in hers the day before in order to calm herself. She blushed again, and hoped he hadn't noticed.

She braced herself as he moved to the edge of the ledge, breathed a silent prayer to the Lady, and then her feet left the ground without any warning at all. She couldn't stop herself flailing her arms and legs as if she were swimming. "Stay still Kaz, this is difficult enough as it is!" She'd rather thought she'd feel something, like a giant hand perhaps, but there was just the air and her, and underneath her feet – nothing. She looked down, and then wished she hadn't as she curved away from the cliff edge and wafted upwards. The river foamed below, spurts of spray pushing up around the bones, and she imagined her own bones joining them.

She dragged her attention away from imminent death, to the cliff face now passing by in front of her at a dizzying pace. She risked another look below, and saw Sendar, his face pale and clenched, as he pushed her higher and higher. She looked upwards, wondering just how high he could lift her. Javon had zoomed around about three or four metres above the ground, she thought, and she was much further up than that, and going higher – and faster. Her stomach swooped and swirled, and although she was going up, she felt as if she were falling into the sky. Her head spun.

The top of the cliff face wasn't far now, but the rocks were overhanging, thrusting themselves out into the vacant air and Kazari's left foot struck one with a stinging impact as she flew past it. Suddenly, she slowed, almost hovering, about three metres below the lip. "Kaz, you'll have to climb from there. I'm going to push you towards the rocks!" Sendar called, his voice tight with strain. She nodded, and then realised he couldn't possibly see her.

"Ready!"

She moved towards the cliff face, and as she approached it, realised that Sendar must have begun to lose control. She sank, and made a wild grab for the closest rock. Her fingers scraped off it, at the full extent of her arms, and she tried desperately to throw herself towards the nearest outcropping – but how could you throw yourself when there was nothing to gain purchase upon but air? Skin tore and a fingernail bent back painfully and then, somehow, she was clinging to a rocky outcropping for dear life, hanging on with all her strength. Upper body strength had never been her strong suit, but her legs were chunky, and she scrabbled for purchase with them, and then thankfully her boots found something solid, allowing her legs to take some of the weight off her arms.

Shivering in the chilly air, she looked around wildly, seeking a path to the top. She wasn't quite as far down as she'd thought, and as reason slowly snuck back into her mind, she slowed her panting and tried to plot a climb that she could achieve. She unclenched one hand, reached sideways and began to climb, trying to spare her arms, as soon as her feet found each new foothold. Still, her entire body was quivering with strain when she finally managed to scramble her way over the edge of the rocks and into the thick layer of snow that girded the edge.

Wary of being seen, she inched her head upwards, trying to figure out where she was, while remaining concealed in the whiteness. Clad in her Hunter Blacks, she'd stick out like a sore thumb if she wasn't careful, but at the same time, she couldn't stay where she was, or she'd freeze to death. Her hands were already feeling stiff, so she tucked them into her armpits, trying to warm them up, chancing a look back down to where Sendar was a huddled speck on the ledge. She took one hand out from her armpit and waved it, hoping he'd see it, and then turned her head resolutely away, trying to figure out where she was.

It took her several minutes, but finally she was fairly certain she knew where she was. The Mayor's house was at the edge of Suborden, and Suborden itself was perched on the shoulder of a mountain. Kazari was about five hundred metres from the Mayor's house, on the edge of the village bounds, just where the mountain plunged steeply towards the river on the border. If she could make her way northwards, she'd be heading in the right direction for the chapel and her fellow Hunters, or at least Androvar. There were no people visible as far as her eyes could see, just the thick drifts of snow, newly fallen in the storm. She wondered if this was the morning after the last day she remembered, or if it had been longer. She had no idea how long she'd been drugged.

Keeping to the cliff edge would be too dangerous. She'd have no idea if the snow was concealing an edge, or whether the ground was solid. She crawled forward, teeth chattering, and limbs shaking. Another problem. If she didn't move faster, she'd be unable to move at all. The cold bit deeply into her arms and legs, and crawling as she was, she was barely able to see what direction she was moving in. At least if she couldn't see, it was unlikely that a casual glance would spot her. She made for another rock outcrop. One of the only features in the white landscape. She couldn't help the trail she was leaving in the snow, but she hoped that anyone searching for her wouldn't think to look above ground.

Then she fell into a deep drift, and the newly fallen snow closed over her head, filling her eyes and nose. She flailed with her arms, trying to swim out, and then came to her senses, and righted herself, then edged upwards once her feet found firm ground. The rocks weren't far now, and after taking a quick look around, Kazari scrabbled her way through the snow towards it, focusing more on moving and less on worrying about who might or might not be following her.

Her hands began to feel the cold almost immediately. She pulled her sleeves down over them as far as she could, and tucked them under her armpits as often as she could, but the snow was so deep in places that she was forever stumbling into drifts and throwing her hands out to save herself. The abrasions on her hands stopped hurting after a while. Initially she was grateful, but after taking a look at her hands and seeing the dead whiteness of her skin, she realised that frostbite was becoming a real possibility. Again she tucked her hands away – this time underneath her shirts, but almost immediately, she stumbled and flung them out again. Apparently healing could only do so much.

She contented herself with alternating them – one to help her balance, and one to warm up. Her fingers felt icy against the warm skin of her stomach, and she wished the exertion would warm her hands too, but apparently the freezing air was too much for her circulation to overcome. As she struggled on, Kazari found herself replaying the hours of pain, her mind full of memories of the old woman's barbed tentacle. As she extricated herself from yet another drift, she found she was shaking – and not with cold.

Fear gripped her. Fear that she'd fall into the creatures' clutches again, and fear that Sendar was already back in that tiny room, being questioned. He didn't have her ability to heal, and the possibility that his leg would become permanently damaged loomed large in her mind. It was very quiet – perhaps the creatures who'd tormented them were quiescent in the daytime. She wondered how many of the villagers really knew what was going on – and who 'The Master' that the old woman had talked about really was.

Step after step, she forced herself through the snow. She remembered following Sendar only a few days ago, grateful for his tall strength, and the thought of him waiting on that icy ledge spurred her on. She was close enough to smell the smoke now, and her breath rasped in her throat as she pushed her way doggedly towards the chapel. Images of hot drinks, pancakes with syrup, eggs and bacon, all tantalised her. Her legs were burning; she was shivering almost continuously now, and her hands had completely lost all feeling. Slowly, the air around her brightened. As if apologetic for the previous weather, the sun flung pale fingertips above the horizon, causing Kazari to cast a long shadow against the pristine whiteness.

She crouched, trying to minimise her outline, but she knew it wasn't much use against the whiteness of the snow. At least she was almost there. Her cheeks burned, and her breath was groaning in her chest as she staggered her way closer and closer to the rocks. She fell again, boots sliding on a slick patch of ice, and the smell of fresh blood added itself to the fear. The bright redness against the snow made her look at her hands again. Her left palm had been sliced open on a piece of sharp ice. Blood welled slowly, and the cut didn't heal as quickly as she'd become accustomed. Then she realised that she was standing still, looking dazedly at her hand, and forced herself to move again. She hadn't felt the cut. Perhaps her hands were beyond saving too.

For a moment, she wished she had the Gift of Ascension. She could have used it to compact the snow ahead of her and thus move more easily. As it was, she floundered through the drifts, caution thrown to the wind, legs pumping and propelling her forward. Finally, she rested, panting, in the shadow of the rocks. She peered out from behind them, hoping that no-one from the village could see her tracks, and then climbed the rocks to gain height, and with a surge of hope, saw the chapel on its knoll not too far away. Smoke poured from Androvar's chimney, and trudging almost directly towards her were the other six Hunters.

CHAPTER TWENTY-TWO: RESCUED

From her perch on the rocks, Kazari waved her arms. "Help!" she called, "Help!" But her voice was croaky and didn't carry. Clearing her throat she tried again. "Help!" This time they heard her, and Kazari saw six heads rise in unison.

As the Hunters forged their way through the snow towards her, Kazari allowed herself to slide exhaustedly down the rocks until she collapsed in a heap at the bottom. It didn't take long before the others reached her, breaths steaming in the icy air.

"Kazari – what happened? Where's Sendar?" Andiss asked.

"Sendar – he's on the ledge," she forced out. "And there are creatures . . . "

"Kaz, your hands!" exclaimed Javon, taking them gently. "Andiss, can you help?"

"Don't worry about them now – Sendar needs help!" repeated Kazari. "Quickly!" She blurted out Sendar's location, pointing to her trail through the snow, and at a nod from Andiss: Mikel, Sherd, Jern, and Kellis were off, moving faster than Kazari would have thought possible.

Javon took Kazari's hands again. "Andiss," she repeated. "Can you do anything?"

He looked at the waxy skin, touching them gently. "Can you feel that, Kaz?"

She shook her head.

"Kaz, your healing will help preserve the tissues for some time, but without circulation you'll be in deep trouble if we don't thaw you out soon. We need to get you back to Androvar as soon as possible."

"But Sendar . . . " she began.

"The others will bring him. Can you walk?" As Javon spoke, she was wrapping Kazari's hands in oversized mittens, and then pulled a warm cloak from her pack and wrapped it around Kazari's shoulders. Andiss put an arm around her and helped her to her feet, and with Javon on her other side, Kazari began to stumble towards the chapel.

It seemed like an age before she was seated inside, shivering, in the warmth and comfort of Androvar's kitchen.

"This is going to hurt, I'm afraid."

Kazari looked down to see Javon's hands gently stroking her waxy looking ones. She'd removed the mittens without Kazari noticing. Her hands were battered, oozing blood in spots, and still numb. Androvar brought a deep bowl and placed it on the table, and Javon tested it with her own hand, then took Kazari's hands and eased them into the water. She shivered violently, and Androvar draped a blanket around her, and then her hands caught fire. She tried to jerk them out of the water, but Javon was too fast.

"Just leave them in there, Kaz. It's not hot enough to burn, but it will feel awful. It's the only way to get them on the mend."

"Hurts . . . " Kazari croaked.

"It does. But it'll settle down in a little while. Now, while you're sitting here, you need to tell us about whatever you meant by 'creatures.'"

Androvar held a steaming cup to her lips, and Kazari tried to stop herself from shivering long enough to sip from it. The warm drink slid down her throat and radiated heat from her stomach. For a moment her shivers intensified, and then it was as if something had suddenly loosened all of Kazari's muscles. She slumped back into her chair with a sigh, eyelids beginning to droop.

"Don't go to sleep, Kaz – Androvar, what did you put in that?"

"She'll be alright in a moment. It won't knock her out, just warm her up, and moderate some of the pain. The rest is just exhaustion, I think." Androvar pulled a chair closer, and placed a warm hand on Kazari's shoulder. "You're safe, Kaz. Now, can you tell us what happened to you?"

Tears came unbidden to Kazari's eyes, and she nodded, although her throat was suddenly tight again.

"How long have we been gone?" she asked.

"It's only the morning of the day after you went missing," Androvar said as she held the cup up again. Kazari sipped again, sighing in relief, and the drink seemed to distance her from the burning in her hands and the immediacy of the previous night's events, and she began to speak, haltingly at first, but then the words were pouring out of her in a torrent.

Finally, when she'd finished, she was allowed to slump back exhausted. The others hadn't interrupted her once, but she'd seen their faces change from understanding to horror, and then back to grim understanding again.

"So, it's even worse than we'd thought," Andiss said. "Androvar, we'll need to send word to the Abbot immediately. Do you have any birds? It has been many years since we've had to deal with those such as these." He looked at Javon as Androvar left the room. "And once we have Sendar back with us, we need to deal with this infestation." He paced back and forth in front of the fire, head bowed and hands clasped, while Javon added more warm water to the bowl. The worst of the fire had gone from Kazari's hands now, but they still throbbed violently when Javon encouraged her to begin to move her fingers. They felt stiff, and twice as big as they should, and she was wondering if they'd ever be the same again.

Now warm, her face had begun to throb again, and she saw Andiss frown as he raised his head to look at her.

"You think the Mayor's whole family knows?"

She nodded, and he went back to his pacing.

"So, the questions: how deep does this infection run? How many malmetal charms did the 'traders' leave here? How many of these changed are there? And who is this, Master?"

"And what will they do when they realise that Kazari and Sendar have escaped?" Javon added. She took Kazari's hands from the warm water and began to pat them dry, very gently. Kazari looked at them. Her skin was mottled purple and her hands were swollen, and the skin now felt tight and uncomfortable. They looked like sausages. But even as she looked, she could feel her Gift begin to help things. However, this time, the healing was slow, sluggish even. She wondered just how much the creatures' torture had taxed her body. The discolouration began to fade, and the tightness eased slightly. "Even with your Gift, this will take some time, and your Gift is exhausted after your ordeal." She began to wrap Kazari's hands in soft bandages. "This will protect them in the meantime."

Kazari nodded, tears springing unbidden to her eyes. She'd never felt this drained in her entire life. The wound on her face throbbed in time with her hands, and the remembered pain stung her back, despite the wounds being fully healed. Javon placed a bowl of soup in front of her as Androvar entered the kitchen again carrying a cage containing two homing pigeons, and clumsily, she lifted the spoon in her bandaged hand and fumbled some into her mouth. The shivering had finally settled down, and the soup tasted almost unbelievably good. Hoping the others would forgive her dreadful manners, she abandoned the spoon and picked the bowl up in her bandaged hands and drank from it directly. The soup warmed her like nothing else she'd ever eaten.

"These are my last two until new birds arrive," Androvar said. Andiss nodded his thanks, while the Intercessor paused beside Kazari, laying a gentle hand on her shoulder. "The memories will slowly pass, Kaz. In the meantime, I will entreat the Lady on your behalf." The words were comforting, and some of the anxiety within Kazari bled away. She sipped more of the soup. *Lady, please be with Sendar.* Her own prayer was desperate and heartfelt. At least her injuries would heal with time, but Sendar's – she didn't want to think about the wound in his leg. Perhaps Andiss' Healing would help more than her own. For the first time, she wished that they had a Healer travelling with them. She remembered how well they'd healed her own injury after the fight with the greater gorgone.

A sudden flurry at the door heralded the others' return. Sendar was being carried between Kellis and Jern. His face was white, he was barely conscious, and the blood on his trouser leg appeared to have frozen solid. With an exclamation, Androvar cleared the chairs out of their way, and they laid him carefully on a pallet closer to the fire. Andiss hurried over, and bent over Sendar's still form. Kazari began to struggle out of her chair, anxious to help if she could, but Javon placed firm hands on her shoulders. "Leave him to Andiss and Androvar."

"But . . ."

"They're much more capable than you are right now, Kaz, your Gift can barely heal yourself, let alone someone else. Rest."

Reluctantly, Kazari did as she was told, but couldn't stop herself from craning her neck to see what was happening. In the background she could hear Mikel speaking. "The village is still quiet. Quieter than normal, actually. Whatever's wrong here, is very wrong. Sendar told us a little, but he was too exhausted to make much sense."

Andiss crouched over Sendar, and Androvar eased his trousers down with Sherd's help. Kazari heard a hiss of indrawn breath, and a groan from Sendar, but couldn't see what was happening. "Can you fix it, Andiss?" Javon asked, and she heard the anxiety in her teacher's voice.

Andiss' reply was too soft for Kazari to hear, so she turned her gaze towards Javon. The woman was intent on what was happening and didn't see her anxious look. "Will he be all right?" she asked, and Javon's head whipped around.

"I hope so, Kaz. It's a pretty bad wound. Quite close to the major artery and nerve."

Jern bustled in with another armload of blankets, and then Andiss was sitting back on his heels and wiping a hand across his brow. He pushed himself up and pulled a chair out from the table. "Do you have some more of that soup, Androvar?" He looked tired, Kazari thought. "I think he'll be alright. The leg's saved, but only time will tell how well saved. He'll probably need the attention of skilled Healers back at the Abbey though."

Tears sprung to Kazari's eyes. His leg was saved? It had been that bad? She found herself sobbing, heedless of how she looked to the others, bent over the table with her throbbing hands and face, an emotional wreck. She wondered how long it had been since she'd slept.

Vaguely, she could hear the voices around her, and then arms wrapped around her and someone picked her up and to her relief, laid her down next to Sendar, on a pallet by his side. She had to know how he was, and after their ordeal, she couldn't imagine being separated from him. Turning her head, she could see his face, pale under his dark skin, and that he was either fast asleep or unconscious. A soft hand – Androvar's? – rested on her forehead, and then she had the impression of song, before she fell into a warm dark well of sleep.

When she awoke, the light was dim. Quiet voices spoke from the table, and a rustle of movement by her side suggested that Sendar might be awake too. Stiffly she rolled over and pushed herself into a sitting position, looking anxiously at her friend. "Sendar?" she whispered. His eyes were open, and he turned his head as she spoke.

"Still alive – and safe, thanks to you."

"More thanks to you!" she replied. "I couldn't have climbed that cliff by myself. How's your leg?"

"Better, I think." She could see him trying to move it under the mound of blankets, wincing. "Yes, definitely better."

"You're awake," Andiss said. "Just as well. We have work to do."

"Work?" Kazari asked.

"We are Hunters," Andiss told her, "and where there are gorgones, we hunt."

"But they were people," Kazari said. "At least they used to be."

"They are people no longer," Javon said flatly. "This is an ancient evil. It has been a long, long time, since we've had to deal with the 'changed', but it doesn't mean we've forgotten what we have to do."

Androvar looked troubled. "But they were people – people I knew. People I liked."

"Androvar, we've been over this. You may have liked them, but they liked evil more. To 'change' they had to *choose* to. You've read the Writings. You know what they say."

"They're in the Writings?" Kazari said, puzzled. She had no recollection of the Changed in the Writings, or at least if they were there, she hadn't read that bit.

"Not in the mainstream books, no, but in the end of each Book given to each Order, you'll find a chapter entitled *The Manifestations of Evil.*"

Kazari nodded her understanding. She'd seen the chapter but had not yet read it. Andiss had encouraged her to memorise the Lady's instructions to her Hunters, and apart from commenting that they'd study the rest of *The Book of Hunters* in much greater depth shortly, hadn't touched on that portion.

She'd flicked through it idly, but with needing to learn how to use her gifts, the ongoing physical training, and the sudden journey, delving into the final chapter of *The Book of Hunters* hadn't been high on her list of things to do. In retrospect that seemed stupid, given what a Hunter was up against.

And now she knew that each of the Order's septs had their own Book. She wondered if she'd ever get to see them. Apparently Andiss had. She wondered if Androvar's was full of songs, or written like her own *Book of Hunters*. Andiss recited from memory. "'There are those who choose the ways of evil. You will know them by these signs. They find joy in hatred, and glee in despair. They mistreat those within their care, hoping to drive them from the light of My love. They rejoice only in darkness. When evil is entrenched, and their wills enslaved to a greater gorgone, their physical bodies reflect it, mirroring the changes within their souls.'"

Kazari nodded in understanding – the words Andiss had quoted described the creatures exactly.

"And how do we overcome them?" Sendar asked.

"As we do any gorgone, because that is exactly what they are becoming," Mikel said. "And with the Lady's help, that is, because there are many of them, by your own accounts."

Kazari sat back, daunted. She was a Hunter, and Hunters hunted. So far, she'd fought several gorgones, but each time she'd fought because she'd been attacked. This time, she'd have to attack – or perhaps 'hunt' was a better word. Hunt deliberately, not just react to something. It was sobering. These 'changed' had been people – people just like her own family. She wasn't certain how she felt about that. Then suddenly she remembered – The Mayor, Clorri – what had happened to them?

"What about the Mayor?" she blurted, "and Clorri?"

Androvar looked troubled. "They're still here. Clorri's in a guest room, and she doesn't know about her father. He's locked in the cellar."

"Is he . . . changed?" Sendar asked in the sudden silence.

Javon sighed. "And that is the question, isn't it? The short answer is that we don't know. That he'd attack a Hunter and be complicit in his daughter's abuse suggests that, he has begun the change, but at this point, we're divided on whether he might be salvageable. His body shows no physical signs as yet."

"Salvageable?"

"Whether he might turn away from evil, and towards the Lady's light," Androvar replied. "He was once a good person – kind, generous and intelligent. This village's prosperity is in no small way his doing. What has happened to corrupt him?" She shook her head. "Perhaps it was the influence of his mother. She was forever a gossip, delighting in the misfortune of others. Perhaps it was the malmetal charms, although he had none on his person. I, for one, am unwilling to let him change without a fight."

Kazari looked at the Intercessor. Her face was sad but determined, and she remembered that Androvar had been living here for some years. Some of those who'd changed were probably friends, or at least had been friends. How difficult would that be, she wondered, imagining Dari changing, becoming one of those they now hunted. She closed her eyes momentarily. Dari would never do such a thing, even with the temptation of a malmetal charm.

"Enough of that," Andiss said. "Kazari, you and Sendar will remain with Androvar. Neither of you is recovered enough to fight with us today. Stay here while we hunt these creatures, and be safe. I have sent messages to the Abbot, and she will send further assistance."

"Stay here?" Kazari couldn't believe what she was hearing. "But there are only six of you – you need us!"

"Kazari, we don't need two injured, exhausted, trainees with us," Mikel replied.

Kazari looked at him with hurt eyes, feeling rejected, like a naughty school child.

"Mikel!" Javon was exasperated. "Think before you speak, would you? Look, you're both unfit enough to hamper the rest of us, no matter how great your gifts are," she temporised. That Kazari could accept, if barely.

"But how will you locate them without me?" she asked.

"We'll be going back in the way you came out," Javon explained. "They may have guards, but we're Hunters." She shrugged. "Experienced Hunters. It's a confined space, and a bottleneck for them rather than us, and we need to discover the extent of the underground network anyway. It also explains why Androvar didn't see any of them earlier – they must have been using it to move around."

"But, I'm pretty good now," Kazari replied. "My hands feel much better." She began unwrapping the bandages around her hands. Her fingers felt a bit puffy still, but there was little pain.

"Kazari, the matter is closed. Sendar can't come, and if anything goes wrong, you'll be Androvar's defence," Andiss said firmly.

Slightly resentful, Kazari finished unwinding the bandages. The skin on her hands was pink, and a bit tingly, but the wounds had all closed and her sensation had returned completely she realised, with a sigh of relief. She looked at Sendar, who looked annoyed but resigned. She could see him moving his leg again, testing it. He winced and stopped moving it.

Unconvinced, she listened, frustrated, as the other six finalised their planning. She took small comfort from the fact that she was apparently the last line of defence for Androvar. Within her, she could feel anger simmering away. Anger at those who'd hurt her and injured Sendar. She realised that hunting them down wouldn't have required too much from her at all.

Chapter Twenty-three: Attack

Androvar's house seemed very empty after the six Hunters had departed. It was late afternoon, and the winter light was already growing dim. Kazari had ventured outside only once before the others had left – accompanied by Javon – to source a change of clothing for both herself and Sendar, and to rearm them both. She was more tired than she cared to admit, even after eating more of Androvar's excellent soup. Still, she felt much better after bathing in Androvar's bathroom. The Intercessor's bath was supplied by water heated in pipes that ran through the back of the fireplace. It did require some pumping on Kazari's behalf, which only served to emphasise her persistent fatigue, but the reward of hot, steaming water was enough to overcome any reluctance.

After drying herself, she paused, looking in the mirror set on the wall above the basin. The scar on her face was still lividly red. It marred the smooth skin, and she knew with certainty that the scar would remain as a reminder of the fight with the suckers, and the words of the greater gorgone. There was a puckered bit near her ear that twisted the skin slightly and pulled as she moved her mouth. She wondered what her parents might say – that is, if she ever saw them again.

Regret stung for a moment. Regret that she hadn't heard from them, that they hadn't said goodbye, and that perhaps she'd never be able to say all of the things she needed to. She'd already come close to death several times, just as her mother had feared. Still, her path was set now. She'd pledged to the Lady, and even now she didn't regret her choice, just her lack of contact with her family. She'd had a number of letters from Dari, and sent some in return, but there still hadn't been a word from her parents. Perhaps there might be one when she returned to the Abbey.

She grimaced at her reflection, and the scar twisted and stretched below her unruly mass of short curls. Her body was harder now – muscled as it had never been before, yet more womanly than she remembered. The constant exercise had toned it, and the new muscle only emphasised her curves. Her chunkiness looked different, somehow – stronger, perhaps. She looked in the mirror again, remembering the day of initiation. She'd regretted the loss of her hair in advance, but she'd never imagined that her face would be permanently scarred.

She snorted softly to herself. She'd never imagined she'd be a Hunter, either. She tried a smile, and the scar stretched even more. She wondered whether it would fade in time. As it was, her face would now draw stares. A sense of loss hovered above her. She hadn't been a beauty to start with, but she'd had a pleasant face, and her skin had been smooth and unmarked. She wondered what Dari would say if she could see her friend now. In her mind, she could hear her mother's voice: 'Kazari, I told you this would happen. You're lucky you're not dead. And who in their right mind would marry a girl with a face like that?'

The imagined words stung, and she dropped her eyes from the mirror, imagining her father's face – he'd be horrified if he saw her, devastated that her choice to serve the Lady had left her marked so early in her career. Then the amethyst at her chest warmed briefly, and even as Kazari wondered if she'd imagined it, she caught a sudden flash of violet from the mirror. She'd been scarred in the service of the Lady, protecting her people from deadly danger. The scar shouldn't be a badge of shame, but an honourable battle wound. It didn't stop the regret for her lost looks, but it did soothe the thoughts of her parents' probable reactions. Perhaps they'd see it as a mark of honour one day. She tried to comfort herself with the thought.

She dressed quickly, and then emptied and refilled the bath for Sendar. The least she could do for him was to help him get clean, and into clean clothing. And then she blushed. Javon wasn't here to help this time. Her mind was jumping around like a grasshopper, she thought. And then she blushed again, organised a chair by the bathtub, composed herself, and went to get Sendar.

His leg had improved, she thought, as he leaned on her on their way to the bathroom. He wasn't limping nearly as much, but he was still struggling. As she helped him out of his clothing, her eyes were drawn to the wound on his leg. Like her face, it was still red and inflamed looking, even if the skin was now closing over. The scar was puckered and rough, even helped along by Andiss' Healing. He followed her eyes to the scar.

"Mars my beauty doesn't it?" he said with a wry grin.

"How much does it hurt?" she asked.

"Well, it's better than it was," he replied, "but it still feels as if the muscle is either bruised or torn. And when I put a lot of weight on it, my leg feels like it might give way."

He looked at her face, and gently touched the scar. "Still sore?"

Kazari nodded, not trusting her voice. His hand was warm and gentle, and his eyes understanding. Finally she was able to force a few words out.

"Throbs a bit, but nothing like your leg." Thinking about his leg made her scar seem minor in comparison. "Would you like me to have a try at healing it again too?"

"Do your worst," he smiled. And then went on hurriedly. "Not that you'll be bad at it or anything, I didn't mean that." He flushed. And then suddenly Kazari was laughing, and he was laughing too, and she felt remarkably better about everything. She sobered abruptly as their laughter stilled and he went on. "It's not like you thought is it?" he asked, tentatively, and she shook her head.

"It's ... more ... somehow. More in all kinds of complicated ways. More difficult, more fulfilling, more dangerous, more better. Which doesn't make sense at all," she replied, and helped him off with his shirt and layered vests as he sat on the chair by the bath.

"I know what you mean. I'm a year ahead of you, but this last six months has been different. Very different. I've seen more, and experienced more than I could ever have imagined, and now both of us have to sit by and wait, hoping the others will be all right, because we're too injured and too inexperienced to help them," he replied. There was a hint of bitterness in his tone, but he shook the words off and continued to help her remove his clothing.

As she went to help him off with his underwear, Sendar shook his head. "I can manage once I'm in the bath. Help me in, and then I'll call when I'm ready to hop out. Then you can try your healing worst." She grinned at him, slightly relieved, and complied with his request, leaving the bathroom door slightly ajar so that she'd hear him call.

While he bathed, Kazari rearmed herself, sheathing her spare knives, and regretting the ones lost, particularly her first knife. She'd become quite attached to it over the last few months. The day had dimmed further while she'd been getting herself clean, and Androvar had lit a number of lamps in the kitchen, and pulled the curtains across the windows.

"No sense letting anyone see in," Androvar said. "Hopefully the villagers still think you're all holed up with me in here tonight." Something savoury was simmering on the stove, and the smell of fresh bread baking filled the air in the kitchen as Kazari slid the last knife into her sleeve under Androvar's curious gaze. "I had no idea you lot carried so much ironmongery," she said.

Kazari smiled. "I'm just a new initiate. This is nothing. I only have the things I know how to use a bit." Androvar rolled her eyes, and took the bread out of the oven and set it to cool on a rack. Then she heard Sendar calling. "Back shortly."

Sendar had draped his underwear with care, to spare her more blushes, she realised, smiling slightly, and helped him out of the bath, wrapping a towel around him as he sat on the chair. She helped him dry himself, and then paused before bringing his clothes over. "How about I give it a go now?" She waved her hand at his leg.

He nodded. "Do your worst."

She made a face at him, but crouched next to his leg, and gingerly touched the red scar. It was hot to touch, and he winced slightly. The palms of her hands tingled, and closing her eyes she concentrated as Andiss had taught her. There was . . . something. Something that resisted her touch. It felt as if the tissue itself was fighting back against her. She frowned, and tried again. It was unlike anything she'd experienced before – not that her experience was exactly enormous, or comprehensive, she reminded herself.

She concentrated again. The amethyst warmed against her chest and the room brightened slightly as Sendar's joined hers, bathing them both in gentle violet. There was a sudden sharp stench, and then a snap, and a hint of lavender washed the stench away. Abruptly her face also felt better, and the wound on Sendar's thigh had lost its angry redness. The scar was still there, puckered and ugly, but he sighed with relief, and put one of his hands over hers.

"Thank you. That feels much better."

She looked up at him. "Really?"

"Really," he repeated. "Do you have any idea how often you say that?"

"Say what?"

"Say really," he replied.

"Do I?" she asked, confused. The healing had left her slightly wobbly and off balance.

"You do," he replied firmly, and then levered himself up onto his feet. "That really does feel better." He looked down. "Feels better, looks about the same, but less red. I think I'll be able to dress myself now." He smiled at her. "See you in a moment."

Shaking her head, Kazari left the bathroom after telling him to call if he needed her, joining Androvar, and to her surprise, Clorri, in the kitchen. She must have looked startled, because Androvar shook her head with a quick jerk, and wiggled her eyebrows meaningfully at her, which she took to mean that she was to act normally and say nothing out of the ordinary. She took one of the seats at the table, adjusted one of her knife sheaths slightly for comfort, and tried to think of something to say.

She didn't think that "I met your grandmother yesterday," would go down particularly well. The other girl looked uncomfortable, and by the way she was avoiding the back of the chair, Kazari could tell that her injuries were still painful. She wondered at that. She was sure that Andiss would have tried to heal Clorri, and opened her mouth to ask, when she heard Sendar limping his way from the bathroom. "Back in a moment," she said and hurried to help him.

He was walking much more easily, still limping a bit, but much less than he had been, and he looked much more himself, garbed in his Hunter's clothing. "Clorri's in the kitchen," she warned him as they approached.

He sniffed appreciatively at the smells in the room as he sat down. Kazari brought him a selection of the weaponry she'd collected from the barracks, and as she had, he began to rearm himself under Clorri's suddenly wide eyes. Kazari noticed that he had considerably more 'ironmongery' than she did. Of course he had been in training a year longer than she had. He winked at Clorri, who looked down, embarrassed.

"Food?" Androvar asked. "It's ready." She spoke a small blessing, thanking the Lady for her bounty, and asking her care on 'all who serve this village' tonight. Kazari silently appreciated the guarded reference to the others, and added her own silent prayer for their safety. By now they'd be on their way down the cliff. She caught Sendar's eye as he dug into the bowl of stew Androvar handed to him. He nodded and launched into a story of their travels and the quirks of their horses. Eventually he won a smile from Clorri. She was so involved in his tale that Kazari could see that she failed to notice when Androvar departed the kitchen with another wooden bowl of stew and a hunk of bread.

Slightly uncomfortably, Kazari wondered if she should have gone with the Intercessor, but then reasoned that she'd have had to excuse herself, which would have been much more noticeable than Androvar's quiet exit. Still, she wouldn't be happy until the woman had returned. And she'd better pay attention to Sendar's story so that she could laugh in all the right places. She felt like a fraud, pretending to laugh, not mentioning the scars on Clorri's back, or the fact that her father was imprisoned in Androvar's cellar, or that her grandmother had tortured both herself and Sendar the night before. In fact she wasn't even sure what Clorri knew, so she pretended that the girl knew nothing, unless she decided to mention the abuse herself. Perhaps it was her way of trying to heal. Surely the fact that the girl had taken herself to the chapel, looking for refuge was a big point in her favour. Still, the old woman's words about Clorri's readiness to change sat uncomfortably in the back of Kazari's mind.

Perhaps the girl had been beaten into agreeing or perhaps she'd been pretending. She *had* sought sanctuary in the Lady's chapel, Kazari reminded herself.

Androvar reappeared within a few minutes, and joined in the conversation, describing her own journey to Suborden in hilarious detail. She did it so smoothly that Kazari was impressed, but it made for a long meal, and she wondered how long Clorri would stay in the kitchen, and slightly guiltily, wished that the girl would retire to her room very soon, so that she and Sendar and Androvar could get on with the real job of worrying and wondering about what was happening under the Mayor's house.

Fortunately, once the meal was finished, Androvar ushered Clorri from the room, with a quick. "I just need to check your dressings, dear."

Kazari didn't miss the girl's stricken face, or Androvar's nod at the cup sitting on the bench. "Will you bring that to Clorri's room in a moment, Kaz?" From her meaningful look, Kazari guessed that it contained more than just tea.

Once Clorri was out of the room, she turned to Sendar. "How's the leg now?"

"Working better," he replied. "Wonder how the others are doing, though." She nodded, and paced to the window, drawing back a tiny bit of cloth to peer out. The moon had risen, and the whole village was outlined in stark black and white. The stillness, even on a freezing night, was uncanny. Kazari was uncomfortable, wanting to pace up and down, but with a shrug, she recognised the fruitlessness of the action. Then she heard a shriek, and the sound of something heavy falling. It came from Clorri's room.

Chapter Twenty-four:
The Master

Without thinking, Kazari ran. Her abused body complained, but the screaming continued, and she acted on reflex, racing down the hallway. Behind her she could hear Sendar's limping tread following her more slowly.

A scene of chaos met her as she burst into the guest room and skidded on the blood on the floor. Whose blood? Flames reflected wetly from the spill, and Kazari barely missed sliding into the spreading puddle. She grabbed at the bed post for balance. Clorri was nowhere to be seen, but Androvar's limp body sprawled bonelessly on the floor, eyes open, staring sightlessly at the ceiling, eyes and lips blue. Her chest didn't move, and the enormous gash in her throat told its own tale. And above her, the source of the flames towered.

Kazari stared open mouthed at the figure as the stench of gorgone assaulted her nostrils, and smoke rose from the floor as the thing's feet burned into the polished wood.

"Sendar!"

Her fellow Hunter limped into the room, and Kazari heard his quick intake of breath as he poised himself by her side. Her hands sought her knives even as her eyes scanned the room, searching for Clorri.

"He is come!" the figure declared. "Come within *me*. See your folly, girl?" One hand gestured towards Kazari, while the other burst into flames, sending flares of light across the room and Androvar's blood. A muffled sob came from the direction of the curtains in the bay window, and the figure turned, the flaming hand engulfing the curtains, sending a gout of fire towards the ceiling.

Behind the curtain, Clorri cowered, shaking.

"Run Clorri," Kazari shouted, "Run and hide."

The gorgone's flaming arm lashed out towards the girl, while it kept its attention on the two Hunters, as Clorri tried to scramble away, but Sendar's thrown knife struck its arm, and it roared in pain, even as the metal flashed to molten, and dripped to the floor, igniting the polished floor boards near the creature's feet. Clorri leaped, throwing herself at the large windows, and crashed through them in a flurry of broken glass. Kazari only hoped that the girl hadn't been seriously injured, but she was glad Clorri had had the sense to leave when urged.

The remains of the curtain exploded in a flash of fire, and Kazari threw up an arm to protect her face. The tough leather of her Hunter's gear took the brunt of the flames, but the tender skin of her hands wasn't protected, and she felt the skin on the palm of her left hand blister almost instantaneously. She jumped backwards, reflexively, and squinted through the glare.

"You defy me?" the gorgone roared.

The voice prodded at Kazari's memory, and her blood ran cold in the face of the flames. It was the same voice she'd heard during the sucker fight. Was this one of the greater gorgones? And if so, why hadn't she sensed it earlier, or at a greater distance? The smell seemed to be filling the whole world with its stink, growing and expanding in a miasma of corruption, smoke, and char.

She looked back at Sendar. His face was set, and she could see that he was still bearing weight awkwardly on his injured leg. She crouched again, and tucked closer to Sendar, even as flames began to take hold in the room, and smoke roughened her breathing.

The thing spoke, and as it spoke, a sneaking suspicion began to dawn on Kazari. Underneath the deep tones, she could hear an echo of a different voice. "See me and despair, weaklings. I have seen your hearts, and you are flawed – imperfect tools that will break under my might." It stepped forward, ponderously, and Kazari scooted backwards towards Sendar, looking around to make sure she wouldn't stumble into the bed.

"You're the Mayor, aren't you?" she asked, trying to distract it.

"I was once the Mayor, but no more. I am fully come within this body. It houses me, feeds my power, and makes me mighty. You are but dust in my eyes." It stepped forward again, and Kazari could feel the heat from its body begin to beat at her face. The scar throbbed under the creature's regard. Mayor or not, this was like no gorgone she'd ever read about. She wondered how he'd concealed such a change. Surely it hadn't come upon him in an instant?

"And we are Hunters, sworn to uphold the Lady, and protect her people," Sendar said, quietly, such assurance in his tones that Kazari was almost startled enough to turn and look at him. He stepped forward to stand beside her, a knife in each hand, ready to fight. She took courage from his stance, despite knowing that they were probably about to die. Perhaps they could distract the monster long enough for Clorri to escape and warn the others.

Then there was no time left. The flaming gorgone charged, and she began to dance. It was easy enough to dodge the creature's flailing limbs. Its size made it more ponderous than the dexterous suckers, but it was much more difficult to dance and keep it away from Sendar, whose mobility, despite his bravery, and her healing, was still compromised. Frantically, she tried to distract it, desperately trying to think of some way to defeat it. She spun and dodged, occasionally feinting a strike with her long knives, wondering whether if she managed to impale it upon one of them, the knife would last long enough to wound it fatally or just turn to molten metal in her hand.

Where Sendar's blade had struck, a steady stream of sparks plummeted downwards, but so far, the creature showed no signs of weakening, and some of its strikes were coming too close for comfort, handicapped as she was by her need to make sure it stayed away from Sendar. It laughed as it swung a flaming arm at her. She ducked it easily, but then realised that it had drawn her away from her companion, and dodged back again. This time, heat burned a hole in her leathers near her knee. She stumbled, shocked, recovered and gritted her teeth. The blisters on her palm had long healed, so she drew a second blade, and used both of them to swipe at the nearest arm. Heat seemed to fry her knuckles, and she wished momentarily that the new skin on her hands wasn't so sensitive as she'd nearly dropped both her knives.

Sendar cried out, and she saw that the creature had thrown a gout of flame towards him. The intense heat forced him backwards, and he stumbled on his injured leg, falling to the ground and rolling under the bed. The bedding went up in a flare of smoke, and Kazari coughed and sputtered as it caught in her lungs. She could hear Sendar shouting something faintly from beneath the bed, but couldn't make it out. The creature's flame burned more brightly, almost incandescently, and she heard its mocking laughter.

"Worms, grovelling before me. Still, shortly you will no longer need to grovel, as you will be ash beneath my feet."

Sendar shouted again. Something about the window? Kazari ducked again, throwing herself sideways around the creature's swing, tapped it with her knife, and saw the blade disintegrate into a rain of fiery droplets. She dropped it before it could burn her hands and flipped another knife from her boot sheath into her hands as she ducked under the other arm. "What did you say?" she shouted above the crackle of the flames and the mocking voice of the flaming gorgone.

"Window! Now!"

What? Kazari had no idea what Sendar meant, until he crawled out from underneath the now disintegrating bed, and ran, limping, to the window that Clorri had crashed through. He knocked out several jagged pieces of glass, and then threw himself through it, vanishing into the snow and darkness. Even then, Kazari didn't know why he'd done it. She'd prepared herself to die to save Clorri, not to lead the monster to her again. She danced, weaving through and around the creature's strikes almost contemptuously now that she didn't have Sendar to worry about, and nearly died as part of the roof of Androvar's house collapsed almost on top of her.

Ah. Belatedly, she realised that Sendar must have noticed. She calculated the distance in her mind, reflexively dancing around the fire beast, and then as it swung a burning fist at her, dropped, rolled and leaped through the window. The cold outside was shocking in its intensity and she was covered in sweat from the fire and the fight. She almost collapsed as her feet hit the snow, but wobbled and retained her balance, then turned just in time to see the whole bedroom wall disintegrate as the gorgone burst through it, writhing tendrils of flames surrounding it. Awed by the sheer power of the thing, she failed to dance, and a burning hand flung her into the air. Leather scorched, and burns traced their way across her chest, adding to the pain and the confusion of her senses. Then the icy snow quenched the burning and added another sensation all its own.

Gasping and winded, blistered, and covered with icy sweat, Kazari struggled to her feet. She'd dropped one of her knives, so she flicked another from a wrist sheath, dropping it into her hands. It was short bladed, double sided, and better for throwing than fighting with. Certainly better for throwing rather than attempting to stick it into a flaming monster.

"Duck, Kaz!" yelled Sendar, and she did, trusting him implicitly, and a burning foot passed just above her. She ran, crouching, towards his voice, her legs struggling with the snow.

She slipped on a patch of slush, and for a moment her mind didn't comprehend how there could be slush when the temperatures were so low, but then realised that it was a place where the gorgone had trod, now melted and wet. Thankful that she'd put her boots on after her bath, still she felt water soak her legs. That could only end one way if they remained out in the snow. The gorgone roared and turned, heat radiating in waves from it. The snow around it melted and slumped away, allowing it to move more freely, and it stomped towards the two of them in a cloud of steam.

Kazari prepared herself to dance again. To dance, hampered by the thick snow, slush and ice that formed where the slush had been. They'd jumped out of the frying pain into the boiling pot it seemed. But then Sendar tugged at her arm. "There's enough room for me to use my Ascension, Kaz. But you'll have to keep it occupied. Here." He thrust an armful of snowballs at her. Snowballs?

"What?" she stammered, clutching them.

"You throw them," he said, and before she could say 'What?' he was off and she was dancing. Sendar wanted her to do what? Pelt the thing with snowballs? Almost disbelieving, she looked stupidly at the mass of compacted snow in her arms. Sendar had fashioned a kind of sling out of – his overshirt? He must be freezing. Again. Still, he must have some kind of plan, she thought, so she sheathed her knives, hung the sling from her neck and shoulders, and picked up the first snowball and lobbed it at the monster.

He laughed as the snow melted in a flash of steam before it even touched him. Kazari lobbed another, and another, dancing around the glowing form. It stood still and mocked her, until the sling was empty. As she passed him, Sendar shoved another shirt full at her. "Keep going, Kaz. It's working."

What was working? Her snowballs had barely touched the thing. At least it wasn't endangering Sendar for the moment, but she was beginning to freeze. The sweat on her forehead had begun to ice over, and her hands were slowly regaining the pale waxy tone that spelled frostnip. Still, she threw the snowballs as Sendar had asked. This time, some of her snowballs struck, and she realised that they were leaving darker patches on the beast's skin. Was it even skin? Or would it be called hide? She had no idea, and realised that she had no business thinking random thoughts while she was trying to kill a gorgone. Or, more to the point, survive a gorgone. She had no idea if they could kill something like this.

It roared, and a stream of embers shot into the sky, but they weren't nearly as bright as they had been, and as she swooped in for another armful of snowballs, Sendar whispered. "Keep it occupied as long as you can. Make every strike count, and when you run out of snowballs, throw your knives. But stick them in this to cool them down first." He wafted her a slightly smoking chunk of what she'd thought was snow, but since when did snow steam? She carefully scooped it from the air with the remains of his shirt. And whatever it was, the stuff burned more coldly than anything she'd ever felt when it touched her skin. She hastily readjusted the shirt. What on earth was it? "When you can, pull the knives out of this and then throw them. Wait until you have no more snowballs," he cautioned again. "Aim for major blood vessels. I've only got one more go in me. Ready?" One more go? What was he talking about?

"Yes." She was, she realised. She felt the effort he was making, somehow, as she danced back towards the monster, but out of the corner of her eye, she saw that the beast had been surrounded by mounded snow, and her mind went back to the snow Sendar had compacted on their walk to the village, and the snow he'd thrown at her on their journey. Somehow, while she'd distracted it, he'd built snow walls around the flaming gorgone. And now those same walls were inching closer to the beast with every second.

With a burst of renewed vigour, she threw carefully, making each shot count, and slowly, the creature's brightness dimmed further, hemmed in as it was by the walls of snow, and her snowballs, until it was a dull, angry maroon, and each snowball left a blackened circle on its body.

Its movement slowed, and Kazari realised that it was struggling to move its feet. Its rage escalated and it roared and snarled, but this time the embers died as they spurted from its mouth. Sendar was tiring fast, though, and the walls moved only infinitesimally closer each second now. Frantically, Kazari threw her second to last snowball, and then pulled her frosty knives from the lump of stuff Sendar had made, still hanging in the remains of his shirt around her neck, burning her fingers and dropping the first knife with clumsy hands. She thumped them on her thighs in frustration, trying to stir the circulation, then scrabbled for the knife, but it was stuck firmly to a chunk of snow. She wrapped her sleeves around her hands, grasped her final two knives, grimacing against the sting of cold that struck her hands, even through the leather wrapped handles and the cloth of her shirt.

She waited, feeling Sendar's fatigue, feeling the rhythm of the dance, waited again, and then threw, both hands at once. The knives flew true, embedding themselves where the creature's femoral arteries would have been had he still been human. As they struck and then stuck, she wondered if it even still had a circulatory system. Somehow this time, the knives didn't melt immediately, but then, as she stumbled in her dance, something struck it in the face in a cloud of steam.

It howled, clawing at its face, and as she fell sideways into a drift, rolling in the soft snow she saw it tremble and shudder. Snow slid down the back of her jerkin in an icy trail. Groaning, she kept rolling onto her feet, forcing herself leadenly through the snow to let the forward momentum propel her forward, and then she was running, or rather, wading through the snow.

Eventually, she burst from the soft snow onto the slippery surface of the ice that mired the gorgone.

Both knives stood out on its thighs, and she bolted forward, ducked under another ponderous swing of its arms, and without heed for her own safety pulled the knives, now her last, from its body and kept running, skating her feet on the icy surface. Her hands burned – from heat or cold, she had no idea – and the thing sprayed sparks, pumping them from the knife wounds in its thighs as though pumped by a beating heart. Perhaps they were. Kazari had no idea. All she knew was that the thing was fading, freezing, and stopped, and then she staggered to a halt, gasping the freezing air, her hands still burning from the knives. She was almost too afraid to let go of them, fearful of what she might see, and afraid that her skin would come off in strips.

The amethyst at her neck warmed again, glowing gently, and as she unclenched her fists gingerly, she realised that the heat she'd felt was the same as when Javon had plunged her hands into warm water all of those hours ago. Her palms were mildly blistered – from the knives or the frostbite she didn't know, but already the blisters were beginning to subside. Almost numbly, she turned towards Sendar. He was standing, shivering, pale and exhausted, but at the same time, his face wore a smile of triumph, even as tears coursed down his cheeks and froze on them. She stumbled over to him, and together they turned and watched the monster turn to a rigid pillar, backlit by Androvar's funeral pyre.

Chapter Twenty-five: Beginnings

The barracks had remained untouched by the fire, separated as they were by just enough distance from Androvar's house, so Kazari and Sendar had been able to hobble together through the snow, and collapse inside their room, shivering. Slowly they'd dried their clothes, tended Sendar's injuries (again) and then, wrapped in cloaks, gloves and layers of warm, dry clothing, gone to search for Clorri.

They'd finally found the girl in the stable with the horses, tucked away in the back of Stumpy's stall. Kazari's sturdy horse had shared his warmth freely with her, and still wide-eyed and trembling, she'd allowed them to lead her over to the chapel, where they'd stoked the stove, set water to heat, and raided Androvar's chapel supplies for sustenance. Then they'd waited. Waited for hours, while not one villager appeared to assist, and wondered what had happened to their fellow Hunters.

Finally, the others had appeared in the early hours of the morning, striding and limping through the snow to stand stunned before the ashes of the residence and the frozen pillar of the dead gorgone. Gore and blood stained their clothing, Kellis had her arm in a sling, and both Mikel and Javon were limping as Sendar and Kazari went to welcome them. Without a word, Andiss wrapped an arm around the two of them and led them back into the warmth of the chapel.

Later, seated together in the warmth, Javon had told them what had happened. "We entered the tunnel as expected, and found it deserted. You were lucky you chose the direction you did when you escaped, because it's a maze in the other direction. We found the 'changed' not far from what we assume is the room they kept you in, but they led us a merry dance. Eventually we split into pairs. It was tough and messy, and they fought hard." She paused and looked at the others, eyes shadowed. "I've never seen anything like them. They were foul, and there was nothing left of their humanity. Nothing at all. No wonder this village has had a shadow over it. We came out via the Mayor's house. That family . . . " She shook her head. "There's a big job to do here."

Andiss turned to Kazari and Sendar. "And to think we left you here to keep you safe – what was that thing?"

"The Mayor, apparently," Sendar said. "Or rather, what was left of the Mayor. It appeared that something else had taken up residence in his body. Some sort of gorgone made of fire."

"And Androvar?" Mikel asked.

"Androvar's dead," Kazari said "He killed her, and then we killed him." Tears trickled down her cheeks again, and from the muffled noises around her, she knew she wasn't the only one crying. "She was so good, and so caring, and he killed her and tossed her aside like a piece of rubbish."

"And that, Kazari, is why we'll continue to fight," Andiss said. "Albatar is under much more of a threat than we believed, but I think we've bought some time tonight. Androvar's death is tragic, but she now resides with the Lady, in peace. We'll hold her funeral ceremony tomorrow before we return to the Abbey." He indicated himself, Javon, Kazari, and Sendar. "There is much to tell the Abbot that can only be told in person." They sat silently before the stove for some hours without speaking, before returning to the barracks.

The following morning, they stood before the ashes of Androvar's dwelling and the frozen hulk of the gorgone. Kazari sniffed the air. No stench remained. It was dead and long gone. The house had taken Androvar's earthly body, but the shapeless hulk would stand forever as a reminder to Suborden.

Andiss stood forth before the assembled villagers, Javon by his side.

"This place has fostered evil rarely seen in Albatar. Somehow it gained a foothold here, was nurtured, and nearly destroyed you all." His eyes swept the crowd. Kazari saw that their faces were shadowed, ashamed, but in places relieved and thankful. Not everyone had been corrupted, or tempted – and these were the ones who'd resisted, or as she remembered Clorri, been abused by those who had chosen to change, and had lived for months in fear and silence.

The assembled Hunters stood out on the field of white. Their clothing marked them as different, and the amethysts around their necks glowed violet in the rising sun. The colour sparkled in the sunlight, reflecting it to shine upon the villagers. Kazari wondered why none had spoken, why none of them had thought to tell Androvar, and why they had suffered so much in silence? But then she remembered her own fear. She had survived, but only because of her training and the grace of the Lady. How would she have fared had she still been the callow teen who'd left home all those months ago?

Slightly chastened, she listened to Andiss' words. "There will be Hunters here, now. Mind them well as they teach you the ways of the Lady once again. Hear their words and teach them to your children. Remind yourselves why your ancestors came to Albatar so long ago. Mikel leads, in Androvar's place, with the help of Kellis, Sherd, and Jern, and when you are tempted to stray, to fall back into corruption, remember Androvar's sacrifice." He turned towards the burned shell of the priory, and inclined his head.

"The Lady takes her servants to herself, wipes away their tears and turns their sorrow to joy," Javon said. "Hear the words of the Writings. Hold them in your hearts and let them comfort you." She opened a copy of the Writings, holding it carefully in gloved hands, and removed the bookmark that had marked her place. *"When one of My servants lays down their life in My service, that servant tastes the joy of My love. Heed their sacrifice, and treasure it in your hearts. Go forth therefore, remembering. Let their sacrifice spur you to service of your fellows, secure in the knowledge that your servant stands with Me forever more."* She closed the Writings and looked out on the villagers, many of whom were now openly weeping.

"Will you hold Androvar's memory in your hearts?" she asked.

"We will," they replied, and Kazari was startled to hear the fervour in their voices. These were a people released from a nightmare.

"Then go in peace, seek love, serve each other, and read the Lady's words."

For a few moments more, the villagers stood, staring at the ashes, the pillar, and the Hunters, and then Clorri stepped forward and laid a delicately fashioned woollen flower in the ashes. She stepped back and walked over to the oldster with the arthritic hands whom they'd met while accompanying Androvar on her rounds that first morning. She'd agreed to take Clorri in. The girl's siblings were to be fostered with various families, while their mother was to accompany Kazari's group back to the Abbey. The woman's mind appeared to have broken under the strain of the last few days, and now, she stood staring into the distance, unmoving. Andiss hoped that with the skilled care of the Healers, she might yet recover. Kazari suspected that they also wished to question her further concerning the gorgones, and the source of the malmetal charms.

Those, the other Hunters had gathered carefully from the corpses of the creatures they'd dispatched, and then melted them in the remains of the residence's fire. Kazari had watched as each bauble had shed a fog of black smoke, before the metal had melted into puddles of gold and copper. "The metal is just metal now," Javon had said. "But there were many of them. Hopefully we found them all."

One by one, the other villagers laid tributes in the ashes, walking back to their homes in silence afterwards. Finally, none but the Hunters remained. Together they approached the remains of the house. It had burned hotly, and there had been little to salvage from the wreckage.

"Honour to you, Androvar," Andiss said, touching his amethyst to his lips. "Honour, and love, and thanks. Be at peace with the Lady."

Kazari swallowed convulsively, as tears threatened again. She'd only known Androvar a short time, but she'd been such a blessing in those few days that Kazari felt as if she'd lost a good friend. She repeated Andiss' words. As one, the Hunters turned away.

Later, as they mounted their horses and farewelled the others, Kazari looked around. The village was peaceful again. And if it hadn't been for the scar of the burned residence and the strange pillar that stood before it, a stranger would never have believed that such evil could have existed in such a beautiful place.

"We leave Suborden in good hands," Javon said as they rode away.

"But what awaits Albatar?" Andiss asked as they rode down the track on the mountainside.

What indeed, wondered Kazari. And then, inside her mind, she heard that voice again – the one from the fight with the suckers.

"You think you've won? Because you defeated a fledgling infestation? Think all you like. This war is just beginning, and Albatar *will* fall."

She looked up, startled, to see shock on every face. This time the voice had spoken to them all.

"You might think so, gorgone," Andiss replied. "But we are Hunters, and you are our prey. You will not prevail." His tone was firm, and confident, but Kazari knew that regardless, dark days were ahead. She looked at Sendar. Together they'd defeated a greater gorgone, but it had been a near thing. Dark days indeed.

About the Author

Originally from Western Australia, Leonie now lives in NSW in the Upper Hunter. She is the author of Frontier Incursion, Frontier Resistance, and Frontier Defiant (YA Speculative Fiction) published by Hague Publishing, and also works part time as a physiotherapist. She dabbles in poetry, and has had a short story published in Antipodean SF, and another in the Novascapes 2 anthology.

The Frontier Trilogy is full of glow-in-the-dark cats who like to sleep on the bed, alien invaders, and a planet out to kill the unwary.

Now, in Amethyst Pledge, she has dipped her toes into the waters of fantasy.

She has a past life as a volunteer firefighter and SES member, and once trekked almost six hundred kilometres with eight camels and several other human beings. She is married with two adult children, two dogs and three cats, one of whom frequently handicaps her ability to use a laptop computer.

Hague

Publishing

www.HaguePublishing.com

PO Box 451 Bassendean
Western Australia 6934